RULE NUMBER ONE

RULE BREAKERS SERIES
BOOK 1

NICKY SHANKS

LIMITLESS PUBLISHING, LLC

Rule Number One

First Print Edition: December 2017

Limitless Publishing, LLC

Kailua, HI 96734

www.limitlesspublishing.com

Formatting: Limitless Publishing

ISBN-13: 978-1-64034-280-4

ISBN-10: 1-64034-280-X

DEDICATION

To my husband…my own personal Oliver Jackson.
Life is always a tornado, but you're my calm in any storm.
If you're lucky enough to find someone you can share your
whole self with…keep them.
Fall for them.
Let yourself be loved.

To Stacy…always my number one fan and supporter.
I can't thank you enough for what you've done for me and
this journey.
This series would never have been born if not for you
encouraging me to try.
For you, I will always be grateful.

ONE
OLIVER

I WAKE myself up from a light sleep, hungover and still exhausted.

A girl with a mess of dark hair stirs next to me and yawns. Her morning-after breath reaches me and I wrinkle my nose. What's her name again? Candace? Mary? Amber? She stretches and *moans*, making me smile as she turns to face me. I close my eyes quickly, hoping she hadn't seen me awake so she won't try to have a conversation. I just want her to leave. Ever since my grandfather and father both died—and my ex, Heather, destroyed my life shortly after—I've lived my life by four simple rules that can be applied to any situation in life.

Rule number one: Don't let your guard down.

Rule number two: Don't take anything for granted.

Rule number three: Keep your secrets safe.

Rule number four: Don't destroy your own happiness.

Four rules. Four simple, easy rules. So far, living by these rules has been blissful. Except for when I'm alone—like, *really* alone—and the silence suffocates me.

I feel the girl move from the bed, and I pop open my left eye to watch her pick up her clothes, piece by piece, and look nervously back toward me before slipping out of the bedroom.

My eyes open all the way when I hear her shut the front door, and I stare at the paste-white ceiling.

All alone again.

I am a *mess*.

I hate Heather for sleeping with her brother-in-law in my bed, but there was no way I could've known she would do that to me. She always seemed so sweet and normal, interested only in me. I finally realized her game when I caught her, but how could you instantly throw three years with someone out the window and forget them? At first, her betrayal didn't make sense to me. How could she cheat on someone like *me*?

Me, of all people.

Now I only have one opinion of her: She's as fake as those cheap "diamonds" she wears.

I want to sleep for the entire weekend, but I know that isn't going to make me feel any better. What's-her-name that just left—she makes me feel better for long enough periods of time that I can turn off the world and indulge a little. I shiver at my shallow-ness, closing my eyes when the doorbell rings. I hope to God it isn't What's-her-name. These women…

they're always leaving something behind to try and come back for more Oliver Jackson.

The doorbell rings over and over, like a song, as I make my way toward it. I'm getting ready to yell at whoever this is. "What?" I growl, swinging the door open before looking through the peephole. That probably wasn't a smart idea in case it *is* What's-her-name.

"Man, *move*." A broad shoulder pushes me to the side and Casey, my best friend, rolls his eyes at me in annoyance as he enters the apartment. I watch him shove his cell phone in his jeans pocket and look at me, wrinkling his nose because I'm only wearing boxers. "Can you put some clothes on? What is this place? Magic Oliver?"

I scoff, but I know I look good; he doesn't have to remind me he's jealous, or that he looks the complete opposite of me. I notice that he hasn't washed his copper blonde hair in a few days. For someone who wishes he were more of a ladies' man, he sure the hell doesn't put a lot of effort into trying to become one. "What do you want, Casey? I need sleep." I yawn and pick up a gray V-neck t-shirt from the back of the sofa, sniffing it for any unknown odors. After pulling it on, I find some sweatpants on the floor and do the same thing, watching the disgust in his eyes grow.

Okay, so maybe he's not the only one with a few issues in the hygiene department.

"Okay, so I have a great opportunity for you, Ollie," he says.

I sigh. *Here we go.*

"Nora—you know, the girl I've been chasing around for three months—finally gave me the green light, man." His schoolboy grin and eager nod make me extra nervous. "There's just one little problem— she wants me to take her camping. Fucking *camping*, Ollie. I've never been camping in my entire life."

I laugh in his face. "It's just camping…what are you so afraid of?"

Casey scoffs. "*Everything*, asshole. Bugs, animals, creepy sounds and shadows—"

"Fine, you big baby. Just use my cabin at Lake Reed; that way it's still outdoors but indoors too. The best of both worlds. Problem solved."

He snaps his fingers at me in enthusiasm. "Good idea! See, *that*'s why I came here." He looks at me and gives me a cheesy smile, but I've been down this road way too many times with Casey to believe that he doesn't want more from me.

"You are such a bad liar," I say to him. "What else do you want?"

Casey looks sick, like he's trying to figure out how to tell me he slept with my girlfriend. "Don't say no—listen to me first."

"What *else*, Casey?"

"Now, just listen first—"

"What. Else. Do. You—"

He cuts me off this time. "I need you to go with us."

I laugh; I really think he's trying to be funny. "No."

4

"Come on, Ollie, she's insisting she bring a few of her friends with her and I want to bring friends too." He's out of his mind if he thinks I'm gonna be paraded around a bunch of vanilla virgins, walking on eggshells the whole time and hoping I don't offend someone by walking around half-naked. Or worse—one of them falls in love with me and I end up getting stalked again. That definitely wasn't the best week of my life.

"Ollie—"

I shake my head. "No."

"But—"

"NO," I say louder, sleepily walking toward the kitchen to start making coffee. "Can't you get a girl to sleep with you without dragging me along? Wouldn't it be easier to get them in bed *without* me there?" The amused smile on my face isn't as amusing to Casey. I know he hates when I point out that we're different, and I know he *really* hates it when I remind him how many women pass through my door while he has to chase *one* all the way to Lake Reed.

I honestly have nothing better to do these days. Since I kicked Heather out of the apartment, I haven't thought about my next move. I graduated from NYU three years ago; my business degree is gathering dust on a shelf. When my grandfather died and left me all of his money, I didn't see a need to spend endless hours sending out resumes.

"Ollie, come on, man. She's bringing three friends, and I have Harley and Victor going with us. I just need one more slightly less idiotic friend than the rest of my options." He clenches his jaw. "I need someone who won't embarrass me."

I shake my head. "I doubt any of those girls will enjoy my company anyway." I take my cup from the machine and add a few spoonfuls of sugar before blowing on the steam. "You do realize that Heather just basically screwed my head up only a few months ago, right?"

Casey smiles wide. "Yes! Exactly, which is why you need this."

"I don't need this." I wave him off. "I need to have sex with random girls, that's what I need to do. I'm pissed off, Casey—no amount of faking a good time will fix that."

"I've known you for over twenty years. I know when you're pissed, and you're not pissed—you're sort of...*broken*." He slowly says the last word. It feels like a hot dagger through my torso just the same, if not worse.

"Screw you, I'm not broken," I retort and cross my arms over my chest.

Casey holds up his hands. "Okay, okay, sorry. I just need you on this, Ollie."

I close my eyes and slowly shake my head from side to side. "Dammit," I hiss. I know I'm making him feel uncomfortable, but I give him what he wants. "Fine."

He pumps his fist in the air and claps his hands. "Okay, we leave tonight—"

"Whoa—" I stop him before he can go any

further. "You want to leave *tonight*?" Casey pouts. "Fine, but no more surprises, and you owe me more than one for this."

He blows out a hard breath. "Okay, good. Yes, I promise I owe you more than one for this."

"*Way* more than just one." I cross my arms again; this time I mean business. I'm sort of a pushover for Casey and his crazy tactics to get women out of his league. Sometimes I get lucky too and they have decent-looking friends, but I never remember their names, either.

"Get out—text me the details." He gets up, salutes me, and races from the apartment before I can change my mind. My mind wanders to Heather again—the way her pale, milky skin glows in the moonlight when she wears those little lacy outfits to bed. I lick my lips and clear my throat, remembering that I'm alone...*again*.

Three months ago, I had it all. Hell, I had more than everything a guy could ever dream of: I had the girl, the popularity, and the money.

Until I didn't have the girl anymore.

I think that's where I went wrong, now that I stop and really think about it. When I say that I had it all, that might be the biggest lie I've ever told. I have no family left after my grandfather died—my mother disappeared when I was five and my father died when I was fourteen. I'm sort of a curse on my family, people dying and leaving wherever I go. When my father died, my grandfather was forced to take me in, twisting me into something I learned to hate, and then he died of lung cancer.

…Actually, no. That's not entirely true—he died from being an asshole and we both knew it. I still miss him sometimes, though. Not often, but times like this—times when I need a swift kick in the ass for being such an idiot. Right now, he'd say something like, "Oliver, I told you that girl was trouble; stop being a waste of a man and take life by the balls." The memory of his raspy voice haunts the walls of my mind and I shiver.

"Seriously…come on, man," I say and shake my head, my dark hair falling into my eyes. Brushing it back, I sigh and walk toward the spare bedroom of the apartment that houses my personal gym, and after a few hours of working off the Heather tension, I shower and change into jeans and a green, long-sleeved shirt.

My phone dings as I put on socks and boots, pushing my hair to the side. Casey's name pops up on the screen, followed by a series of texts.

CASEY

Thank you so much for doing this, Nora and I are already on our way to the cabin.

Can you pick up her friend?

She lives in Rockford, 411 South Avenue.

> Her name is Julie. She's expecting you around three.

> Can you also get snacks?

I scoff and throw the phone onto the bed. "Great." I start packing my things. That jerk only gave me an hour to pick the girl up and that was thirty minutes ago. I pick my phone back up, typing a reply.

> The master bedroom is mine and mine only.

I send it to him and start throwing stuff into my suitcase without any real organization. As I close the suitcase and click it shut, I start wondering what Julie looks like. No matter what, she's probably going to talk my ear off the entire drive about makeup and who's dating who in Hollywood, and I can't think of anything worse.

The suitcase has a brochure sticking out from the side, so I snatch it and look at the cover. It features the waves of a blue ocean behind a group of women with leis around their necks, swaying their hips side to side.

Hawaii with Heather.

My face grows red with heat.

I *hate* her.

I hate packing too. Heather always does—did—it for me.

I'm going to be late if I don't leave soon, so I grab

the suitcase and the small bag with other essentials in it, lock my apartment door behind me, and stick a note on my across-the-hall neighbor, Mrs. Atchley's, door, reminding her to feed my fish for me. The building fades in the distance as I race toward the black dot that the GPS is taking me to.

Julie.

It's taking me toward Julie.

The houses look the same in the cookie-cutter neighborhood, and I stop when the GPS lady tells me to, in front of a large red-bricked house. Biting my lip, I don't see anyone waiting for me, so I sigh and leave the car, my long legs shuffling to the front door.

I want to get this over with.

I push the doorbell and wait. Nothing. I push it again.

The door finally opens, slowly, and a small boy with wild red hair and freckles looks up at me, his eyes covered by thick glasses. "What?" he snaps.

I frown. "I'm here for Julie?"

"And?"

My laugh is quick and cold. "Look kid, can you just get her for me? Is she your mom or something?"

The kid scoffs, loudly. "You're a stranger, you idiot, like I'd ever tell you anything. You could be a spy."

My lips flatten. "Seriously, kid, get Julie."

The kid crosses his arms over his small chest. "I don't know a 'Julie.'"

"Clyde," I hear a woman say from out of view,

"let him know I'll be out in a few minutes, okay? I'm almost done packing. I didn't have much notice."

The kid snaps his fingers. "Hear that?"

"I can help you with your things," I call through the open door.

Clyde snorts. "Wow, what a loser."

I shake my head at him. "I'm not a loser, trust me."

"You sound like a total douche." Clyde mocks me: "*I can help you with your things.*"

"Clyde, leave him alone," the woman says from inside the house. "Okay…" Her voice gets louder and she finally appears. "I'm ready, sorry. Nora never gives enough notice for anything she does."

I grunt and try not to stare at her. I swear to God I could have a damn heart attack right here. Julie's electric blue eyes lock on mine and she blushes. I can get used to that. Her honey blonde hair is thrown into a messy bun on her head and her pink-and-black flannel shirt skims the top of the light denim cut-off shorts she has on, displaying her curvy frame for all to see. I can see goosebumps forming on the alabaster skin on her legs as a breeze kicks up. I bite my lip as my eyes stop at the top button of her shirt; it's undone and flirting with the top of a lacy black—

Clyde snickers. "Dude, be any more obvious?"

I clear my throat and reach for her bags. She's a little taken aback by my boldness. I'm pretty sure she can tell I was instantly attracted to her, but I try my best to fight it as I brush past her and throw her bags next to mine in the back of the Jeep. I don't wait to open her door for her before throwing myself into the driver's seat and taking deep breaths. She even smelled delicious as I passed by her; the breeze caught her sunflower perfume and it's going to drive me crazy.

Well, this is unexpected.

Once she gets into the Jeep and waves at Clyde, he waves back and then gives me the middle finger. I gotta admire his attitude—he obviously doesn't trust too many people, which I can relate to.

I make sure her seatbelt is on before speeding off toward the grocery store to get the snacks, my mind racing and palms sweating against the steering wheel. She's making it *really* hard to concentrate.

"I'm Julie." Her voice is velvety and fills my head with sunshine, making it hard to focus and drive. I've gotta stop this. I nod my head in acknowledgment, my hair falling into my eye. "I guess that makes you Ollie?"

"My name is Oliver," I snap at her on accident. "*Oliver.*"

I hear her gulp but don't bother looking over at her. I do feel bad a little as the tension in the car rises between us, and I dodge several cars in the parking lot of the grocery store. After parking the Jeep, I don't speak to her as I step out and shut the door behind me. My phone buzzes before I even make it to the front doors.

CASEY

Dude, what the hell?

I stop on the sidewalk.

What?

Julie doesn't want to come, what did
you do to her?

I raise my head and look back at the Jeep. I can
see her staring out the window in the opposite direction of me, her forehead pressed against the glass,
and I growl. I type to him, smashing my fingers on
the pad.

I'll take her home.

His response comes quickly.

No! Please fix this!

I shove the phone into my pocket and walk back
to the car, making sure I don't startle her when I open
the passenger door. My head's still a little fuzzy as
she lifts her huge blue eyes to meet my gaze. "Come
on," I say. "Let's get some snacks."

She rolls her eyes. Her thick, pouty lips form into
a frown and I find myself wanting to bite her bottom
one. "I'm staying here. I have someone coming to
get me."

"Hey, look, I'm sorry—"

"Leave me alone," she barks. "Just go, and when
you're done I'll be gone."

A few women pass us and give me dirty looks.

13

They eyeball Julie to make sure she's okay before moving along. "Just call off your ride." I grit my teeth and narrow my eyes at her, hoping my dominant attitude will make her squirm. "Just come in with me and help get snacks, and we can get through the next three hours as easily as possible and then be around people we actually like."

She snorts. "*Wow*, nice talk."

I watch her bite her bottom lip and my insides twist a little, like a fire is raging through my veins. She's sexy, about six inches shorter than me, with a small waist and curvy hips—and she's a few years younger too, which excites me even more. I want to trace her hips with my thumbs.

Heather is nothing next to this girl...and now I'm growling again, pissed that my cheating ex has entered my thoughts for the millionth time today.

Julie's eyes widen. "Are you *growling* at me?"

I shake my head. "Of course not. Look, I'm sorry. Really, can we just forget I was an ass and go in for the snacks? I'll let you pick them out."

She smiles at me, taking her hair down and throwing the thick mass over her shoulder. "Deal."

I nod. "Deal."

She texts someone—no doubt to cancel her ride—and once again, this time with Julie in tow, I make my way back to the grocery store. Julie grabs a shopping basket, trying to pretend we didn't arrive together. My cart is full of junk food like cookies and chips when she looks seriously at me for a few moments but doesn't say anything.

"You think we're missing something?" I ask.

Julie nods, soft blue eyes still holding mine. "Beer?"

I raise my eyebrows. "*You* drink beer?"

She smiles and nods again, batting her eyelashes.

"Okay, girl. Beer it is."

I'm impressed.

After all, it's so like me to make the best out of a weird situation, right?

TWO
JULIE

I MAKE a mental note to thank Nora for her wonderful trip to a luxurious cabin in the woods.

Thank you, Nora.

Thank you so, *so* much.

The guy that picked me up is pretty much the biggest ass ever. To be fair, she *did* warn me. Oliver and Nora had met a few times before Casey even came into the picture, but Oliver didn't remember her when Casey introduced them. If someone that looks like Oliver Jackson forgot about me, it would sting just a little.

I feel so out of place as I walk next to him toward the checkout counter. Several women around us all but drooled when Oliver walked past them, and I honestly couldn't blame them because throughout this entire shopping trip, I've been sneaking peeks at his tall, muscular frame and drooling a little myself.

Until he opens his mouth to speak.

Regardless, I can tell what those women are

thinking; it isn't like I haven't thought these things myself before:

I wonder how she got a guy like that.

They do not look like they belong together.

She is one lucky girl.

I shiver as the jealous women hover over us like vultures.

"Hey, Julie, do you want some candy or anything? I need some Skittles more than you *know*." He smiles quickly at me and turns his gaze toward the candy choices even quicker. "Something to drink, maybe? We do have a long drive ahead of us."

For a moment, I find myself drawn to his wide smile and bright eyes. There's something about him that makes me feel weirder than I usually do—his green eyes look like they're made from fire and brimstone as his hooded gaze watches me squirm. He knows what he does to women; he knows he gets underneath their skin.

"Plus, I'm not stopping again."

And there it is.

I snort and roll my eyes at how pathetic he's making me look. "Better watch out, your chivalry is showing," I say, and he grabs an iced tea from the small beverage fridge, shaking it for my approval. I nod and he places it on the belt with a handful of candy bags, including his Skittles and an impulse cupcake purchase. Now the women are *really* judging me; I'm sure of it. Since he clearly looks like he doesn't even know what candy tastes like—his perfect body doesn't scream Skittles around the waist —the tons of junk food just *have* to be for me.

I blush from embarrassment. I know they aren't really thinking that—it's all that low self-esteem that Brandon has instilled in me. Honestly, I shouldn't even have said yes to Nora when she begged me to go on this trip, no matter how much she cried and pouted. Doesn't she remember the relationship I just broke free from? Brandon is my kryptonite, and the grip he had on me was no doubt superhuman.

The pain is still very raw as I scratch the scars over my heart.

I don't hate him, though.

Oliver takes out his wallet and pays for the snacks. As I watch his muscles bulge, he lowers the bags into the cart and looks up at me for a quick moment—making sure I hadn't run away yet, probably. I know, in this moment, no matter how small it is, all those jealous women want to be me. They want to be the one getting that quick smile he's flashing at me.

"Ready?" His deep voice cuts through my thoughts.

I nod. "As I'll ever be, I guess."

He nods at the cute little cashier that bats her eyelashes at him and winks back at her. I shake my head at the two of them. I mean, okay, I'm right here. When I pass her, she glares at me and then rolls her eyes. Oliver laughs a little as I storm off ahead of him and the cart of food. "Hey, wait up!" I hear him say, jogging lightly to catch up with me. His long legs finally come to level with my short ones, but that doesn't stop me from pushing harder and trying to ignore him for the crap he just pulled inside.

I let myself into the Jeep and buckle myself in, waiting for him to load the groceries into the back with our luggage and put the cart away. He's making sure to take his sweet time. Even for July, the air is stickier than usual and makes my skin crawl; it's begging me to just take myself home and bury my head under the covers like I usually do.

"Hey, are you okay?" he asks me when he gets into the Jeep, his breathing heavy. I nod and mumble a quick, "I'm fine," but he isn't buying it. "Maybe I should just take you home; we're still close enough."

I scoff. "Yeah, maybe you should."

His mouth opens, then closes slowly. "But, I thought—"

I wave him off. "Sorry, I just changed my mind. I'm not really ready for this."

"What's 'this'?"

My throat is dry and itchy. "This, this whole—" I wave my arms around in a small circle. "—trip. I shouldn't have said yes...I'm just not ready to be around people, I guess." I lower my head and hear him let out a small sigh, followed by him shoving his hands into his jeans pockets.

"Hey." His voice is low and I can feel myself start to get awkward and push myself away from his sadness. "I'm sorry for being an asshole."

I scoff. "You were fine. It's not you, it's me."

He laughs at my cheesy reference. "No, seriously.

I know I was giving attitude and being a jerk. I'm sorry, I shouldn't have acted that way. But this week means a lot to my friend because he wants to be with *your* friend, so maybe we can both just..." His lips purse and he blows out air. "Pretend to be happy for their sake?"

I fake a huge smile. "I *am* happy."

Oliver isn't amused. "About the same as I am, I imagine. Look, I don't know you or anything about you, but Casey is my best friend—he's been there for me when no one else has been. I owe him a lot more than some weekend trip."

I look out the window and sigh. "Fine."

Oliver laughs, making my stomach drop a little. "Good." I make a weird agreeing noise and he starts the Jeep. I don't know what I'm even doing here; I told Randy I'd start looking for a new job. Now here I am, in a car with a man I don't know, going out of town.

I can hear my phone start pinging after the Jeep lurches onto the freeway, heading out of town.

Nora's name pops up on the screen.

NORA

How far are you?

I glance over at Oliver, whose gaze is dead ahead. He probably forgot I'm even here. I most definitely haven't forgotten about him as I glance out the corner of my eye so I can look at him without getting caught.

> Just getting on the freeway, we aren't even half an hour in yet.

She sends me back a sad face.

> Okay, drive safe. We had a change in rooms, just FYI.

I gasp a little louder than I probably should have.

"Is everything okay?" Oliver asks me without looking away from the road…not that he wants to even have a conversation, let alone make eye contact with me.

"Fine. I guess there's a room issue; not quite sure of the facts," I say coldly, listening to him suck in air between his teeth.

Oliver looks annoyed. "No, there shouldn't be. There's eight of us…a few of them can sleep together, right?"

"From the sound of it, some of them *want* to sleep together." My mouth dries from having to say that sentence.

"Should you call her? I mean, we need to figure this out before we get there, don't you think?" His voice is strained and nervous, but I hardly want to let Nora know this guy thinks I'm not worthy enough to sleep next to him. "You'd better call her before we lose service—before we're all alone out here."

I open the tea he's grabbed for me and dial Nora. When she answers, I put her on speakerphone, which I can instantly tell is a big mistake. Once I realize that her voice is raspy and she's out of breath I want to hang up the phone, but Oliver's lips are turned up into a sexy, slight smile so I stay on the line. "What?" she breathes into the phone.

"Um, Nora? Your boyfriend's friend wants to ask a question." I am totally mortified.

"Okay?"

Oliver keeps his eyes forward. "What's the problem with the rooms?"

Nora laughs. "Oh, *that*."

"What do you mean, '*Oh, that*'?" His voice is thick with frustration.

"I mean..." She giggles and drags out her words. "...that it's under control now. You guys will have to just room together, okay?"

I can feel the tension in the Jeep rise a little as Oliver thinks about sleeping in the same bed with me and gets annoyed. "I guess that will be okay," he says in a low voice. He gets lost in his own thoughts as we drive down the dusky, winding roads.

"What happened to all the rooms?" I don't want to sleep in the same room with him; I don't even *know* him, and I'm not about to share a bed with a man who could crush me with a single bicep curl. Not to mention the fact that Oliver is so against even breathing in the same space as me.

"Well, there are four bedrooms," Nora says and giggles again. We hear Casey's voice in the back-ground. "Casey and I are taking one, and there's only one bed in each room, so the other guys are taking one and then Staci and Amber are taking the other one. That only leaves one—"

"I know how to do basic math, Nora," Oliver says. "Never mind, I guess we'll just be sleeping together, then."

I'm so embarrassed that I start to tear up a little. "We'll figure it out, okay? I can sleep on the floor in the girls' room or on the sofa in the living room…*something*."

I know that Oliver is just trying to make me feel comfortable, but a rush of heat washes over my body as I hang up the phone and bite my bottom lip, trying my best not to take it personally. Brandon didn't want me, either, so I can't expect that a stranger would.

Stupid Brandon.

I still don't hate him.

"Hey." His voice is smooth and sweet. "Look, I'm sorry. I didn't mean to hurt your feelings. We can sleep in the same bed—we're adults, right?" I shake my head. I don't dare take my eyes away from the window, even though I'm a little cold and really want him to turn on the heat. I doubt he would anyway, so I tuck my hands underneath my legs to try and keep them warm, my eyes locked on the outside world passing us by.

He finally looks over at me. "Are you cold?"

I shake my head again. I'm not exactly comfortable speaking to him right now.

"Are you going to ignore me the entire way there?"

"No," I finally say, "I'm shaking my head, I'm not ignoring you."

Oliver sighs and runs his fingers through his shaggy dark hair. I want to study him more, but he's rude enough with me doing nothing to antagonize him, so I don't want to muck up the waters any more than they already are. I do know that he smells delicious: manly and spicy, woodsy and strong.

"*Are* you cold, though?" he asks again.

I nod and blush. "A little."

His lips curve into a small, sexy smile. "Well then, why didn't you say so?"

I shrug my shoulders. "Didn't feel like it."

He lets the heat warm up the Jeep in a subtle way before turning it down again. "Better?"

I nod and smile warmly at him, but he doesn't look back over.

"Better." I pout and return my gaze to the window. Anything is better than sitting in awkward silence with a man who puts me off so badly. In the corner of my eye, I follow the length of his jeans, trying to be subtle. He has muscular legs and even more muscular arms, small bulges outlined underneath his olive-green Henley.

And the first two buttons are unfastened.

Crap.

My stomach flutters with excitement. *No, Julie, no.*

"We have about an hour left; you can sleep if you want," he says. The sky around the Jeep looks like it's on fire from the sun setting as we race over the deserted road.

"Okay." I bring my knees up into the seat with me, nearly kicking him on accident. I blush. "Can you wake me before we get there?"

He nods and I close my eyes.

Sure, anything for you, Julie.

Says no one.

Ever.

I can smell the cookies baking when someone says my name in a deep, sexy voice. Oliver appears in my dream, his jeans unbuttoned. He's shirtless, lying on a bed and smiling at me, his dark hair falling into his eyes. "Hey, Julie." He winks, biting his juicy bottom lip and sheepishly smiling. I saunter over to him and he pulls me onto the bed before pinning me underneath his hard, warm body and kissing my neck gently.

"Julie?"

Oh, crap.

"Wake up, sleepyhead, we're almost there," I hear Oliver say.

"Okay." I rub my eyes and look around. It's already dark and I can barely see anything outside now. "How much longer?"

"About ten minutes."

Wow, he did what I asked.

"Thanks for waking me." I fake a sweet smile that he returns with a genuine, warm, and gentle smirk from what I can see in the moonlight.

"Did you have a nice sex dream?" he asks me, laughter in his voice.

I gasp. "What?"

25

We pull onto a long, creepy road with trees hanging in a thick canopy over it. I smell the lake water and inhale it deep into my lungs.

Oliver smacks his lips. "You were making some interesting noises before I woke you up, Jules."

Jules.

Oh. My. God.

"My name is Julie." I stiffen my jaw. "Just like your name is Oliver, right?"

He nods. "Noted. So, your dream?"

"Wouldn't you like to know?" I mumble.

"Actually, I just might." He purses his lips. Once the Jeep pulls into the parking area of the cabin, my eyes widen. It looks like a lit glass beacon on the otherwise dark and damp lakefront. My stomach grumbles and Oliver snickers; I know he hears it too. "I'll get our bags—you go ahead inside and see if they have dinner started."

I shut the Jeep door behind me and trot toward the glass double doors of the front entrance. I hear laughter and crude comments coming from inside. Following the cheers and bottles clinking together, I enter the white-tiled kitchen. Six pairs of lips stop moving and six pairs of eyes fix on me.

"*Finally,*" Nora says, snorting. "We thought you two stopped off somewhere."

"I'm not her type or we would have," Oliver says from behind me, dropping my bags at my feet. "We had to get your snacks." He groans and shoves the shopping bags toward the group, then nods at his friends in a silent greeting. "Maybe you assholes can help me get the rest of my stuff." The three guys instantly stand up and follow Oliver outside while the three girls look at me in confusion.

"Meet Oliver Jackson, girls," Nora scoffs. "Just as I remember him: crude and self-absorbed."

Staci licks her lips. "I think he's sexy as hell."

Amber giggles. "Yeah, maybe I'll sneak into *his* room one night."

I gag. "Let me know since *I'm* sleeping in there too."

The three of them look at me with narrowed eyes. "Are you, now?" Staci smiles and smacks her lips together; her lip gloss looks like glue and that makes me want to laugh.

I nod and roll my eyes at them. "You other jerks pretty much smashed us together, taking up the other rooms. We basically don't have a choice." The guys come back in noisily and Oliver raises his eyebrows at me.

"I'll take your stuff up for you—you can thank me later in any way you see fit," he says. "Nora, always a pleasure." He nods at my friend and ignores the other two girls, but they don't mind.

I shake my head and look at Nora, my eyes narrowed in disgust. "Thanks for a *great* weekend, Nora."

I follow Oliver's heavy footsteps until I reach the doorway of the biggest bedroom I have ever seen. The walls are a sea foam green color and the dark-stained hardwood floor is slick and shiny under my feet. There are two light oak dressers, a medium flat-screen TV, a golden-colored chaise, and…the bed.

The.

BED.

"Go ahead," I hear him say as he walks out of the master bathroom. "Jump."

I roll my eyes. "I'm not going to jump on the bed, I'm twenty-two, not five."

His lips spread into an innocent smile and he walks up behind me, his hot breath on the back of my neck and ears. "You know you want to."

"I'll just unpack my stuff," I croak. My mouth is dry and I can smell his manly scent again.

Crap, crap, crap.

The dresser drawers creak when I open them and I shove every article of clothing I brought with me inside. It should've taken all of ten minutes to unpack everything, but I'm still exhausted from the drive, so I'm only halfway done after what seems like forever. Oliver has relaxed on one side of the bed, his shoes kicked off and his huge feet wiggling in the air underneath bright white socks. The hardness of his stomach and chest ripple as he stretches out and watches me flutter around the room, making sure everything is in the most logical place.

Everything in its place.

Except for me.

Right now, I have no place.

But I have my sadness.

And that counts for something…right?

THREE
OLIVER

ONE THING IS for damn sure: Julie is extremely frustrating to me.

I watch her bounce around our bedroom, putting things away and fretting over if I'd seen her panties before she throws them into a small dresser drawer. The entire dance she does turns me on. I admit, I'm a little frustrated that she isn't trying to show me her panties *on purpose*. I avert my eyes when she flicks her gaze toward me. I hope she doesn't know that I've been looking the whole time.

Not that I won't try and check those lacy things out while she's still wearing them.

My legs ache when she bends over. With the way her jean shorts hug her hips, I can just imagine how soft her skin must feel, but I stop myself. She still flutters around the room, her chest bouncing with her every move, and I fake a yawn and stretch out on the bed, shaking my head at her demanding one of my dresser drawers for her pajamas.

"What's mine is yours." I yawn for real this time, remembering that I haven't gotten very much sleep in the past few days because of my extracurricular activities at night. But Julie doesn't need to know about that.

She closes the drawer gently and leans back on it. I get a perfect view of the curves on both sides of her body and the way her slender, pointed nose turns down at me. "You can sleep for a while, if you want. I can cover for you downstairs."

How about I cover myself with *you, instead?* I clear my throat. This is getting out of hand already. I hadn't done the whole girlfriend and mushy feelings thing ever since Heather, and I'm not trying to start doing it now with a random girl I just met.

Still, she smells like strawberries and sunflowers —it makes me want to cover myself in her scent, but I take in a deep, sharp breath and she looks at me with bewildered eyes. "I should be okay, thanks though."

Julie makes a small noise and turns back to her suitcase. "That's all of it." She closes it, zips it up, and looks around for a place to put it. I close my eyes and let her think for a few more minutes, then stand up, taking the case from her. I push her onto the bed and my body's on fire now thinking of her pinned beneath me. I hurry and put her suitcase in the closet and rush from the room before I get any other stupid ideas.

What is wrong with me? I have to get out of here. **Now.**

"I've gotta go," I mumble and leave the room. I don't bother looking back at her; I know she's aware of my issues.

"Hey, bro," Casey says when I enter the living room, "did you want to grill some meat tonight? I had the caretaker go shopping before we got here."

I grunt. I'm glad that he's steering my attention away from someone I can't have. "Sure."

His eyebrows rise in suspicion. "What's wrong with you?"

I wave my hands. "Nothing. Where's the stuff for the grill?"

Casey points toward the back patio where everyone—except for Julie—is laughing, drinking, and hanging out around the large fire pit. I think about running back upstairs to grab her, but I tell myself that if she wants to be down here with me, then she will be.

I want her here.

"Oh, so you guys—" Nora snorts through her hysterical laughter. "—Is it okay if I invite another friend to come up in a few days?" I throw the large plate of turkey legs and steaks on the grill, slowly turning them.

"Sure, babe," Casey answers her. "Anything for you." I hear them sloppily kiss and a pain twinges in the bottom of my stomach. There is no way I'm going to turn and look at that while everyone else gushes over how cute they are.

"Awesome, you are so amazing. She's going to

love it here." Nora coos and I want to be sick all over the food.

"Food is done," I mutter after a few more minutes and look around behind me.

No Julie.

"I'm going to get Julie," I mutter again and leave the group. As I search the house, I finally find her tucked away on the chaise in our bedroom, a thick book open in her hands and a smile on her face. The soft light from the floor lamp next to her warms her face and her golden hair glows around her like an angel.

Whoa.

My heart races and I can feel the blood rush to my cheeks. I make sure to quickly turn and look away before she can catch me staring at her. It takes every ounce of strength I have left not to close the bedroom door and lock everyone else out.

"What the fuck?" I mouth.

"Hey," she says. "Did you need something?"

"Yeah—yes." I choke and turn back around, hoping that my face isn't red. "Are you hungry?"

Julie smiles and stands. "Actually, yes. Thank you."

"Okay." My body's frozen in place.

She rolls her eyes. "I can't walk *through* you to leave the room, you know."

My body is still frozen as my eyes focus on her lips. I *want* them; they're thick and pouty, and the bottom one is slightly pink from the way she bites it when she focuses on something—like she focuses on

32

her book when she's lost in the pages. I'm so much taller than her that I'm sure she feels uncomfortable, but I can't make myself move out of her way.

"O...kay." Her mouth moves into a perfect O-shape and my stomach drops. "I'll just find something to eat later. I want to finish my book before it gets too late."

Move, Oliver!

I finally gain control over my legs and walk toward her, furrowing my eyebrows. I'm angry at her for making me want her, and angry at myself for not being able to have her. "You're only like halfway through that thing," I say and snatch the book from her hands, smiling. "And at this rate it'll take all night long. Why not come and eat with me now?"

Her little nose twitches with annoyance as she grabs for the book, which I wave in my hands. "I'm not going to fawn over you, so you can forget about that."

"What is that supposed to mean?"

She sighs and grabs the book back. "It means you are very aware of your charisma and what you look like. I'm not here for some crazed, casual sex weekend with a stranger. I'm here because life sucks and I want to look at pretty trees and nature. Okay?"

Well, okay, then.

"Just come on," I demand, my eyes burning into hers.

She doesn't bother to look back up to me, sticking her nose back in her book and ignoring my demands.

What the hell? This won't do.

"Julie. Come. On."

Finally, her eyes meet mine again. "I'm not a child —you can't order me around to do what you want. I told you—"

I growl loudly and before my mind can catch up, I scoop her up, clutch her body hard against my chest —with only a small bit of want dripping from my skin—and storm out of the room with her fingernails digging into my neck and her feet kicking against my abs. She's frustrating me on purpose. "Put me down!" she squeals. The pressure of her sharp fingernails excites me, but it's the tone of her voice that ruins it.

There's no delight in her voice.

She *fears* me.

I put her down when we get to the bottom of the stairs.

"You are such a major jerk." She scowls and punches my arm, the book still in her hand. "I'm not some girl you have to save—I don't need you doing things for me."

"I'm sorry." I bow my head. "I'm not trying to be a jerk."

Julie isn't buying it. She taps her foot against the floor in annoyance.

"And I definitely don't think you need to be saved."

A small smile creeps across her face, and the knot in the pit of my stomach grows a little when she bites her lip.

She's thinking about me.

All my blood rushes to the lower half of my body.

"Can we just go eat?" I snap a little at her, annoyed with my inability to control myself.

Julie rolls her eyes. "Fine, but only because I'm actually hungry."

I smile and place my fingers lightly on her back, gently nudging her toward the back patio. The others are already helping themselves at a long table of food and laughing at something Casey had just said. He waves at us, then motions toward two empty seats at the end of the table.

I don't bother pulling out her chair for her, so I just sit down in my own and start filling my plate with meat and the steamed vegetables the girls have prepared. Julie hungrily eyeballs the steaks and turkey legs as I shove food into my mouth, but she just nibbles on some steamed asparagus and a few cheese cubes.

I cut a small portion of my steak off and plop it onto her plate, narrowing my eyes at her.

"I don't want that." Julie pouts and whispers, "Take it back."

"Is it not cooked the way you like it?" I frown. "How *do* you like your meat, Julie?" The girls giggle and Julie's eyes are wide. *There she goes, biting that lip again*. I'll have to make her stop doing that or it'll drive me crazy. "Do you want a beer?" My gaze never leaves hers for a second. She nods and starts to stand, but I hold my hand out to stop her. "I'll get it." I run off into the house, my tail between my legs.

At first, I drown myself with a few glasses of

cold tap water, letting the chill fill my insides and settle the little twinges in my stomach. I slam the glass down on the counter when the feeling starts to come back, throw the fridge door open, and grab three bottles of beer from the top shelf. I pop them all open and guzzle the first one instantly, tossing the remains into the recycle bin and letting the liquid fill my insides. "This isn't working." I'm starting on the second bottle when Julie walks into the kitchen.

Her honey blonde hair is braided down one side of her neck, exposing the other side of her pale collarbone. It's perfectly defined beneath her smooth skin, taunting me. I think about pressing my lips against it and find myself angry that the arousal has come back ten times worse than before.

"What isn't working?" she asks. She bends her head a little so her collarbone is exposed even more. My teeth start to grind; they want to sink into the skin there.

This isn't going to work for me.

Oh, no. Oliver, you are in trouble.

You *like* her.

"Oliver?" Julie's voice cuts through the silence. I nearly drop the bottle I'm holding at the way she says my name.

I gulp down the rest of the second beer. "Yeah?"

"I can get my own." She takes the third bottle from my hand. "Is this mine?" I nod and don't dare say a single word. Her lips touch the bottle and my skin starts to rage with fire. I slam my empty bottle down on the table in frustration, but she hardly notices my tantrum.

"So, a little information about me…" Her teeth play with the underside of her lip. "I don't usually eat meat and I'm actually talking about the food topic, not the…other one." She blushes a little and I want to reach out and run my thumb along the bottom of her lip, just to see how soft it is compared to what I think. "But it's sweet of you to care."

I choke when she says that.

Sweet. There's that word.

Heather used to call me sweet.

My bones grow cold and my smile stiffens. "I'm not sweet—don't say that. *Nothing* about me is sweet."

Julie's lips turn down, and without saying another word, she takes her drink back to the patio where the others are enjoying life. I grab a third beer and follow her back outside.

"Hey," Julie says to me, her voice dainty and faint, "are you sure you're okay?"

"He's fine," Casey chimes in, his voice booming in the backyard like he's speaking through a megaphone. He's slurring. "He's just brooding over his ex. Trust me, he'll be fine." He glares down the table at me. I know I'm putting a damper on the good mood —I just don't care.

I shoot him an I'm-going-to-kill-you look, but he doesn't notice. Now, his tongue is so far down Nora's throat that I want to vomit. The twins, Harley and Victor, hardly notice either, as they've intensified their moves on the other two girls that Nora brought with her.

And then there's Julie.

I like it when she blushes; it pulls at my insides and sets me on fire.

Stop thinking about her, man. What is wrong with you?

Julie starts reading her book again while sipping her beer and nibbling on the baby carrots that litter her plate. I look down at my lap, lost in my own thoughts and not even listening to the other conversations floating around the space between us. My hair falls into my eyes but I don't bother pushing it away this time.

I am sad.

I miss Heather.

I hate her, but I miss her.

Maybe I can forgive her.

"So, Oliver…" Nora clears her throat. "Do you remember that you and I've actually met before?"

I stare at my plate. "Before what?"

"Before Casey. You and I met at a few parties. We have some mutual friends."

I hardly care what Nora is talking about. I certainly don't care enough to ask her any further questions. Once the silence drags on, Nora takes the hint and stops talking to me. I have a lot of "friends" and she could be talking about any of a hundred people.

Julie giggles at something she read and I get nervous, sitting so close to her. She's sexy, in her own nerdy way, and that isn't going to stop me from wanting her so damn bad. I stare at her for longer than appropriate and I haven't even noticed that Casey and Nora have gotten up to disappear into their bedroom. After the conversations die out, the other two girls yawn, finish their pink wine, and giggle their way back into the house.

The twins drink more beer and Harley leans his body onto the table. "So, why are you still driving that shitty Jeep when you don't have to, man? You've got money—you should be investing in something with a few more zeros behind the price."

I blush, hoping that Julie's too involved in her book to listen. Another rule I live by: Don't let the women I sleep with know that I'm loaded. Not that I'm sleeping with her—yet. "Don't worry about that —just worry about the money I keep spending at your body shop fixing the damn thing all the time. I'm keeping you in business."

When Julie yawns and stretches, her chest moves with her and Harley and Victor stare at her with their tongues out, practically drooling. I want to jump them for even looking at her.

"Hey, I'm going to head upstairs and take a shower—can you light the fireplace when you come up?" I say in my best smooth Casanova voice. Julie's eyes flutter with confusion, glassy from looking at book pages for over an hour. One thing Casey managed to do before whisking Nora up here first was call the caretaker to get the cabin ready. I noticed firewood already stacked neatly in our bedroom fireplace earlier.

"Sure." She nods and rubs her temples. "Oh, shoot. I forgot ibuprofen when I packed earlier...do you think there's some inside?"

"Hey, you want to get into the hot tub?" Harley asks her. "It does wonders for headaches."

"Yeah, I'll go start it—you should join us," Victor adds.

Julie brushes them off and starts to stand up, taking my plate in her free hand. I growl at them and then glance at Julie, who stifles a laugh and picks up her plate too. "No thanks, guys." She faintly smiles and then without even looking at me, walks the dishes into the house and leaves the three of us in silence.

"Dude, if you want to fuck her, just say so," Harley whispers. "You don't have to act like a little bitch."

"I don't want to fuck her," I blurt. I try to lower my voice so she can't hear me from inside the house. "Quit being little creeps."

They look at each other in disgust. "We aren't creepy."

We hear dishes clanking in the kitchen. "Yeah, you are," Julie says loudly through the open patio doors. I raise my eyebrows at the twins and cock my head like, *See? I told you so.* I leave them arguing with each other and join her in the kitchen, but she's already left to go back upstairs. My heart sinks a little. I wanted to share that victory with her.

When I get to the bedroom, she's bent over, rummaging through a smaller backpack. "Oh, sorry." She blushes and sits down on the bed when she notices I've come into the room. "You wanted to take a shower? You can go ahead; I have to find my toothbrush anyway."

I have to force myself not to pick her up and take her into the shower with me. I grunt and mumble something that even I don't comprehend, but she doesn't bother to even look up at me. Her honey hair is loose now—she'd taken out her braid and the soft waves frame her body. As she sifts through her bag, I watch her carefully. I don't want her to know, so I pretend to be going through my suitcase for clothes.

"We can get you another one if you forgot it," I say. "I have to go into town later this week."

Julie smiles at me and holds up her purple toothbrush. "Again, sweet of you, but I found it."

Sweet. You're so sweet, Oliver.

I don't want to be sweet.

I wait as she slips in to brush her teeth and smile innocently when she returns. "All yours." I find so much pleasure in those two words that it's hard to keep calm.

"I'm going to shower now," I flatly say and leave the room. I have to go before my body totally explodes and I do something I'll probably regret later. When I stand in the shower, the hot water rushing over me, my mind goes back to Heather.

Talk about someone who I thought was perfect in every single way. Her jet-black hair shimmered when we showered together, and her lips are thin and powerful, making her smile light up the room. I start to get aroused, so I turn the heat down a little bit, letting the cooler water wash over me and help settle me down.

There's a small knock on the door. "Oliver?"

Shit. It's Julie. And I'm hard as hell.

"Ye-yeah?" My voice cracks so I allow water from the shower to loosen it. "What's wrong?"

The door opens and she lets cold air into the room. I hear her walk toward the shower. I *really* hope she's going to open the door and get in with me, but instead she lifts up the toilet lid and stands facing away from me like she could see through the glass. I smile and wonder if she can.

"I have to pee and Staci is in the hallway bathroom losing her pink wine," she says. "Don't look."

I scoff and decide not to tell her about the other two bathrooms inside the house. "Not my thing, baby."

She says nothing, and I hear her feet shuffling around. I know she can see my silhouette through the frosted glass of the large shower. I smile at the thought of her sitting across from me, watching me and wondering what I look like on the other side.

The room is silent until I hear her clear her throat in the awkward air. Suddenly I realize that if she pushes the lever down, my world is gonna be on fire. Before I can say anything, she flushes the toilet and I dance around the scalding hot water until I feel the cool breeze of the door opening and then closing. I quickly jump out of the heat and hop around the steamy bathroom.

I blow out hard. That was too fucking close.

The door opens suddenly and the cold air hits my naked body. Julie and I both freeze in place. Her eyes widen and she quickly fixes her gaze on mine. Embarrassed, she covers her eyes and squeaks, trying to run from the bathroom—but she runs into the wall instead. Her head makes a loud thump against the hard surface.

I spring into action, twirling her body around and moving her hands from her eyes so I can inspect her head for damage.

"Y-You're naked!" she squeaks. "*Naked* and I just burst in here—"

She's right.

I *am* still naked.

I immediately reach for my towel and wrap it around my lower half, almost definitely too late because I catch her glimpsing down there. Her face brightens, then almost immediately falls. "I-I'm going to change while you finish your shower," she says as she quickly leaves the room.

I stand in confusion for a moment. What the hell was that? Something switched inside her head—something put her off of me—and I don't think I like it. I return to the shower to think about what just happened and where I went wrong.

You're falling for someone you hardly know.

That's where you went wrong.

FOUR
JULIE

HE.

Is.

Naked.

So very naked.

My insides are squirming with pleasure as I stand in front of Oliver in the steamy bathroom, his... everything...just *out there* for me to see. This guy irritates me more than anyone ever has, and here he is, his huge muscles and huge—well—and I can probably reach out and touch if I want to.

Do I want to?

Yes!

But I don't dare move a single inch to give him any indication that I want to touch him. That's what a normal person would do in this situation, but that's not me. Staci would have jumped on his naked, wet body and rubbed herself like soap against his skin. Me? No, I cover my eyes like a little schoolgirl and apologize, then try to run and flee from the bathroom. I can't see where I'm going and run into the wall, bumping my forehead against it with a loud, hard smack. I feel the breeze change around me and a pair of rough hands twirl me around, but I won't let go of my eyes because if I can't see it, then it isn't real. "Are you okay?" Oliver asks me. I can smell the musky scent of his body wash and he brushes my hands away from my eyes.

I freeze at his touch.

"Y-You're naked," I stutter. "*Naked* and I just burst in here—"

I watch him grab for a towel immediately and wrap it around his lower half. I drop my gaze to the towel and then slowly move my eyes up his body. Droplets of water race from his hard chest and broad shoulders down to his stomach. Oliver towers over me—he could swallow me up if he wanted to, and I whimper silently under his hard, green-eyed glare. I can't tell if my mouth is open or not. I want him to devour my mouth with his; I want him to push me against the wall and just do whatever he damn well pleases, but instead, I think about Brandon and my body cools off almost instantly.

Oh, crap. What a mood killer.

I paste a weird smile on my face and make some odd remark just to get out of here. "I'm going to change while you finish your shower," I say and immediately leave the room, shutting the door behind me. I hold my breath, careful not to make a sound until I eventually hear him slide the shower door open and step back in.

What's wrong with me? It couldn't have been any easier for me than in that moment. I could've had him with almost no effort if I'd really wanted.

No, not me—I'm not the type of person who takes chances like that anymore.

Quickly changing, I choose the least sexy pajamas I brought with me: black leggings and an old t-shirt of Brandon's with some rock band's logo on it. I have to make sure I am in the bed before Oliver is…I want to get into a good sleeping position facing away from him as fast as I can so I don't have to look at him again after what just happened.

Oh, crap.

I forgot to light the fireplace.

I jump out of bed and find some fireplace matches on the mantle. I light one and throw it inside before shutting the gate and watching the ember grow slowly on the neatly stacked logs. I hear some rustling in the bathroom, so I race back to the bed and snuggle into my warm spot, which just happens to be facing the bathroom door that Oliver is now coming out of, towel around his waist and his hard, lean body displayed for me to see.

"Sorry, forgot to take clothes in with me," he says, opening his suitcase and pulling out some sweat-pants and a light blue V-neck t-shirt. He's combed his shaggy dark hair back and his lips are light pink from brushing his teeth. I touch my mouth as he looks over at me, and the smile on his face fades into a frown. He throws his towel into a large, wicker laundry basket and looks back toward me.

It takes me a few seconds before I finally realize I'm watching him. No...I'm *studying* him. My eyes lower to the perfect lines of his naked ass and it makes me blush that he notices my gaze hovering over it, but I...can't...look away. *Uh, wow.*

"You like what you see?" he asks, his emerald eyes burning into mine. He can trigger every nerve in my body with the way his gaze meets mine and washes all the bad feelings away. "I can show you a lot more than this if you really want to see something amazing."

I chuckle nervously. "No, thanks."

Oliver's thick lips curve and he bites his cheek. "Are you sure? It can be our little secret; I won't tell anyone that you secretly dream about me." Even his whisper jolts my insides, and he laughs when a shiver down my spine rocks me to my very core. "So, are we both sleeping in the bed, then?" His words are slow and drawn out as he examines me lying near the edge of the mattress. "I can sleep downstairs if it bothers you, you know...sleeping in a bed with a strange man and all. I wouldn't want anyone to think my intentions with you are less than honorable."

I know he hears me gulp.

"Just keep your hands to yourself and it'll be fine," I tell him, only half-serious, but the desire drips from my tongue. The bed moves underneath his weight as he slides his warm body under the comforter, dangerously close to mine. My mind starts to spin a little too fast. I think seriously about inching my body back a few centimeters, but decide it'd be too obvious that I'm trying to get away from him.

Oliver turns his body to face mine, but I don't do the same. There isn't anything for me back there. "So, who's the kid?"

"What kid?"

"That redheaded kid—is he your son?"

I laugh. "Oh, Clyde? No, he's my nephew."

"Oh, does he live with you?"

I finally give in and turn to face him. Is he trying to get to know me? The fire snaps and crackles, making the cool lake air coming in through the open window warm around us. "No, I live with *him*—and my brother, Randy. He's a detective for the Rockford PD." Even with the lights off, I can see his big eyes looking at mine, and he smiles when he catches me looking at him for too long. He knows that he's slayed me already; I just don't know how my mess of a self will be able to handle it when he makes a move.

"So, are you in college, then? You're twenty-two, so shouldn't you be graduating soon?"

My eyes narrow. "No, I never had the chance to go. I worked right out of high school."

He grunts. "That's a shame. But you have a job?"

"Not anymore. I lost it when I moved in with Randy to get away from—"

"You don't have to finish that sentence." His voice is rough, but he looks conflicted.

"What's with all of the questions?" I snap and roll my eyes, trying to push annoyance on him instead of desire. "Are you writing a story about me?"

Oliver laughs and it feels like warm syrup down my throat on Christmas morning. "That depends. What am I in your story?"

I swear I don't mean to literally gulp aloud for the millionth time. I know it's showing my hand every time, and I know that my face is beet red from blushing too. What's happening here? I try to catch my breath, but at the risk of being too obvious, my breathing becomes raspy and shallow as I catch a whiff of his woodsy scent and my brain almost melts. Breathing Oliver in must be like what the forest smells like after a microburst of afternoon rain.

"I guess we're friends," I say, swallowing the lump in my throat before it chokes me and I need mouth to mouth.

Oliver doesn't look amused. "You *guess* we're friends?"

"I just met you today." I laugh, and I can see that I've hurt his feelings. "We aren't really even friends."

Now I've *really* hurt his feelings. His expression darkens.

"What about you?" I blurt out, trying to keep the conversation light. "College, job?" I say when I see confusion in his eyes. He smiles a little; it seems like he can feel the need to change the subject too.

"I graduated from NYU a few years ago. Then my grandfather died and he left me some money. I haven't exactly been worried about finding a job yet."

His answer is so matter-of-fact, it sounds rehearsed. I think of other ways I can get to know him without stirring up his manhood—or thinking about his naked, juicy ass.

Oliver's eyes wander over the parts of my body that aren't covered up by the blanket we share. A few inches closer and our bodies will be touching, but I won't allow myself to do that.

I think about Brandon again.

That always kills the mood.

"Do you have a boyfriend?" His voice cuts through the darkness.

I gulp again, a little softer this time. "Not anymore."

"Oh, what happened? Bad breakup?"

I say nothing and hope he just lets it go.

"Me too." He sighs. "Mine was sleeping with her sister's husband."

I raise my eyebrows. "*She* cheated on *you*?"

He chuckles, which turns into an even weaker laugh. "Several times. In my bed. Why—you don't think someone like me can be cheated on?"

"It's hard to imagine." I turn away from him, hiding my face so he can't see the embarrassment. He doesn't say anything at first—he just lets me lie with him in the darkness while our thoughts race through the room, surrounding each other and picking fights about who was the worst at showing their hearts underneath all their locks and chains.

Oliver sighs and I can feel him inch toward me. "Hey, are you okay?"

"I'm fine, I'm just tired." I shiver from a deep yawn. He gives me a few more inches of his side of the blanket and lets me drift off to sleep, drunk off my own terrible thoughts. It doesn't even seem like I've fallen asleep when a noise outside wakes me and I stare into the pitch-black bedroom, listening to Oliver lightly snore next to me.

I can't believe how easy and safe it feels to be next to him.

I smile and shift my weight to get a better look at him in the moonlight. His eyelashes touch his cheeks and when he exhales, the strands of hair that had fallen in his face look like feathers in the wind. I can see his perfect teeth when he opens his mouth for a moment, but his full lips hide them quite well. He has some stubble on his face, but I imagine the scratchy whiskers brushing against my face and I have to press my legs together without moving the bed too much.

Suddenly, his snoring stops and he adjusts himself, so I gently roll away from him, but somehow, in his attempt to find comfort, he brushes against my arm and then it's like a magnet. I squeeze my eyes shut, careful not to show that I'm awake as his warm, rough hand slides down my side and finds the curve of my waist, squeezing it gently before resting there.

I don't move.

I *can't* move.

I don't want to move.

I let him lie with me like that for a few minutes until he groans in his sleep and mumbles something. I don't much care to even listen because if I move an inch on my own, it could all be over. I like his outdoorsy smell and how it surrounds my entire body.

His body stirs as his muscular arm slides around my stomach and tightens its grip. He flexes and pulls me into him, burying his face in my hair. My chest burns as he tucks me into his warm cocoon, softly moaning into the thick mess of my hair. He nuzzles his face against it.

"You smell so damn good," he whispers.

Wait, is he awake?

His soft snoring starts again, and I realize he's talking in his sleep. Okay…I'm safe. His grip around my body is so tight it's paralyzing. I can't move…not that I want to, really. I nestle my head into the pillow and close my eyes.

———

I MUST HAVE DOZED off again listening to his heavy breathing, because next thing I know I'm smelling cookies baking and I'm in a completely different place than a dark bedroom. The kitchen is huge—it has everything I could ever want to use for baking, wrapped up in one room.

I smile.

"Are they almost ready?" someone asks.

I sniff the air. "Almost."

Two arms pull me backward into a warm body and wrap themselves around my waist, giving it a squeeze. "Good," the voice whispers in my ear.

I lose control of my neck first—he brushes my hair to the side and kisses the tender part of it, his hot breath on my skin.

"I love you, Jules."

Brandon? I whip around.

Brandon. I must be dreaming. I *have* to be.

"What are you doing here?" I snap at him. "Get out."

He sits down at the kitchen table and laughs. "You obviously want me here or else you would be thinking about someone else."

I growl deep in the back of my throat. "I thought it *was* someone else."

"Yeah? The guy you've lucked into sleeping next to? Jules, come on. He's way out of your league." He chuckles.

My face heats. "He's better than you."

Brandon acts scared and waves his hands in the air. "Even if that were true, I was even out of *your* league. I only moved in with you because we'd been together so long. I felt sorry for you."

Before I can pounce on him and tear his eyeballs out, he's gone and I'm alone with cookies that need to be taken out of the oven before they burn. I set the tray on the cooling rack next to me and sigh. Besides the gourmet kitchen, I can see an overbearing dining room doorway a few feet from me. The longest dark oak table sits in the middle of the room with eight matching chairs around it. A glass chandelier reigns over the table, its twinkling lights illuminating everything below it.

I sigh. I can't stop thinking about Brandon now. His wavy, chestnut hair was a little too long when I left him. I think about his eyes: the darkness in them is what makes them that shade of brown. He isn't much shorter than Oliver, but he definitely lacks the muscle definition. Tall and thin with a permanent scowl. Nothing compared to the man lying next to me—hard bodied with a strong jawline.

"This is what you want but can't have," Brandon says.

"You again," I mutter. "Can't I just flick my fingers and wish you away?"

He laughs. "I'm not a genie, Jules. I'm just in your mind."

I'm starting to actually hate him now.

"Well, then, just go away." I blow air at him like that'd be strong enough to make him float away. "I don't care what my mind or my heart say. I don't want you here, so go. Away."

Brandon holds up his hands in surrender.

"Whatever you say."

I nod. "Yeah, whatever I say. Leave."

And he's gone again.

Every room I go in is magical in its own special way; I didn't want to leave the huge bathroom with the Jacuzzi tub and vaulted ceilings with skylights, but the last door I reach calls to me. It looks so familiar.

It's the same door that's on the bedroom I'm sleeping in.

Same fireplace.

Same bed.

Empty bed.

"There you are," he says as he comes out of the bathroom. "I was starting to worry that you lost your way back to me."

Oliver.

I gulp and look nervously behind me at the closed bedroom door, as if someone would come rushing in. "Brandon is here."

He doesn't look angry. "I know. I can keep you safe." He notices my face fall a little and walks over to me, hooking his index finger underneath my chin and pulling my face up toward his. "Don't worry; he can't do anything to us in here. This is our room." Oliver lowers his thick, warm lips to mine and kisses me with such passion, I feel the air being sucked out of the room. I gasp when he lets go of me, fall into his hard chest, and smile.

"Oliver," I say his name gently, careful not to burst the dream bubble, "why are you here?"

His face falls. "I thought you wanted me here."

"I do!" I squeak, panicking. "I really do. I guess I'm just a little confused."

His long, lean body inches closer to mine. "Don't think—just do." I leap at him and Oliver's tight arms flex around me; I'm eager and filled with all of the bottled-up longing that I've been saving just for him. In the real world, it's been six months or so since I've even seen a man naked, and I desperately want Oliver to be the first man to ravage me something fierce.

But as he presses my body into his, it's more gentle and romantic than I imagined it would be. He laughs into our kiss and picks me up, wrapping my legs around him and squeezing my ass as he walks toward the bed. "You are crazy beautiful, you know that, right?" He doesn't wait for me to answer as he lays me on the bed and examines my body before taking off his V-neck t-shirt.

I bite my bottom lip and smile. "I didn't know, but thanks for telling me."

His eyes lock on my lips. "Your smile fills my head with sunshine—how do you do that?"

My throat is so dry I have to swallow a few times before I can speak. "I-I'm not sure…"

Oliver licks his lips and lowers himself down next to me. His fingers play with the hem of my shirt. "It's almost morning." He yawns and stretches against me.

I yawn too. "I got no sleep."

He smiles and kisses my forehead. "Baby, stay with me and you'll *never* get any sleep."

Even in dream world, I am in way over my head.

FIVE
OLIVER

THE LIGHT of the new day blasts into the room like fireworks. It doesn't feel like I've been asleep that long; my eyes are still sticky and thick with leftover bits of dreams dancing on my eyelashes. Yawning, I close my eyes again and snuggle back into the pillow, the aroma of sunflowers and strawberries filling my head. It's so nice that it makes a wide smile spread across my face.

Oh, right.

I'm not alone.

Julie's curvy body is tucked into mine—I can feel my hard-on poking her ass gently, but that doesn't bother me as much as it probably should. When I open my eyes, I see a mess of honey blonde hair and I feel my hands sliding around her body without my consent or my direction. Julie's body is real and it makes my head spin. I like that she's softer—that I don't feel bones when I slide my hands around her.

She's curvier than I'm used to. It's exciting to think about her warm, thick thighs—exciting in a way I've never felt before. My hands finally stop a few inches short of her breasts, and now she's gonna know for sure that I'm turned on because I'm getting harder. I have to let her go before she wakes up and kills me for touching her like I am.

I slide my arms out from around her and squint, watching her bite her bottom lip and smile into her pillow.

Oh, no. I have to get out of this bed.

Don't look at her Oliver, just get up.

I manage to leave the bed without stirring her, but I tower over her body, assessing what I've just woken up to. I don't even bother to dress before I open the bedroom door and sneak into the hallway, pushing the hair from my face so I don't miss a step down the stairs. When I walk into the kitchen, I let out a huge, relieved sigh.

I didn't make it without anyone else seeing me, though. Casey and Nora both raise their eyebrows at me over their coffee mugs, throwing knowing stares. "Good morning, Ollie," Casey says and snickers. "You have some serious bedhead, brother."

I growl. "You try sleeping next to a stranger."

Nora giggles and slaps Casey's hand away. Their PDA makes me want to gag—I wish they'd turn that crap off. "Oh, sometimes it's not that bad," she says.

"Coffee. I need coffee before I listen to all of this," I grumble and push my hair back. "Then I'm going to work out."

Casey scoffs. "No surprise there."

I shake my head and pour the coffee. The steam tickles my nose as I blow on it—I don't want to burn my mouth just in case I need it later for something exciting. Not only do I need to release tension about my hate for Heather, but now I need to add my lust for Julie to the list. I feel like my brain is tugging me in sixteen different directions and the two lovebirds making out in the corner aren't helping me think any clearer. I know I have to go back into the bedroom to get workout clothes, so my heart skips a little. I hope I can sneak a peek of her sleeping again.

I enter the room and she's cuddled up with all of the pillows, a sweet smile on her face.

Damn.

She's cute.

Oh, dude, come on, get your stuff and get out of here.

I strip naked and throw on different sweats, a clean t-shirt, and a pair of socks, but finding my sneakers is a much harder task. That requires moving a bunch of stuff next to the bed and then sifting through a suitcase with a loud-ass zipper, but I succeed and nod in victory to myself.

My weight on the bed makes her stir a little. I pick up the coffee cup from the bedside table and swallow some before she rolls toward me. I freeze, thinking I did all that quiet maneuvering for nothing. Julie looks like she's at such peace that it makes me smile. I wonder what she's dreaming about—

No.

No, Oliver you don't.

"Fuck," I hiss. The weight of keeping myself from thinking about her is finally taking its toll on my mind. "I'm a fucking mess."

I hear her yawn behind me. "You can say that again."

Forcing a smile on my face, I turn to face her. "Well, good morning."

"Yeah, morning." She stretches out and she's still small enough to fit into my pocket. Her hips call to me as the blanket uncovers them. Her teeth sink into her bottom lip as she fights sleep and tries her best to wake up. "Is that coffee?" She bats her eyelashes.

I hand her the cup without question. "Do you need anything else?"

Oliver, you aren't her boyfriend…

She shakes her head and smiles. Her hair is a mess too. "I'm good, thanks for asking. That's—"

"I have to get out of here," I blurt before she can call me "sweet" again.

"Okay, see you." She says it with such breeze that it actually feels like it annoys her that I don't want to stay and talk. I'm probably blowing this entire thing out of proportion—I tend to do that with things—women—I want. She snuggles back into the blanket and closes her eyes, shutting me out and forgetting all about me.

I don't like that at all.

I leave her and lock myself inside the basement gym, where I push my body harder than I probably should, but I'm so frustrated that it feels good to have the distraction. It's temporary, though. The weights, the treadmill, the pull-ups, and the countless other body-numbing things I could've done... nothing makes me forget about the confusion inside my head.

Heather.

Julie.

I hate Heather.

I do not hate Julie.

I miss Heather.

After a few more minutes of killing myself and realizing it isn't going to help me, I give up and wipe the sweat from my eyes, looking at the clock.

Eleven o'clock.

I've been in here for two hours.

The mini-bar has bottled water on top, so I grab one and drink it, then open a second and down that one too. My shirt is soaking wet, so I pull it off and almost do the same with my sweats but remember there are other people in the house. I'll just have to suffer until I reach the bedroom.

"Whoa, hey," I hear someone say behind me as I try to sneak up the stairs. "Sweat, much?"

I turn. It's one of the other girls.

"Staci," she says. I guess it's obvious I don't remember her name.

I click my tongue. "Yeah, sorry, I was working out."

She bats her lashes—heavy with eyeliner—at me. "I can see that." The growl in her voice grosses me out but I do my best to hide it. Okay, down girl. I definitely don't need any of that.

"Working off some sexual tension?" She giggles.

You can say that again, a million times over.

I fake a laugh. "Sexual tension from who, exactly?"

She throws me a weird expression and it makes me uncomfortable to be alone with her.

"Okay, well, I'm headed up to shower now," I blandly say.

She smiles. "Do you want company?"

"No thanks." I smile at her.

Staci giggles and kisses me on the cheek. "Rain check, sexy?" I say nothing as she climbs the rest of the stairs and disappears.

"Propositioned by Staci on the second day," Julie's voice, amused, says from behind me. "I'm surprised it took her so long to try and snag you. Can you pick up your jaw from the floor and move so the rest of us can go about our days?"

I look at her with annoyance. "Jealous."

Her laugh is loud and real. "Nowhere near jealous."

"You know," I growl and stand my ground, not letting her pass, "you're frustrating as hell."

Julie nods and her hair falls in waves around her face. "Tell me lies, tell me sweet little lies. Can I pass now?" I give up and move my body over and she brushes past me, making damn sure she touches my arm with hers as she passes by.

"I'm heading up to shower, okay?" I call after her.

She ignores me—she's already in the bathroom when I make my way upstairs and into our bedroom. Once again, I call out what my plans are, but she says nothing. I wait a few minutes before the annoyance builds up so much that I bite my cheek and open the door, not caring what she's doing or what I'm about to see.

"Oliver!" she screams my name.

I mean—*Screams. My. Name.*

"Get out!"

Her body is stretched out, her right leg hoisted up on the sink. A towel is wrapped around her—*I assume*—naked body and she has knotted her honey hair on the top of her head. White shaving cream is lathered down her leg, and if she raises it any higher, I'm going to be able to see all of—*everything*. I startle her so much that her hand slips with the razor and she clutches her chest, catching her breath.

I'm the one to see the blood first.

"Oh, shit." I run over to her, grab her slippery leg, and hold it firm. The remains of the shaving cream run down my hands and my mind goes blank. "You're bleeding." Her whimper makes me spring into action, scooping her up and getting into the shower with her to wash off the remaining shaving cream from both of us, but I quickly realize—when the water hits her open wound and she lets out a guttural, primal scream—that it's the wrong thing to do. "I'm sorry," I say as I pick her back up and start to panic a little more with each passing second.

Okay, Oliver, just calm down. Look at her leg.

The gash in her leg is pretty deep.

"I am *so* sorry," I say again.

Julie blows out a deep breath. "It's okay; it isn't your fault."

After placing a towel over the gash and pressing down, I carry her to the bed and sit down next to her. I keep applying pressure the best I can without hurting her. "I shouldn't have scared you—I really am sorry," I blurt out.

"Hey…" She tilts her head so she can look into my eyes. "It's really okay. Let's look at it."

I suck in air through my teeth to brace myself. "It's bleeding pretty badly; should I take you to the hospital?"

Julie laughs and I feel a little better. "I hardly think it's that bad." She pulls back the towel and a green look comes across her face. "On second thought, maybe we should go just in case."

I groan. "I really am sorry—"

"You can grovel on the way to the hospital." She waves me off. "Can I borrow one of your shirts and a pair of boxers?"

I instantly get hard when I see her slip into my clothes, careful not to get the blood on them, but I don't care about that. I definitely didn't want the first time I saw Julie naked to result in a trip to the ER. My clothes are wet from getting in the shower with her, so I change quickly while she's distracted. Before she can protest, I pick her up, grab my keys and wallet, and carry her all the way through the house and to the Jeep. No one even notices us as I put her in the passenger seat and pull out of the long, gravel drive.

"Are you okay?" I ask her.

She doesn't look at me. "I'm fine."

You are not fine.

"Julie, I really am sorry."

"You say that an awful lot to me." Her voice is thick with ice and I know it's to freeze me out. "I think I'll sleep in the girls' room and let you have the bedroom…it's your house, after all."

"No, I don't want that," I say, concentrating on the road the best I can.

Her sadness matches mine completely for the first time since we met. "I do."

Oh, man. Dagger to my chest.

I'm seething now. I don't know what else I can do to make her believe I'm a better person than this. I want her to see me how I see her so badly. "You have to believe that I didn't mean to hurt you, right? I don't know what it is we have between us, but the bickering and shit has to stop."

Julie smiles when we arrive at the emergency room entrance. "You think we have something between us?"

"I don't know, do we?" I smile at her. "I don't want you to move rooms."

"Then I won't."

She lets me help her out of the Jeep, then lets me throw one of my jackets over her as we walk through the emergency room doors. We check in and wait for what seems like forever. I offer her soda and candy as bribes, but it really seems like she's okay when we finally get called back by a big, surly looking nurse. She moves Julie's leg to the side and she winces in pain. Julie reaches for me and grabs my hand, squeezing tight enough where I feel a little pain. The nurse uses her forefingers to open the wound wider, making Julie bury her head into my chest and cry.

"Hey, you're making her cry," I snap at the nurse.

She rolls her eyes. "She needs stitches—how did this happen?"

"I cut myself shaving," Julie sobs into my shirt. "Can you hurry?"

The nurse isn't amused. "I'll give you something for the pain and the doctor will come in and stitch you up. Be right back."

I let Julie clutch onto me as long as she needs. After all, this *is* my fault. "Hey, Julie?" I say in a soft voice. "Do you want anything?"

Her small giggle excites me. "No, I'm still good. I'm sorry for wetting your shirt."

My hair falls into my face as I look down at her, snuggled in my chest and—"Uh," I mutter, slightly moving so she'd move her head, "I think I'll go see where the doctor is."

Before I can do anything, there's a knock at the door and a doctor comes in, making a few corny jokes as the nurse gives us a bottle of pills for pain. Ten minutes later, we're headed out the double doors and back to the cabin. Julie had taken one of the pills before we left and I notice her eyes starting to glass over a little, so I help her into the Jeep and shut the door behind her.

"Oliver?"

Oh, shit. Her voice drives me fucking crazy.

"Y-Yeah?" I croak.

Her honey hair is next to me now…her sunshine is breaking into my head. "Thanks for taking care of me. I'm glad I met you. You're not self-absorbed and crude like Nora says…not really." Her words slur as she snuggles into my side. The smart thing for me to do would be to put her back on her side, buckle her in, and go home.

"Nora said I was—?"

Her eyes are closed and I shake my head as she falls into a deeper sleep. Her body is cuddled into mine, so I wrap my right arm around her and pull the Jeep from the parking lot.

The rest of the drive back to the cabin is silent as she dozes off from the pills. I like her when she sleeps—she looks peaceful and at ease, like she knows something the rest of us don't. I admit, I steal a few glances at her as I drive back to the cabin, unaware that both of our phones have been ringing off the hook the whole time we've been gone.

"Where the hell have you two been, and what the hell is wrong with her?" Nora screams at me when I carry Julie's limp body into the house. She runs over to us and dramatically checks for a pulse. "Put her down! What did you do to her?"

Julie yawns and snuggles into my chest. "I had to get stitches."

I raise my eyebrow at Nora. "Right leg, check it."

She looks at her friend's leg and then back at me. "And you took her to the ER?" Nora thinks for a moment. "Okay, that's—fine, I guess. Thanks."

"Wow, way to be sincere." I snort. "Can you move so I can put her ass to bed? Someone self-absorbed and crude wouldn't make sure she got there safely, would they?"

Nora blushes. "Oliver, I—"

I roll my eyes and blow hair from my face. "Save it. I don't care what you think of me."

Nora moves out of my way and I stomp, on purpose, all the way to the bedroom and lay Julie on the bed, collapsing next to her to catch my breath. She breathes softly and I know she's asleep, so I don't bother telling her to take off my jacket. I stand up and gently move her body horizontally, cover her with a light blanket at the end of the bed, and swiftly lie back down next to her.

I want her to roll over and lie on my chest.

Maybe I could give her a nudge.

No, don't. Leave her alone.

Then, a knock on the door makes Julie stir and almost wake up.

"What!" I hiss toward the opening door.

It's Casey. "Dude, is she really okay?"

"Shut the hell up!" I hiss again. "You're going to wake her up!"

He holds up his hands in surrender. "Okay, okay," he whispers and eyeballs the two of us, lying in the bed next to each other. "Is she okay? I see the bloody towels."

I nod. "She's fine. Twenty stitches, pain pills, and this—" I wave my hands over her body. "She's a zombie."

He stifles a laugh. "A cute zombie."

"I'm going to try and take a nap; did you want something?" I snap.

"Just checking on her, man." Defeated, he turns to leave the room. "Look, I'm sorry about what Nora thinks about you, okay? She knew you before she and I met, and I really like her. I thought bringing her here with you would change her mind on it."

"I don't remember meeting her, Casey," I tell him.

He shrugs. "I know that, man. Look, don't worry about it. I'll leave you two alone."

I salute him as he walks out, then get up to light the fireplace. I poke the wood until cozy warmth fills the chilly room. It's always cooler at Lake Reed no matter what time of the year it is.

I slide back in next to her and relax, making sure I don't touch her in any way. The fire snaps and I smile; I like that sound.

Julie softly moans in her sleep.

I *definitely* like that sound.

Heather.

I thought Heather was cute too.

And sweet. Kind. Loving. Wife material, maybe.

Turns out, she isn't.

I drift into a light sleep.

———

As I ENTER my front door, I think that it's weird that Heather's Audi is home in the middle of the day. I'm pretty sure she has a standing mid-afternoon social event every day, so coming home at two o'clock on a Thursday and seeing her car here is a bit odd. I know I haven't been home much; my grandfather had some business I needed to tie up in New York. I was pretty good about keeping tabs on the woman sharing my bed, but still, maybe she invited some friends over that she neglected to tell me about.

You know better than that, Oliver.

Turn back.

I put my keys in that stupid ceramic bowl Heather insisted on paying three hundred dollars for and scowl.

Dude, turn back.

I hear her. She giggles and moans.

TURN. BACK.

She moans louder. My heart races because I haven't heard that moan in weeks.

I want her.

I want to burst into the room and take her—she must be watching a dirty movie.

I hear her moan again, louder, as I get to the bedroom door.

You don't want to go in there.

I go in there because I want her.

I go in there and see her with someone else.

They don't see me.

She moans and calls out his name.

Suddenly, the room is empty and they're gone.

I smell bacon and my mouth waters. I follow the scent downstairs into the kitchen at the cabin.

Julie.

Her face brightens when I walk in. I'm confused, but watching her twitter about, humming to herself and mixing some large bowl of batter, my heart sings.

Yeah, fucking sings.

"Hey, don't just stand there." She giggles. "Lend me a hand."

I smile down at her as I approach her side. She giggles again and hands me a wooden spoon and the bowl, mouthing the word, "Stir" at me. I do what she says; I'm afraid to disappoint her. Her long honey hair is braided down her left side and I feel my legs start to shake from excitement. She dips her finger in the batter and puts it in her mouth, sucking off the tan glob. Her eyes roll to the back of her head. "Perfect."

I groan. "Why do you like to tease me so much?"

She smiles around her finger. "Why do you like it so much?"

"I think you mean why do I love it so much?" The smile that spreads across my face is instant and feels good...it feels so damn good to be happy. I can't remember this feeling; I'm not even sure that I've felt this kind of happiness before I met Julie. I don't even know what it is about her that makes me happy, not that I care to question it.

I raise my hand to touch her face, bringing my lips down to meet hers. She kisses me with so much longing that it's hard to breathe after a few minutes. I press her body against mine and lift her up, placing her on the

71

kitchen counter and losing myself, kissing and nibbling on her neck and collarbone.

Julie whispers my name.

"My head is going to fucking explode." I try and catch my breath as I nuzzle her ear and my lips graze the curve of her neck. "I don't know what you're doing to me, Julie."

"It's okay to let go and feel something," Julie tells me as she tangles her long fingers in my shaggy hair. "We can be like this, you know. We can have this."

"I don't want you to hurt me," I admit to her. "I'm done with that."

Her giggle is sexy. "I won't hurt you unless you want me to."

"When did you get so bold?" I ask, pressing my body deeper between her open legs. She lets me in without restriction. She wants me too.

"Another time. It's time for you to wake up."

And sexy Julie is gone.

———

MY EYES OPEN SWIFTLY. "What the hell?" I whisper.

"Did I wake you?" Julie asks, still half-asleep next to me.

I shrug my shoulders and shake my head. "You could say that."

Right here.

Right here is where it started.

I have a series of pissed-off moments where I wish I could go right back to sleep and back to my dream, followed by several screw-it moments where

I want to ignore my mind completely and do something stupid. There is a war waging between my head and my heart.

My head wins.

"Screw it," I say out loud.

Julie looks over at me, confused. I don't let her speak—I pull her toward me and devour her lips. I'm hungry for her after that dream; I want her more than I've ever wanted anyone. I can feel her relax her body into mine as I kiss her, our lips parting and rejoining as we breathe shallowly together. She lets out a small moan into my mouth and I tighten my grip on her, pressing my hard-on into the bare flesh of her thigh.

This is everything I thought it would be.

I am *kissing* Julie.

My thumb finds the corner of her mouth and rests there. I am leading her lips on a roller coaster ride; her mouth tastes like mint.

I make myself pull away from her and look down. Her eyes are on fire.

"What—what was that?" she breathes.

My eyes close and I shake my head. "Fuck, I'm sorry."

"For what?" she says, touching her lips. "That was…intense."

"I shouldn't have done that."

Julie's face falls. "Oh, I see."

"No, it's not you," I assure her and run my fingers through my hair. "I just don't want to give you the wrong idea."

"By kissing me?" she hisses. "Oh my God, just when I thought you couldn't be any more of a jerk."

She leaves me on the bed alone, everything short of slapping me in the face. I deserve it, I really do. I want her so bad, but I'm not willing to lie to her to get it. I don't want to take her home—I want to sleep with her for a week and then leave her behind, right?

Keeping it casual.

See, there I am.

SIX
JULIE

I LITERALLY WANT to punch Oliver in his smug face.

I made a silent point and slept in the living room last night, in protest of his shameless kissing fiasco, and the only thing that got me was a half-chilly Monday and loneliness. Everyone else had plans— they'd all coupled up and did sweet little things, then howled like animals at night. So, even if I wanted to sleep in the girls' room, I couldn't. It was no longer the girls' room—it's Harley and Staci's room.

And they are *loud*.

Oliver and I lie in the firelight, trying not to think about the loud moans coming from them just across the hall. I blush, using the darkness to hide my embarrassment because it's sort of turning me on. "They are so damn loud," Oliver growls, his arms covering his face as if that would drown the two of them out.

"Just tune it out," I say and turn away from him

on purpose. "You're good at ignoring the obvious anyway."

He laughs at me with such gusto that it makes my skin tingle. "Is that so?"

"You don't have to be such as ass all of the time, you *do* know that, right?" I blurt out and suck in air. "Sorry, I shouldn't have said that."

He waves his hand at me like a white flag. "No offense taken. You of all people have every right."

You're absolutely freaking right, I have the right. If kissing me and then telling me you didn't want to kiss me ten seconds later was any indication of how badly I need to punch you in the face, then green light's a-go, mister. I bite my bottom lip and stare at the ceiling. It's just ridiculous how close he is to me yet how far away he makes himself.

"Hey, I was thinking about heading into town tomorrow." He's trying to talk over the loud sex noises down the hall. "Do you want to go? Might do both of us some good to get out of here for a day. Maybe we can escape the escapades across the damn hallway."

I fake a loud gasp and roll my body over to face him again. A boyish grin spreads across his handsome face. "Me? Be seen with *you*? Are you sure that's okay?"

Oliver isn't amused. "I said I was sorry. What else do you want?"

My lips flatten into a thin, frustrated line. "You say that a lot. It loses its meaning after the first dozen times."

"What do you want from me?" His voice grows gruff and scary—it vibrates up his throat and reaches out to grab me.

I sigh and roll back away from him, this time fully focused on not letting him get to me again. "Nothing, I'll let it go."

"Thank God," he murmurs, but I hear him mumble something under his breath. I don't care, I don't care, I hardly care at all….Okay, I want to know what he said, but I don't want him to know I'm thinking about him…

"You're thinking awfully loud over there." His deep voice sends shivers down my spine.

"I'm trying to sleep," I mutter. Oliver's breath is hot as it reaches the bare flesh on my shoulder and I shiver more noticeably this time. His breath smells like whiskey, the remnants of his several nightcaps with the boys floating in the air for me to breathe in.

"So, the mall with me tomorrow?" He pokes my side playfully, making that burning feeling inside of me return in the pit of my stomach each time his warm finger meets the soft part of my hip. I make a point to take a few lengthy seconds to answer. "No, I think I'll take a hike tomorrow."

"Hey, I can come with you if you want." He starts to sound like he's moving closer to my ear, inch by inch, and the bed shakes from my skin trembling in the darkness. I make a weird grunting noise and allow him to collect his thoughts—maybe take back what he just said to save a little face and back down.

"You don't want me to come with you." He blows

out hard air, making strands of my hair float in the sudden breeze. "Okay, then, I get it: I'm a jerk and you don't want to be around me."

The air grows cold between us. I can feel it from behind me, folding my body into it. I don't like being mean to him just for the fun of it. "You can come with me," I say into the dark night air. "I want you to come."

He scoffs. "Yeah, sure you do."

I groan aloud and turn my body, this time with such velocity, that the bed shakes a little more than I wanted. It tosses me toward him, my chest resting against his hard, warm torso. He makes a small, sexy, agreeing noise and doesn't bother pushing me away. His rough hand squeezes my hip, his green eyes sparkling down at me. I place my palm on his chest and try to push myself away from him, but his grip isn't letting me go anywhere.

"How much do you want me to go on your hike with you?" His voice shakes with laughter. "Bad enough to kiss me again?"

I scoff. "Kiss *you*? You kissed me! *You* practically attacked *me*!"

Oliver's grip tightens, his thumbs moving inside the fabric of my pajama shorts. My legs lose all feeling in seconds as the rough edge of his finger leaves a mark on my hot skin. "Oh, yeah? Maybe I can do something to redeem myself."

My eyes narrow. "I can't take this back and forth anymore. You should let me go."

"And if I don't?" A wicked smile flashes across his face and he lowers his lips onto mine.

My entire body feels like jolts of electricity are rushing through it at the speed of light. I allow myself to relax into his grip and he takes charge, caressing my tongue with his and melting my anger into putty. Even for our second impromptu kiss, he completely tangles my insides. I let myself glide toward him; his hungry, low growl lurches from the back of his throat and I know it's time to stop.

I pull away gently and don't look at him. Oliver sighs and runs his finger down my collarbone. "I still hold a grudge for my ex." His voice is shallow but stable, as if he's choosing the right words to say before committing to them. "It's been hard to let her go...she messed me up really bad, I won't lie." He trails off and runs his fingers through his dark, chocolate hair. "I guess...I mean, we can both feel the attraction, right?" I watch his large hands motion between us. "*I* can definitely feel it."

I giggle. "I can feel it too."

He smiles and I smile back. "Good, so it's not just me. I just don't want to hurt you, Julie, you know. I want to figure out what this is, if I'm into you for the wrong reasons or—"

"I get it, Oliver," I snap. "No need to explain."

I can feel his heart beat through my t-shirt. "No, come on, don't do that." He lifts my face to his and lightly kisses my lips. "I just don't know what I'm doing when it comes to you."

I scoff, annoyed. "Seems pretty obvious to me."

Oliver's laugh feels like silk bed sheets against newly clean skin. "I'm going on that hike with you tomorrow."

"Yeah? What makes you think you're still invited?"

"Well, if you get eaten by bears I would never forgive you." He smiles at me and we both burst into laughter, the bed shaking beneath us. In this moment, as he stifles his laughter and locks his gaze with mine, I feel *sexy*.

"Okay, you can go with me under one condition," I say as he lowers his head toward mine, no doubt going in for another kiss.

Oliver clears his throat. "And what's that?"

My mouth is suddenly very dry. I don't want to ruin the moment by trying to have a real conversation, but I'm growing weary of the hot and cold thing he loves doing so much with me. I notice him looking at me, puzzled. "You can't be a jerk to me anymore."

His sadness feels like a heat wave on my skin, slightly burning me. "Okay, look. We're both coming from bad situations," I say. "We both deserve to be happy. Let's just enjoy this week and be happy together, enjoy each other, and once we go home, we can see where life takes us." My mouth always moves ten seconds faster than my heart.

His hair falls into his face and he smiles down at me. "Does that mean I still get to kiss you whenever I want?" He glides his tongue across his teeth and smiles. "I could use some of that in my life."

My cheeks slowly heat. "You never had that to begin with—don't push it."

He groans playfully and grips my hip, pulling me closer to him. "I can't spend a lot of time with you without touching you, Julie." His voice is so matter-of-fact, it makes me shiver. "I want you—there's no secret about that." His warm index finger traces the spaghetti strap tank top I'm wearing and butterflies flutter around my ribcage. His lips lightly graze my collarbone as my breath thickens and I grip the back of his head. He pulls me on top of him, pressing his lips to mine and holding me against his body with force. "I want you." He breathes the words and then we hear it.

Staci cries out Harley's name.

Oliver's face twists in horror. "Sorry, that killed it for me." He slides me from on top of him to his side and shakes his head. "They need to shut the hell up!" he screams so they can hear him, then huffs, crossing his arms. I giggle at his pouty lips and roll back over, turning off the bedside lamp. In the darkness, I wait for him to slide his rough hand over my hip and graze my curves, but after a few minutes, I let my body relax into the soft mattress in defeat.

"Hey," he whispers dangerously close behind my ear, "I like how you see me sometimes, you know? I haven't had someone look at me like you do in a long time."

My breathing deepens. "For someone as ice cold as you try and pull off being, you sure do wear your heart on your sleeve, Oliver."

There it is.

His hand.

Oliver's fingers tug at my side and he gently forces me toward him. I can feel the heat of his hard chest on my back and again, my body stiffens and I wait for more. I feel the ember inside of me growing, getting hotter the closer he gets to my center. Instead of ravaging me, he nestles himself into my blonde mess of hair and breathes in, satisfied, as his hands grip my side gently. His fingers start to slide down my thigh, and before I can push his hand away from slipping in between my legs, he swiftly turns my body and pulls me on top of him again. He presses my lips to his; he moans into my mouth, and as he holds me against him, his warmth is the most incredible thing I've ever felt.

"Why do you like teasing me so much?" he growls and kisses my forehead, releasing me and putting me back down next to him. "It's frustrating."

"I'm not trying to be." I gasp for air, the walls closing in around me. "This is all confusing for me."

"Why am I so addicted to you?" He cradles my head to kiss me, looking into my eyes with such intense desire that it makes me shiver. "Do I make you feel safe?" he asks me.

"Safe?" I breathe out slowly, my eyes halfway closed.

Oliver laughs low. "Yes, safe." I can barely hear him over my own thoughts, which are racing around me faster than I can catch them. "Do you trust me?"

"Yes," I instantly say, swatting my brain so it will shut up.

He makes that sexy agreeing sound and releases me, my body still shivering from whatever the heck he just did to me. "Good, now get some rest for our hike tomorrow."

————

"JULES." I hear a voice like nails on a chalkboard. "How many times have I asked you not to go to bed without me?"

Brandon.

I cringe and I can feel myself cower. "Sorry."

His scratchy voice sighs and I feel his weight on the bed behind me. "I just wish you were better, that's all." I silently cry, but the bed shakes anyway. "Come on, Jules." He throws his arm around my chest and lightly squeezes. "Don't cry. All you have to do is be better, okay?"

"Okay," I say in a soft voice. "Sorry."

Brandon is annoyed. He hates it when I constantly apologize. His grip around me tightens and I wait for it— wait for the first blow. Instead, he lights a cigarette and lets go of me. I hear him breathe the smoke in and out. "Stop always saying, 'I'm sorry.' It's pathetic." He undresses and purposely misses the laundry basket. I can feel his smirk from behind me, imagining me slaving over his dirty clothes. "I'm going to take a shower; come with me," he demands.

————

"JULIE! COME ON, WAKE UP!" Oliver's smooth and safe voice cuts through my dream and I wake up to him shaking me, terror in his eyes. He gasps and clutches me to his chest. I feel the wetness where my tears were staining his t-shirt. "What the hell was that?" He breathes into my hair and tightens his grip. "That was really scary."

"Sorry," I say and wince, waiting for the annoyance from him. I'd gotten his shirt wet yet again.

Oliver strokes my hair gently. "Sorry? For having a nightmare?"

No, sorry for being a mess when you want a princess.

SEVEN
BRANDON

GOD, *where the hell is she?*

I dial her number, and again it goes straight to voicemail.

"Hey, this is Julie."

She laughs and it makes me want to reach through the phone to at least touch her—or grab her. That rich jerk she's hiding out with doesn't know what he has—he isn't going to appreciate her until it's too late, either.

"Well, you know who this is, since you're the one who called me."

I smile. One of the reasons I fell for her in the first place is her ability to be such a complete nerd, but still manage to captivate the people around her.

"So, leave a message and I promise I will call you back."

I growl and hit the end call button on the phone. I'm going to find her. I text my friend Nate, telling him to come over, and while I wait for him in the apartment I used to share with her, I stop and look around, trying to find something of hers so I can feel normal again. I've done some questionable and horrible things in life, but cheating on Julie with my boss' daughter is the worst.

The. Worst.

I hate myself for even starting it.

Julie probably hates me too.

I was horrible to her the four years we were together. I want to make up for that, but she has to answer the damn phone, doesn't she? I know she's been living with her brother, Randy, and his little demon spawn, Clyde, over in the rich part of Rockford. Her pool house is probably bigger than this apartment. Randy and Clyde both hated me before all of this happened and would probably like to see me dead now, so I know they won't help me find her. I have to find someone that has a big mouth and actually likes me somewhat.

Nate comes through the door, shaking his head. "Just let her go, man—don't do this to yourself." He's just gotten done with a pick-up basketball game; it makes me cringe when his sweat pours over my favorite leather armchair. I can see the glisten of the wet spots as he brings his foot onto the seat to tie his shoe.

I violently shake my head. "No, I know she went somewhere with some rich guy…I got that much out of Nora, but I need to find out where they are and how to get there."

He sighs like he thinks I'm being pitiful and I

don't like that. I mean, this is Julie we're talking about here. Nate and Julie never got along well, but he knows how I feel about her.

"Dude, come on. Let's just go downtown or something, get your mind off—"

"No!" My yell booms through the living room. "I need to find her."

"To do what?" He sounds fearful. "What are you planning on doing, exactly? How are you going to talk your way out of this one? You've made a huge mess this time, Brandon."

I think about what I'm going to say to him very carefully. The truth is, I was more than horrible to Julie, but that's behind me. I don't want...whatever her name is, the boss' daughter. Rachel.

I want Julie.

And I want her to come home now.

When it comes to Julie, I *always* get what I want.

Nate sends a few texts out—one of our mutual friends has to know where she's gone with him. Better yet, they better find out where she went, if they're true friends at all. A few minutes later, Nate's phone pings and he sucks in hard air through his teeth. "Okay, Christian says that she went to some guy's lake house for a few weeks." His voice is annoyed. "They left on Friday, he picked her up, and they stopped at Rogerson's."

I start to laugh almost immediately. "I already knew that."

Nate shrugs his shoulders. "Well, Lake Reed is where they are."

"Lake Reed? That rich people lake in the middle of the forest?" My voice rises, but he's used to my frequent outbursts so the hard look on his face doesn't change. "So, she's with that rich guy up in the forest?"

"I don't know, man," Nate says. "That's all he knew."

Lake Reed isn't a big place—maybe fewer than twenty ritzy houses litter the lakefront or nestle into the thick forest around it. But it'd be like finding a needle in a haystack. A very rich, well-hidden, and heavily secured haystack with forest rangers frequently patrolling the areas and the residents heavily armed with shotguns and hunting rifles.

Nora.

I can only imagine that Nora is with her.

Or at least she knows where Julie is.

I pick up my phone and text Nora. I wait a few minutes before texting her again when she doesn't reply. When she hasn't responded for over an hour, I know I've crossed a line. If I had just told her I wanted to apologize to Julie, she would've given up the information I want. Either way, I took a few days off of work to find Julie so I can bring her home.

She's mine.

Nate frowns as he reads another message. "Christian got the address."

I don't bother packing—I'm bringing her straight home anyways. How can she know how sorry I am for cheating on her if she won't let me tell her? I honestly thought I'd broken her down enough to where she wouldn't leave me if I ever got caught, but she's stronger than I imagined.

"Coming?" I ask Nate, not looking up to see his expression because I fully expect him to say yes. "Come on, don't make me drive up there alone."

"No, dude. I'm not coming. You're not dragging me into this craziness again." His bushy eyebrows come together when he frowns, and he pushes past me to leave. "I told you to leave her alone...I mean, I damn near *begged* you. We're friends, Brandon. I'll always have your back, but this has just gotten out of hand, man."

I sigh angrily. "Fine, but don't go telling anyone I'm coming. Don't scare her off."

Nate laughs in my face. "*Me* scare her off? Brandon, listen to me for a minute, okay? Julie left you—it's over. You haven't seen her for three months. *Three months*, dude. Haven't spoken to her, haven't even seen a new picture of her...you've been too busy porking the boss' daughter."

"Her name is Rachel," I growl and push him away from me. I don't need to be anywhere within arm's length of him right now.

"Whatever," he groans. "You made your choice and she made hers. You each need to live with that. She doesn't want to see you, so don't go looking for trouble, Brandon."

I wave him off. "If you're not coming, then move out of my way."

Nate waits a few moments before stepping aside. "Don't say I didn't warn you, and don't call me to bail you out of jail. I'm not doing it this time." I hardly hear what he says as I leave him behind in the apartment, shuffling my feet as fast as they can go to my car parked outside. I don't bother using the GPS to find Lake Reed—I know where it is, and it's a long-ass drive from here. I'll get there around midnight, so I check my wallet for my credit card before speeding off into the night, just in case I need to stay somewhere close if she says no to me.

Rachel. I think of her halfway through the drive and groan.

She's sexy, all right. Her large, perky tits and the way she licked her lips whenever I did something she liked…it haunts me. Pair that with the way she dresses and the fact she let me do things to her Julie never would, and my desire for her was unstoppable. I knew she was trouble…I knew it, but I didn't care. Julie was boring me at the time; it wasn't like Rachel was the first one. She was just the first one Julie found out about—or more like, walked in on. In my defense, Rachel and I *did* try to get her to join us.

Maybe that was bad.

I think about Julie's body. She's shorter than me— a lot shorter, and rounder around the hips than Rachel. I was a loser when Julie found me, but that isn't stopping me from having my cake and eating it now.

Screwing the boss' daughter was definitely a mistake, though.

To be fair, she seduced me. Every time our team worked late and she brought us takeout Chinese food for dinner, everyone scattered to their offices to eat and she followed me to mine, basically ripping off my pants and having her way with me. Initially, it was just at the office, but eventually we moved to having sex at my apartment when Julie wasn't home. It escalated to me spending the night at Rachel's apartment and not coming home for days on end, losing time as I pounded myself repeatedly into a girl who always wanted more.

I smirk thinking about it, but I still feel bad. I'm *going* to get Julie back, so I need to stop thinking about what Rachel looks like naked and start thinking about what *Julie* looks like naked.

At first, when we met, I was faithful to her. She was all I was ever looking for, until she wasn't for reasons even I didn't understand. I somehow always ended up wanting more—whether it was more than she was giving me or more than she *could* give me, I didn't know or care.

But all I know now is that Julie is mine.

Not his.

Mine.

If she doesn't want to come back and be with me, I'm not sure what I'll do. I do know that whichever rich snob she's shacking up with can't stop me from dragging her home.

Kicking and screaming if I have to.

And I might have to. But it'll be worth it—I can still remember the moment I fell in love with her. We had just started dating; it was halftime at our high school football game, and I watched her leave the sidelines with the other cheerleaders. I placed myself where I could see her when she passed me, then grabbed her arm. "Hey, Jules," I said and kissed her cheek. She gently pressed our palms together. I liked the way she held my hand and smiled at me—it made me feel like I was the only person in the world. The cheers of the crowd roared through the stadium, but I hardly cared about any of that. I didn't come to the football game to actually watch it.

I came for her.

"Hey, yourself." Her blonde hair was braided into pigtails down both sides of her head. The short blue-and-white cheerleader skirt she wore grazed the tops of her curvy thighs, and all I could think about was how good her skin was going to feel on mine. I thought about how warm her body was going to be when she'd finally let me go all the way with her, and it chipped away some of the ice around my heart that had been gathering over years of such a shitty life. "I see you've put aside your hate for organized sports to watch me cheer."

I'm sure I was blushing; my dirty hair fell into my face and I was embarrassed to even look into her endless blue eyes. She was absolutely gorgeous: everything I ever wanted in life, wrapped up in a tight little cheerleader uniform. Except there was just one huge problem.

The entire school was against us because we didn't have the same social status. Julie didn't care, but she was popular. And I was a loser.

I wasn't in a good place in life—my parents were

strung-out addicts and it was public knowledge. We were dirt poor and sometimes I went days without eating—or talking to anyone, for that matter. People in Rockford just loved to gossip about my family.

"It's okay to be shy." She giggled and brushed my hair back into place. My insides stirred when her fingertips touched me; I was so much better when her *grace* touched me. "Some of the best people are the ones who can't always find the words to say." The world exploded in fireworks as she intertwined her fingers with mine and nestled herself against my lanky body.

"Julie, how can you be like this?" I whispered. "How can you be this real? You're a cheerleader."

Her bright smile set my insides on fire. "I don't throw people into categories, I don't believe that anyone's the same. You wearing black t-shirts all the time and always having a sour look on your face doesn't define who you are." She winked and stood directly in front of me again. I got too much bold courage for a moment as my free hand found the bottom of her skirt and I rubbed the fabric between my fingertips.

My head was going to explode.

"I like you," she whispered into the air between us. "Why is that so hard to believe? That someone like me would be into someone like you?"

My hand slid under the bottom of her skirt carefully—she didn't swat me away or get flirty. Instead, her eyes burned into mine as I gripped the flesh underneath the bottom of her perfect ass. I could tell she wanted me to tear into her—her eyes were begging me to take her home.

But I wanted much more from her.

"Julie…" My voice was rough and strained from trying to fight the need for her in my chest. "We graduate this year. What happens if you fall in love with me? I can't go to college—"

Her soft lips pressed onto mine and I latched onto her, sliding my tongue against hers and squeezing her tight. "Don't worry about things in the future you can't control." She played with my bottom lip. "I know you need me, Brandon, so just let yourself need me."

She was right.

I *did* need her.

I needed someone to show me a better way.

I was so tired of always being alone, not trusting anyone.

"You can trust me," she whispered, and her curvy little body fit against mine like a puzzle piece. "I will never leave you."

I laughed as she tightened her grip around me, her arms reaching toward the back of my shoulder blades and holding me against her as best as she could. It was in that moment that I knew Julie was going to be the one to fix me. That was the exact moment my entire soul fell in love with hers. All of the bad shit in my life—my parents getting high every night, my friends ditching me one by one, and now, finding out that I might not graduate on time because of one bad grade—

She knew I needed her.

She knew I needed her to help me heal. I didn't want to be broken anymore.

"Don't hurt me, Julie," I said. She wrapped her arms around my neck and smiled. She had the answers for everything that was, and still is, wrong with my life. I knew she could fix me; I knew she could make me feel better.

"I will never hurt you."

EIGHT
OLIVER

JULIE WALKS several feet in front of me, her pale legs glowing in the sunlight as we follow a small trail into the forest on our hike around the lake. I can't stop thinking about her dream the night before—it startled me from sleep enough to rattle my bones. She screamed so loud and thrashed around so hard that she ended up punching me square in the jaw before I was able to calm her down and wake her up.

I know she can feel my eyes on her—wherever her body went, my tired gaze followed. "I don't remember my dream," she says without turning around. "I can hear your loud thinking from up here."

I try not to blush, but her body turns suddenly and she catches me. "It was pretty scary; I was concerned. It's not every day that a girl wakes up screaming next to me."

She waves me off, giving me a pretty good show of her fake annoyance. I know that she likes when I fret over her—I can see it in her eyes whenever she lets me. "Don't be worried; it must have just been a random nightmare. Nothing to write a book about."

I don't want to press her as she struggles on her wounded leg—her stitches look worse than before. She needs to rest, but she isn't going to listen to me about anything. Instead, she enters a small clearing and waits for me. I can sense her smile from several feet away. Breathing in deeply, she softly says, "This will do." I breathe in the thick forest air, the smell of pine and salty lake water filling my head, no one around for miles.

It's just me and her.

Alone.

"Let me help you," I say. She swats my hand away when she manages to finally lay out a blanket for us to sit on. She lowers her curvy body softly, careful not to hurt her leg, and she holds onto my hand so tight it tingles a little. I sit next to her and put my hand on her left knee, and the smile she paints on her baby pink lips makes me rage with fire.

"Smooth," she says, offering me an apple, but I wave it away. *I'm hungry for you, not a fucking apple.* After a few moments of taking in the scenery around us, she clears her throat. "I think this is in my top ten favorite places now."

There is wonder in her eyes. I've seen this forest dozens of times; the greenery doesn't captivate me like it does Julie. Her small sigh whispers in the wind around us—I can't imagine myself anywhere but here. If my grandfather could see me right now, here with Julie in this place, he'd pick me up by my collar and slap me silly for being so soft. Her eyes follow mine into the darkness I've created in my mind and she takes my hand, squeezing it to let me know she cares. "Do you want to talk about your ex?" she asks. I instantly shake my head.

"Not really, no."

"Are you sure? Maybe talking about it will help you move past your anger—talking about my breakup with Nora really helped me." The sweetness in her voice jams itself into my jaw and I rub the stubble on my cheek, trying to hide the pain. "I know it might be a little weird to talk about it with me—"

"A little weird? Look—" I snort and reach for her, brushing a few stray hairs behind her ear before she pulls away. "I'm the kind of person who looks forward…there's no point in crying about the past when you don't have an endless future to live. I don't chase people and beg them to love me, either." The fabric of her silky blouse touches my arm and I can feel the burn marks it leaves on my skin from the jolt of excitement.

Julie's eyes shimmer beneath the tears looming in the corners of her bright eyes, ready to fall on her cheeks like a waterfall. "You don't sound like you trust in love anymore."

"Love isn't real—it's an illusion we create in our minds to tell ourselves that we're happy with what-ever life choices we've made. It shields us from truth and reality." I shake my head and frown. "That's my grandfather for you."

She places her body closer to mine and rests her head on my shoulder. "I'm glad you came with me—it would've been lonely without you."

I kiss her head and snake my arm around her waist. The truth is that I like sitting here with her, just the two of us, where no one can ruin our good mood. "Likewise, baby." I pause for a moment and cringe at my choice of nickname. It just spilled from my mouth; I tend to word vomit a lot around her. She doesn't notice and leans back, soaking in the sunlight around us. "You really don't remember your dream?"

Julie sighs, annoyed that I've brought it back up again. "Brandon wasn't very nice to me in our relationship. I guess I have remnants of that in my mind still."

Okay, settle down, Oliver.

"Like, what? Would he hit you?"

She bites her lip. "Let's just change the subject."

I want to scream. I want to find that jackass and punch his damn lights out. She's perfect—maybe I didn't see just how much at first, but no woman deserves to be abused, physically or mentally. The rage builds inside of me and I have to use everything I have to not lose my temper.

"What would he say to you?" I demand. My jaw tightens and starts to throb; no matter what she says, I am going to kick this guy's ass.

"Let it go, Oliver," she warns me. "This isn't your business."

I scoff. "You and I are trying to start something

here, or so I thought, and it's not my business? What did he say to you?" I regret asking as I listen to her tell me all of the things he would say and do to her.

"You have to know it didn't start off all bad, okay? We met in high school, we fell in love. I followed him on a path that didn't lead to college." Her voice is barely above a whisper. "It wasn't always bad."

"Julie…" My jaw hurts from the tension. "Tell me what he did to you."

She sighs. "At first, it was fine. The first six months or so, it was actually perfect. But once he got an internship at a law firm, things started to change. He would snap at me, lash out at things I would do wrong…or say wrong. He broke me down a lot, called me names, and took advantage of me even if I didn't want him to. He only put his hands on me a few times." She sucks in a hard breath when she sees my face. "And I know it was a few times too many. I loved him; you have to understand it's different when you love someone."

"No, it isn't. He hits you—shit, even if he mentally abuses you—you leave."

I honestly don't know what I'm talking about. I've never hit a woman, no matter how angry I was. I haven't been in her situation, but I'm so pissed I can't see straight. "So, what you're telling me is that this guy not only smacked you around and made you feel less than human, but he *raped* you?"

Her small body shakes. "He didn't rape me."

"It's rape if you didn't want it," I murmur. I try to

force down the anger; I don't want her to feel like I'm attacking her. She's dealt with that enough. "Did you say no?"

She shakes her head; I can tell she isn't comfortable talking about it anymore. "I never said no. I was afraid to."

"Oh, Julie." I want to rip my hair out. I want to kill this guy and I've never met him.

He had better hope I never do.

The look in Julie's eyes is heart-wrenching, and I know it's up to me to take her mind off the damage he's done to her. As we sit in the clearing, with the breeze caressing our skin and her wounded leg intertwined with mine, I think about how much I wanted this with Heather. I can feel my body tensing—I'm getting ready to stand up and push Julie away from me—but I manage to hold on with every fiber of my being just a few more minutes before she breaks us apart first. I'm not sure if she can feel my mood shift or not—I don't really care.

She tugs at my arm. "Hey, let's not let that ruin today, okay?"

I nod. Of course, I do what she asks. I'll always do what she asks.

"So..." The silk in her voice ties around my throat. "What would you be doing right now if you actually had to work?"

"Probably working for my grandfather, shaking people down for money," I joke. "Actually, at one point, Casey and I wanted to open a bar downtown in Rockford."

Her eyes light up with bright blue waves of happiness. "You should do it! Nora and I could be waitresses, and you can kick all the drunks out who grope us."

When our laughter meets, it warms my entire body. The only feeling that has ever come close to this was the relief of knowing my crazy mother had left town when I was a kid. I pull her close to me and breathe in her strawberry scent. "I wouldn't want you as a waitress—too many creeps out there," I mumble.

She allows herself to lean into me. "You can say that again." Her wink is so playful that it makes me growl and nibble on her earlobe. This is crazy. I literally can't believe I'm sitting in the middle of the forest with someone like her. When she stands, I stand. When she walks, I walk. Our movements are like a symphony.

She totally gets me.

"Let's skinny dip," I say, my voice low just in case anyone might be near without us seeing them. "In the rock pool at the south end of the property."

She whips her body around and looks from left to right, her honey hair falling around her shoulders. "You mean…we're still on your property?"

I smile. "Of course we are. We—*I* own several acres."

As Julie processes that, she allows me to inch closer to her and push her hair behind her ear: the few strands that keep falling from her braid. "Come with me," I whisper and kiss her bottom lip. She blushes. "No one is out here but us." I look around once more just in case. "And even if they were, they'd be trespassing." I can tell I'm making her nervous because she leans so hard into me I have to hold her up. I kiss her to steady her.

"I don't think it's a good idea." Her voice is very small.

Nudging her with my nose, I go in again. "Please? It'll be fun, I promise."

"I said no, okay?" Julie snaps and her blue eyes catch fire. "Can we just head back to the cabin now?" She doesn't wait for me to answer before turning the way she thinks the cabin is and storming off. I let her walk a few paces ahead of me for ten minutes before she realizes that we're heading in the wrong direction. "Are we lost?" She huffs and places her hands on her hips. "It's starting to get dark."

Holding my hands up in defeat, I close in on her. "What's your problem? I'm sorry I say the wrong things sometimes—"

"Nothing." She pouts and looks around for the right way to go. I nod slowly for a few moments and give her the chance to let off some steam, but she can hardly look at me. Am I pressuring her? "Hey," I say and gently grab her arm. "I'm sorry, I didn't mean to be aggressive back there."

Eyelashes.

Her long, flowing eyelashes touch her cheeks as she frowns.

Another dagger in my chest.

"You weren't," she says and frowns harder. "I did learn how to say no, you know."

I nod in agreement. "I'm proud of you." We're both smiling now. She slides her small hand into mine and I guide her back onto the right path toward the cabin. We're still a good ten-minute walk away and she's getting cold, so I throw my jacket over her and bathe in the feeling that regardless of what I thought Heather was going to be, it doesn't matter now.

I want Julie.

The firelight in the large backyard welcomes us and the others are sitting around, making out and laughing when we join them. I place Julie in front of me and let her relax her body into mine as Nora watches us with eagle eyes.

Good job, Nora and Casey.

You brought me Julie.

She's healing the parts of my heart that Heather destroyed.

"And where have you two been?" Nora clicks her tongue.

Julie and I are hardly listening to her as I smile down at her; the pockets in the corners of her mouth are making me come unhinged. I bend down and kiss the corner of her lips. "I don't kiss and tell, Nora," I say.

Casey hands me a beer and offers one to Julie, who declines but doesn't move an inch from my side. "Well, it seems like you two are getting along," he whispers.

She nestles her warm body into my thighs and there isn't any time for me to adjust. I know she feels my hard-on against her back. But she doesn't move her body away—instead, she places her hand on my knee and squeezes, letting me know it's time for us to move our own little party inside. Swiftly, I stand up with her in my arms, then throw her over my shoulder and fist pump—yes, fist pump—into the air before playfully carrying her back into the cabin. Once the bedroom door is closed behind us, she searches my face for anything that might give away something she hadn't noticed in me before.

"Oliver?" Julie says. "Can I tell you something?"

I don't hesitate. "You can tell me anything, you know that."

She does hesitate. "I haven't been with anyone since Brandon."

Good.

"Oh?" I fake a surprised voice. "Well, that's good for me, right?"

Julie scoffs, embarrassed. "I guess."

"What I mean is…" I press her body flush against mine. "I don't want anyone touching you that isn't me." I lick my lips before I press them to hers. Her skin vibrates from my rough hands moving over every inch of her body. I turn her to face away from me, parting her legs with mine. I try my best to be gentle, even though I want to rip her clothes off. "You smell like strawberries and sunflowers…it's very…*intoxicating*." I kiss her shoulder and nip at her collarbone. "You know once I start I won't be able to stop, don't you?"

"I know," she whispers, her eyes tightly shut. "I don't want you to stop."

I lay her onto the bed and take off her shorts, tracing the pad of my thumb along her panty line to feel her squirm beneath me. Her nails rake my shoulders with excitement as I tease her and each time she lets out a billowing breath, she whispers my name into the air. I grip the sides of her panties and rip them off her; there isn't anything in my way now.

"Wait," she says, catching her breath. "Do you have anything?"

Shit.

"I-I don't know." My head spins. "Let me check my wallet." I leap off the bed and find my jeans. The wallet is the last thing I graze my fingers over. I say a little prayer in my head before I open it and find the silver wrapper of a condom peeking out of the smallest flap. I don't know how long it's been in there, but I don't care about that now. I tear off my clothes and rip it open; I slide it on and rush back to her.

She giggles as I kiss her neck. By the time my tongue has reached her stomach, the giggles have turned into moans and I am ready to go. I kiss the insides of her thighs and she aches for me. I have to do this now before I lose all control. Losing myself between her shaking legs, our bodies lock together and our thrusts rock the bed several inches from the wall. The marks from her nails scratching the headboard motivate me to push harder. I'm pulled to her like a magnet as her breathing matches mine and I bury my face in her hair before we both explode and our bodies go limp against each other. She catches her breath and looks up at me with innocent eyes, so I lower my head and kiss her, transferring whatever energy I have left into her.

Julie bites her bottom lip and blinks a few times, bringing herself back to reality. She looks even more incredible than she did with her clothes on. Her hair is wild and yet I still find my fingers tugging at the ends as she looks into my eyes. I can see how quaint she really is.

Small. Fragile. Satisfied.

Maybe even tearing up a bit.

"Shit, are you okay?" I check her expression, then her body, for any unwanted marks.

She smiles up at me and quickly kisses my lips. "I'm fine. It was perfect."

Perfect.

There she goes, throwing those words around again. It makes me smile big and goofy. "O-okay, well…" I have to clear my throat of the lump that's risen in it. "Do you want to shower with me?"

Her eyes laugh at me. "You shower a lot for a guy."

"Hey, I like to be clean. Are you sure you don't want to join?"

She shakes her head and I don't push it—not after what she and I just did. "If you change your mind, you know where I'll be." I kiss her forehead and nuzzle my nose into her hair, which is matted with sweat but still smells like strawberry shampoo from her last shower. Before I can devour her again, I make myself get up and slip the condom off before she notices. I look back at her and smile. I don't bother to put on clothes as I walk across the room naked. I can feel her watching me disappear into the bathroom.

When the door closes, I let out a deep breath. "Holy shit. That was…that was *intense*."

As I wait for the water in the shower to get warm enough, I think about what just happened. The water is a little hotter than I wanted, but I don't really care. I'm not focused on that. Julie's blue eyes burned into mine at the end and our worlds exploded and collided at the exact same time.

My Julie.

I shake my head in the shower, letting the water hit the walls. I need to get a damn grip; this chick is doing a number on my head. I think about her soft, thick thighs and get hard again. There's a small knock on the bathroom door—I can barely hear it over the running water. After a few moments, the knock on the bathroom door comes back, a little louder and more frantic this time.

"Yeah?" I call out.

A muffled female voice says something behind the door.

I smile. "Come in here, I can't hear you."

The door opens and I stick my head out of the steamy shower and frown. It isn't Julie, it's Nora, blushing and looking at the floor the best she can. "I think you better come downstairs," she says in a worried voice.

"What is it?"

Nora backs out of the room. "Just hurry."

When she closes the door, I stand in silence for a few minutes. I haven't finished washing off the soap, so I hurry, turn off the shower, towel off, and carefully open the bathroom door to make sure Nora isn't waiting for me.

The room is empty.

Where's Julie?

There's a sinking feeling in the pit of my stomach as I rush into some jeans and a stone-colored V-neck t-shirt, not caring about shoes or combing my hair. When I open the bedroom door to step out, I hear muffled yelling and someone sobbing so I run down the stairs, frantically looking around for Julie.

The house is empty.

"Let her go!" I hear Nora yell outside.

"Dude, I'll kick your fucking ass—don't touch her!" Harley booms.

"Julie!" Staci cries.

"You told me you'd never leave me!" a man screams.

"Oh, shit! Is she okay? Harley—get him!" Casey shouts.

"I said don't fucking touch her, man!" Harley yells again and I hear loud thuds; someone is punching the shit out of someone else.

My brain twists in fear as I open the front door and push outside. My friends are littered around the gravel driveway, the only light coming from the front patio, but I can still see the fear on their faces.

Harley and Victor are scuffling with another man on the ground who keeps reaching for Julie, crumpled up like a paper bag on the ground next to them.

"Julie." I gasp and start running toward her.

"Oliver, watch out!" Nora calls my name and I feel a blow to the side of my head, bringing me to my knees. Julie's tears hit the ground as I try to catch my breath and look up at her.

"I'm sorry," she mouths to me.

The man who'd been scuffling with the boys is focused on me now. "You think because you're a rich playboy that you can have her?" He screams and kicks me in the stomach, making me cough and fall to the ground completely. "Have you been fucking her this entire time? Huh? No one gets her but me!"

Oliver, get up and kick this guy's ass.

One more kick to my side and that's it. I growl, jump up, tackle the man, and pin him on the ground before punching him in the mouth. "Don't talk about her like that!" I spit. Harley and Victor have to pull me off of him before I kill him. The man gurgles and sits up, spitting out blood and looking at Julie. "Don't even fucking look at her," I yell. "Who the fuck are you?" I almost break free.

"I'm her boyfriend." He spits out more blood.

"Ex-boyfriend." Nora glares at the man and then looks at me. "Brandon Whitehouse."

Oh, this asshole better run.

My chest is on fire. I leap on him again and hold

his shoulder down in the dirt. "Did you fucking hit her? I should kill you!"

Brandon laughs and spits blood in my face. "Screw you."

I smirk and lean down; my voice is so scary that even *I* shiver. "No, screw *you*. I should kill you for hurting her. If you ever, ever, touch her again, I will fucking end you."

"She's mine," Brandon croaks under my weight.

Before I know it, my hands are around his neck and he's gasping for air. Harley and Victor try to pull me off of him and Nora screams my name; she begs me to stop, but I don't care.

I see red—it's blinding me.

I want to erase all of her pain.

I am going to kill him for hurting her.

NINE
OLIVER

HE ISN'T BREATHING.

Wait, there he goes.

The color in his smug face drains and I can't help but smile as he gasps for air. "Oliver, stop," I hear Julie say and it makes me let him go.

"Get the hell out of here before she changes her mind," I growl at him, crawling off his body and clutching my side as I try to start making my way toward Julie.

Brandon rubs his throat and chuckles, picking himself up from the ground. "You can't protect her forever—she *will* come back to me, you'll see. She's mine...she belongs to me."

"Not as long as I'm around." I point toward the car parked behind him. "Leave before I do something I can't come back from."

Brandon turns toward Julie. "You'll come back, just wait and see. You need me, Julie." I push him and he nearly falls over.

"Dude, you better go before he really kills you," Harley says next to me, keeping a tight grip on my t-shirt to hold me back from pouncing on him again. Brandon doesn't look impressed but he decides against talking to Julie again and gets into the running car and backs out of the long driveway. It takes me a few minutes to catch my breath and calm myself down before I can look at her. The tears stain her cheeks but I can't move.

What the hell was she thinking, coming out here with him at night?

Nora gets Julie on her feet and hugs her, brushing the hair from her eyes. Man, she actually does care about her. Again, I need to apologize to Nora for being such an ass, but Julie sniffles into Nora's frizzy hair and I want to tuck her into my pocket and run away with her to make her pain go away.

"I can take her inside," I say, and Nora nods at me. Julie lets me pick her up and carry her inside, nestling herself into my chest and silently drifting off to sleep. "She was tired when I left her to go shower —what the hell happened?" I whisper to Nora once I place Julie back in our bed.

Our bed.

Nora motions for me to meet her downstairs where the rest of them wait. Everyone's trying to calm down after the display of fireworks Brandon caused outside. The girls are shaken up and the guys all still look pretty pissed off and ready to take action. No matter how big sleazebags Harley, Victor, and Casey can be, they still treat women with respect and don't like when someone hurts one, especially right in front of them. I sit down across from them in an armchair and breathe deeply. "Okay, explain to me what the hell just happened out there."

At first, the girls are silent. Then, Staci nudges Nora and she finally breaks. "Brandon wasn't the best boyfriend to Julie, but I guess you can see that." I narrow my eyes at her and nod slowly. "They were high school sweethearts. She was a cheerleader and he was...pretty much a lost cause. Well, after high school, Julie worked a lot and Brandon took a lot of her money...she never really had anything of her own and then Brandon met his boss' daughter, Rachel, and he started sleeping with her behind Julie's back."

"And then Julie found out and he started abusing her, mentally and sometimes physically, so she stayed and he kept sleeping around," Staci adds. "Mainly with Rachel but with other girls too." Her words slice through my anger like a knife.

Oh, I am pissed now.

"Dude, calm down," Casey says to me. "It's over now."

"Calm down? Are you fucking kidding me? You —" I point toward Casey. "—You *brought* me here and you—" I move my finger to Nora. "—What kind of friend are you to let her go through something like that? Why didn't you make her leave?"

Nora doesn't like when she's in trouble. "I-I tried, Oliver, I really did."

"Not hard enough, apparently."

Casey snaps his fingers at me. "Hey, now. This isn't her fault—don't blame Nora for something that she had no control over." I don't take his one-sided bullshit anymore. I've had enough with dancing around sensitive subjects and playing it safe.

"This is probably why I don't remember you," I say with a scowl. "You weren't someone worth remembering." Even I know it's harsh. Nora's eyes well up with tears, but she doesn't let them fall. Casey looks like he's about to kick my ass, but I don't care.

Okay, I care. Julie makes me care.

"I'm sorry, Nora." The words feel bitter in my mouth. "I didn't mean that. I'm just really pissed off. It's hard knowing I give two shits about her and you both act like this isn't a big deal. It's a big fucking deal!" My voice booms throughout the living room. The anger rises again; I do nothing to stop it. "So now I'm stuck giving a shit about this girl when I really don't want to!"

Nora looks sick as the group notices someone behind me. "Nora, can you take me home?" Julie's voice is strained. "I'd really like to go home now."

"No, you're not going anywhere tonight," I say to her and turn around. My heart races; did she hear what I said?

Her face is pale and scared.

She heard me.

"Okay," she whispers and disappears back up the staircase. I can't take hurting her...I groan and bury my face in my hands. The feeling of a thousand

115

hands pulling me in different directions creeps into my stomach and rips my insides apart. "I can't believe you guys have done this to me."

"What exactly did we do to you?" Nora snaps, the bangles of her earrings swaying with her fierce head shake. "It's *your* fault you slept with her. It means more to her than it does to you."

"You don't know what it means to me," I growl, and Nora looks a little freaked out by the rage reaching out to get her.

Casey whistles between his teeth and waves his arms in front of us. "Okay, okay, let's all calm down. Ollie, man—your ex did a number on you, okay? It's natural to get scared when you start feeling things for someone else."

Nora's eyebrows raise. "Do you have feelings for Julie?"

Something isn't right here.

I don't feel like myself.

"I don't know what the fuck is going on anymore," I groan. "But yeah, I guess I do."

"Then get the hell upstairs and go talk to her." Casey points toward the staircase. "She's vulnerable, scared, and embarrassed. I doubt she lets anyone in but you right now." I nod and do what he says, patting him on the shoulder as I pass him. Sometimes Casey can be the best friend anyone could have.

The fire is the only light in the room when I slowly open the door. I hope she isn't asleep. Her small body sits in front of the fire; she's still curling into herself like she's on the defense.

"Hey, you," I say softly and almost tiptoe toward her. I can hear her quietly sniffling, trying not to let me know she's crying, but I can feel it even if I can't see it. "I'm sorry...I shouldn't have yelled at you down there." The room is warm, but that doesn't stop me from sitting next to her and reaching for the strands of hair around her face before she sobs into her hands.

"You don't owe me anything; we're basically strangers," she says through her quiet, heaving sobs. "I don't expect anything from you; I told you I didn't need someone to fix me."

She *did* hear me.

I sigh. "There's nothing wrong with you, Julie. I don't want to fix you because you're perfect just the way you are. This is you and me, now. Here. Together." Before I know it, she's climbed into my lap and kissed me, her lips salty from her tears. I lift my hands to her face and wipe the rest of them away, letting her snuggle into my chest again. I listen to her fractured breathing from the remnants of her cries, and I can still feel the conviction in her bones: She doesn't trust me.

I close my eyes and regret what I say to her before I even let the words past my lips. "Okay, you're worried that we hardly know each other." She nods. "And that I can be a total ass." She nods again.

Her eyes are filled with darkness, but that doesn't stop me from wanting her as much as I do. "The past is the past—why spend any more time on it? What do you want to know?" She stays silent. "Fine, I'll start. Where did you grow up? Where are your parents?" I nudge her and smile. "I want to know every single thing that makes you who you are."

While she decides on what she wants to do, she bites her inner cheek and stares at me. "My parents live in Oakland; I haven't seen them in a long time."

"Why?" I push her, but she shakes her head. "Julie, come on. How can I know anything about you if you refuse to tell me?"

She gulps and it makes me uneasy, so I push her again.

"Okay, they aren't good people, all right?" she says. "They like to steal things and manipulate people into getting what they want. I'm pretty sure they'd opened up a half dozen credit cards in my name—and dozens of other people's names—before I was old enough to drive."

"Seriously?" My eyes grow wide. "Did you turn them in?"

She nods and looks flushed. "They were caught, they went to jail for a while and I came to live with my Aunt Shelly in Rockford, then I met Brandon our senior year of high school and Shelly died a few years ago from a heart attack."

"That's tough luck." I frown. "My grandfather died from lung cancer."

Julie wipes away a tear. "I'm sorry, Oliver."

I laugh and wave her off. "Oh, don't be, he was a cranky old bastard who hated everyone and everything. He just didn't want the state to take his money, so he left it to me."

She smiles at my aloofness. God, she's beautiful. I'm not sure why I fought it so much before. The way the corners of her eyes crinkle when she smiles and her full lips tuck into each other when I know she's thinking about kissing me—and she thinks about kissing me a lot—I can see it. I am losing myself in her and I'm in so much trouble when it comes to her, there's no turning back now. "Julie, I don't know what you're doing to me, but when I'm with you, I get this burning in my stomach and I feel like I'm falling in space, like I can't get a grip on myself."

She giggles and feels my forehead with the tips of her long fingers. "You need sleep, or maybe some vodka."

"No, I need you." I lift her chin to look her in the eyes. "I need you, Julie."

She searches my eyes with confusion. "Oliver, are you okay?"

"I'm fine, just don't ever forget that, okay?" She nods in silence as I pick her up and place her gently on the bed, making sure she doesn't get up this time. I tuck myself in next to her and hold her against me as I let what happened run through my mind. Brandon isn't ever going to lay another finger on her as long as I am alive to protect her.

My Julie.

I wait for her to drift off to sleep and when I hear her breathing slow and she snuggles deeper into the cocoon of my body, I think about Heather and realize that I hate her for making me wait to be with someone like Julie.

I deserve Julie.

―――

"HEY, OLIVER?" *I hear a woman call to me from another room. "Baby, can you come in here?" I feel myself smile and jump out of a chair, following her voice like a puppy dog until I find her standing in the middle of a bedroom, wearing a cocktail dress that is a few sizes too small, but I don't dare say a word. Julie's honey blonde hair falls down her back as she frowns into the full-length mirror in front of her and says, "Can you see if you can zip me up?" I wasn't going to ask her why her dress wouldn't fit, but instead I run my hand down her back and squeeze her ass gently, making a low growl.*

She swats me away and giggles. "Be serious―you have to zip me up, okay? We have that charity dinner in an hour and this is the only dress that hasn't betrayed me yet. Not to mention, that―" She points to the lower half of my body and smiles. "―is how we got this." Her short fingers rub the large, round bump on her torso.

I manage to zip up the dress and she looks miserable in it, but the ring on her finger suggests that I spent a good chunk of change making her happy, even if she sobs into her hands about a cocktail dress not fitting her.

"Oh, God," she sobs and runs into my arms. "This one is too small now too…what am I going to do?"

I stroke her hair and comfort her. "Why don't you just buy bigger ones, baby?"

The glare she gives me sends shivers down my spine.

"Is that the solution? I'm sorry, I didn't realize." She

lets herself free from my grip. "I guess each time the baby gets bigger when he's born, you're going to suggest that we just…what? Get a smaller baby?!" Her tone is frantic.

"Baby? What baby? My…baby?" I choke, focusing on her growing stomach. It's the size of a perfectly round basketball.

"Are you okay? You should probably get ready while I find a bigger dress that isn't hideous on me." She frowns and looks at me. "You're pale as a sheet—are you sure you're okay? Oliver?" She waves her hand in front of me. I stare blankly at her and pull her down onto my lap, placing my hand on her stomach. A small kick scares the shit out of me. "That's a baby in there!" I squeak and she laughs.

"His name is Colin, remember? Not 'A Baby.'"

Colin.

My father's name was Colin.

"I don't want to wake up from this," I say, but she doesn't hear me as I watch her saunter from the room, humming a nursery rhyme and closing the door behind her.

I can hear her struggling with another dress as I look around the oiled and shiny office. I smile at a picture of us on the desk behind me.

Me and Julie.

Together in this moment.

I never want to leave this place.

TEN
JULIE

"HUMP DAY, hump day, what day is it?" I hear Harley chanting downstairs, the rest of the group laughing and talking loudly, not caring if Oliver and I are still asleep or not. "Hump day!" Staci giggles and no doubt smothers him with lip gloss and her slobber.

"My friend will be here tonight!" Nora's excited voice bleeds through the others. I can feel Oliver's large, warm body behind me and when I move to sit up, he pulls me back down into his embrace and locks his arms around me tight.

"I can't wait to meet her, babe," we hear Casey say, and their lips smacking together echoes through the stairwell and into the room. Oliver breathes in so deeply that I can feel his chest expanding into the small of my back before he lets the air go and his rough fingers slide down my arm, traveling toward my hand. His fingers twist around mine.

I open my eyes and let the sunlight into my sticky

eyelids. I feel so stupid for answering Brandon's phone call—thinking I could make him go away on my own—that I do want to make it up to Oliver somehow. I think about the possessiveness that Oliver showered me with...the glint of rage in his eyes scared me when he towered over Brandon, about to choke him to death.

He would have killed him if I hadn't stopped him.

"Good morning, sunshine." I can feel him smile against my hair. His sleepy voice weaves through the chills he sends shivering down my spine. "Apparently it's hump day." The grip he holds on my fingers tightens and he moves closer to me, nearly flush against my shoulders. My entire body is numb. Each time he closes in on me, it's like something locks me in place and I'm unable to break free and run from him.

"You tossed and turned a lot last night—did you have a nightmare?" I say, my lips trembling around a yawn. Oliver never lets go of his hold on my body as he brings our locked-together hands up to my chest and rests them there. When he finally lets me go, I can turn to see him holding himself up on one elbow, his brow strained and confused. "Not a nightmare. More of a...*surprise*." His tongue glides across the outside of his teeth, making me squeeze my legs together almost instantly.

"Let me take you to breakfast." He smiles and kisses my forehead quickly, before I can protest. I hardly want to open the curtains to let the full sunlight inside, so going somewhere is out of the question. "Come on, get up." He winks and then disappears into the bathroom, running water in the sink and brushing his teeth.

I take a long time getting ready, brushing my hair and trying to make some kind of sense out of it before I realize that it's going to be a mess no matter what I manage to do with it. I pick out my best jeans and a red sweater before frowning at myself in the mirror. I hear the bathroom door open and Oliver walks through the bedroom, naked and dripping wet from his shower.

"So, are you always going to walk around naked?" I ask him playfully, my hands on my hips while I squint my eyes. "Do I need to get a different room? There seems to be too much nudity in this one."

He laughs as he pulls on a pair of black boxer briefs, making a point to face me so I have a full-frontal view. "You wouldn't dare do that to me." He winks at me, pulling me next to him on the bed and locking his arm around mine. "I'm not letting you go until you promise to stay."

"I'm staying, I'm staying." I raise my hands in surrender. "But it's not fair when you walk around like...*that*."

He lets me go to pull on his jeans. "Like what?"

I roll my eyes. "Like a Greek god or something."

Oliver snickers. "I'm no god. I'm just me."

"Yeah well, *'just me'* is pretty intimidating sometimes."

He frowns. "So, what? Do you think you're not good enough for me?"

I snort. "Oh, I know I'm not good enough for you."

"Dammit, Julie," he growls, angrily pulling on an ocean-blue sweater. "If anything, it's me that's not good enough for you."

"Oliver—" He looks like he's going to cry so I close my mouth, rushing through ways I can fix this in my head. He sits on the edge of the bed and pulls me to his side. "This conversation ends here, okay? You have nothing to worry about; if you hadn't noticed, I am totally into you."

There isn't anything I can do now about the way I'd just made him feel, so I pull on my shoes and join Oliver downstairs, where he's greeting everyone and letting Nora know our plans so she won't worry. He laces his fingers with mine and squeezes to let me know it's going to be okay.

"So, there's a small cafe in town," Oliver says a few minutes after we pull out of the driveway of the cabin. I watch it get smaller and smaller by the second as we drive, then it disappears. A lot has happened there in just five days that running through everything in my head makes me dizzy. I'm in way, way over my head. "Is that okay?" I hear him say.

"What?" My voice cracks and I blush, embarrassed that I got caught not listening...but for a very good reason.

Oliver laughs. "The cafe? Is that okay?"

He parks the Jeep and we sit in silence for a few minutes, breathing in each other's air and frustration. "I don't know what you want from me," I say in a low voice, my gaze still fixed on the small, ritzy cafe ahead of us. Oliver finally takes the key from the ignition.

"I want to eat breakfast with you," he answers me matter-of-factly. "I assumed you want the same since you came with me. You can eat whatever you want."

I scoff. "You know what I mean."

He smiles and turns his tall body so he towers over me. "I know what you mean, I just don't think this is the time or place to discuss it." My mouth opens and closes as I search for the words to knock him off his feet, but find none. He smiles again and nods, pleased that for once he's succeeded in rendering me speechless. "Come on." He pats my leg gently and leaves the car, walking around to my door and opening it for me. He pulls me out into his grasp. "Let's eat."

I allow him to escort me inside without too much of a protest. The hostess, a small brunette, big-chested model, melts at the sight of Oliver when we enter the building. There's a small wave of silence as everyone notices him, and when they see me next to him, I can hear murmuring. The hostess frowns when she sees my hand in his.

"Hey, Kate." Oliver waves weakly at her. "Table for two, please."

Kate smacks her lips. "Only two?" She snickers as she looks around us, obviously hoping we had friends and this wasn't a breakfast date. I think about Brandon and how he never took me on dates—he *did* use my money to take Rachel on dates, however. My grip tightens and Oliver notices. He pulls me into the booth next to him and places his warm hand on my thigh, tugging me back into the moment. "Hey, you okay?"

I nod. "I'm fine. *She's* a pistol." I point to Kate and he laughs, not even bothering to look at her.

"We were friends for a few weeks." I can feel the heat flush to my cheeks, but he's already one step ahead of me. "Look, you'll find that out a lot about me. After Heather—" He cringes when he says her name out loud. "—I had a lot of friends like Kate." His face falls a little and I know that even though I don't share this with him, I understand that it's in the past.

"Do you think we're crazy for being this comfortable together?" I ask. "You know, we just met—"

He cuts me off. "Why are you so fixed on how long we've known each other? Why does time even matter? I like you, you like me, right? So, what does a few days have to do with it?" His voice grows angrier by the second, and then he looks saddened by his outburst. "I just really wish we could get past whatever it is holding us back and just be together and not care what other people think."

"I'm just a little scared," I tell him. "This is weird for me. Brandon wasn't exactly nice toward the end of our relationship, and I'm conditioned to think the worst."

He claps and smiles. "Okay, new rule. No more talking about exes. We're moving forward with each other: Oliver and Julie, okay? Now, let's eat." He calls Kate over and tells her to bring us pancakes and eggs, fruit, and biscuits and gravy. My mouth waters when they bring us all of the requested food and Oliver digs in like a hungry wolf.

I pick at the pancakes and eggs and gobble down a few small pieces of fruit, and the entire time Kate and a few other women are eyeballing the two of us, gritting their teeth and gossiping.

Oliver squeezes my leg and smiles at me; he can see what the vultures are doing too. "What do you want to do today?" He pushes his plate away and downs a glass of milk. "I haven't worked out in a few days, unless you count what we did in the bedroom." His eyes twinkle as he thinks about our night together. "But I can do that later. What about shopping?"

I make a sour face. His mouth forms an O in surprise. "No shopping? Well, that's a first. What about renting a boat and going out on the lake for a while?"

"Okay." I raise my eyebrows in intrigue. "But I get to drive the boat."

He laughs. "Oh? You know how to drive boats, do you?"

"I guess we'll see." I smack my lips like Kate did. After paying the check, Oliver tips Kate very well and basically pulls me to the Jeep, tosses me in, and revs back onto the road.

The marina smells like fish so badly it makes my nose crinkle. He laughs at me as he escorts me inside and pays for the rental. He places a life jacket on me and I frown.

"Where's yours?" I demand and cross my arms over my chest. "Am I the only one that's supposed to be safe?" Groaning, he takes one for himself and holds it in the air for me to see, but he doesn't put it on. Once we're in the large pontoon boat and slowly drifting away from the docks, I watch Oliver in silence. He has such grace when he steers the boat, his gaze fixed on the calm morning waters.

His eyes are blissfully *happy*.

"There's our cabin," he says to me over the quaint lake breeze. His voice is only a little louder than a whisper. "I bet everyone else already went back to sleep."

I giggle. "Jealous?"

Oliver shakes his head immediately. "Not at all. I am exactly where I want to be."

I freeze.

He wants to be here with me, looking at *our* cabin.

No. Don't let yourself open up too much more or he's going to swallow you whole and spit you right back out, tearing your life to shreds more than it already is. I smile to myself because he already has.

Oliver lets the boat drift on its own while he joins me on the long backseat just above the now-quiet motor. He smiles over at me, gently intertwining our hands. "I've never been this relaxed in my life." His face brightens as we soak in the scenery around us.

"It's perfect out here; this whole thing is perfect. You're perfect, the air is perfect."

My entire body buzzes with weird emotions and hope.

This can't be real.

Oliver is gorgeous. Like, *really* gorgeous. He looks like he's been kissed by the sun and blessed by something—not humanly possible. I watch him push his dark hair from his eyes and let the lake mist graze his face. His thick lips curve into a smile as he squeezes my hand and looks up at the silky blue sky. We soak up the morning light for a long time, stretched out next to each other, making sure we're always touching. I'm nearly asleep when I hear him stand up. He kisses the top of my head, starts the engine, and swiftly drives us back to the boat docks.

————

"GET IN HERE!" I hear Brandon yelling at me from the bedroom. "Don't make me come and get you."

I go to him, crying.

"Stop crying," he demands and pushes me on the bed, sitting down next to me. "I'm sorry for losing my temper."

I nod. "It's okay."

He sighs. "I didn't mean to hurt you."

I nod again. "It's okay."

Brandon scoffs. "You just make me angry sometimes… you don't listen to me and it frustrates me. Didn't I specifically ask you to pick up my dry cleaning at noon?" He doesn't wait for me to answer. "And you didn't pick it up until three. I needed that jacket for a meeting."

"I'm sorry," I say in a small voice.

Brandon sighs again. "I love you, Jules. You know that, right?" *He pulls my body into his.* "You are so lucky I'm a reasonable man."

I nod and let him take control over me.

"Do you remember our first date?" *he asks. I frantically think so I can give him the right answer.* "It was at that stupid bowling alley arcade place on Barney Road, remember?" *He continues without giving me a chance to speak.* "And we got drunk in my car that night, remember? Peach schnapps and apple ale." *His nose wrinkles in disgust.* "And I took your virginity in the backseat of that old thing, remember that?"

"Yes," I say.

His eyes glitter. "What do you say we relive the memory?"

I scream.

———

"HEY, IT'S ALL RIGHT." Oliver's smooth voice comforts me. He strokes my head and cradles me in his lap. "Did you have another bad dream?"

My eyes feel sticky from the fresh daylight. "Must be just the boat ride," I say and swat his hands away. "I'm fine."

He lets me go free and doesn't push me, which I silently thank him for.

What am I doing here?

I don't belong here; this entire thing with Oliver is crazy.

Mr. Oliver Jackson.

That's all I know about him.

I have to end this somehow.

I know it's going to be hard.

"Oh, good—the Inn employees brought our lunch for us," Oliver says, motioning toward the dock. A thick, flannel blanket and a picnic basket full of snacks has been spread out for us. My jaw drops and I instantly draw back into him. "It's just a light lunch with some chardonnay, no big deal." It's as if he were reading my mind.

I swallow, and my throat is so dry I think I could rip it to shreds. "This is really sweet of you."

His smile is huge. "There you go, using that word again. Sweet."

"Just help me off the boat." He laughs and helps me onto the dock, and we talk about the water and how he's always wanted a house right on the lake so he can jump into it from his backyard. When he speaks about life, he has such a childlike presence about him, and that puts me at ease a little as the afternoon goes on and my heart warms back up to him.

He holds my hand almost the entire time.

After we end our conversation about fantasy vacations, he's quiet as he studies me. "You're really beautiful—I wish you knew that about yourself." He raises his left eyebrow. "I plan on telling you every damn day too."

I squint to see him—the two o'clock sun hovers behind him. "What exactly is the plan once we return home?"

"I plan on seeing a lot of you."

"My brother and Clyde, they're very protective of me since…you know." I lower my gaze to the ground, but he picks me back up with two sentences.

"Well, then I guess I'll have to win them over, won't I? They'll see that I want to love you, not hurt you."

Crap. Crap. Crap.

I just keep getting deeper into a world I don't belong in.

With a man I don't belong with.

ELEVEN
OLIVER

JULIE PICKS at the food waiting for us when we dock the boat like it's tainted with poison. I can tell something is on her mind, but I really don't want anything to take away from the time alone we have, just the two of us. I enjoy being alone with her; I don't have to be anyone but myself. And I can be whoever I want to be. Not Oliver Jackson, grandson of a legend. Not Ollie. Just Oliver. I can't imagine what she thinks of me: rough around the edges and rude one minute and then sleeping with her and kissing her fingers the next.

I don't know what the hell I'm doing here with her, either.

She bites her bottom lip and it makes me smile. She's amazing; I'm getting addicted to the small things that she does like twisting the ends of her hair when she's deep in thought or the way her smile gets wider when she laughs at something stupid I've said.

Six days.

Six days is all it took for me to forget about Heather completely and actually focus on someone better—someone I've been waiting to meet for a very long time.

"Are you getting cold?" I ask when she tucks her hands underneath the place where her thighs meet her ass. I lick my lips when I see her do this and she blushes, noticing the predatory grip I have on her. "We should head back, anyway; Nora and Staci are arranging a date night for all of us. Cheesy couple games and all." Her eyes darken a little, but when we talked about it earlier, Casey and I decided that it'd be good for us to mingle with the other people in the house.

My phone starts to ring and I look at the caller ID —Casey's name pops up, so I hit the ignore button and shove it back into my pocket. Almost immediately, it rings again and a wave of adrenaline rushes over me as I look at Casey's name once more. "Yeah?" I answer it as I help Julie to her feet and keep her from falling off the dock and into the cold lake water.

"Dude, are you planning on coming back here today?" Casey's voice shakes. "You should take Julie to that hotel you've always wanted to stay at. You know, the one down Wickermaker Road."

I look at the Lake Reed Inn standing in the distance, and the Inn workers—identified by their bright white uniforms—are trickling out to tend to us. I hold up my finger toward Julie and walk a few feet away from her. "Down Wicker...The Lake Reed

Inn? Why, what's going on?" Girls squeal in the background and I hold the phone as far from my ear as I can. Julie's eyebrows rise in suspicion. "Casey, what the hell is going on over there?"

I hear him shuffle away from the screaming and shut a door behind him. "Dude, Heather is here." I laugh instantly. "No, really. That's Nora's friend she invited up here. God, Ollie, I had absolutely no idea —I don't even know how they know each other."

My entire body freezes in place. He isn't kidding. Heather is Nora's friend? The friend that she basically invited to stay with us at the cabin? Now I have to try harder to remember Nora. I never made much of an effort to know Heather's friends—since she has so many—but I would have remembered Nora by seeing her a second time. Right? "Oh, shit." I say it a little too loudly and fearfully, keeping my eyes on Julie as she acts like she isn't trying to hear my conversation. "Casey, tell me you're bullshitting me."

I can almost see him shake his head in my mind. "I'm not, Ollie. I had no idea."

"You said that already," I growl at him, then hang up. I sigh loudly. "Julie?" I turn around and watch her fold up the blanket like it's her job, helping the group of people wearing uniforms clean up our mess of food and dirty glasses. She smiles as they chat with her; I don't hear or care what they're saying, but the entire scene is just so…*simple*.

As far from complicated as I want to be right now.

And then there's Heather.

"Julie, we have to talk," I say in a low voice as she finally notices me and waves goodbye to her new friends. I smile at her and capture her hand. "Let's head back to the cabin; there's something I have to deal with." I don't wait for her to say anything before whisking her back toward the parked car, but I take my time opening the door for her, placing her inside, and walking around to my door. Breathing heavily, I have to get inside or she'll know something weird is up with me.

She can't meet Heather—she just can't.

Does she already know Heather?

"What's the matter?" Her honey hair falls around her shoulders, escaping the braid it had been tied into all day. The strands are like curly rays of sunshine. "I could feel the tension our entire walk back to the Jeep."

I don't wait to figure out an answer. My hands find her waist and I pull her toward me, devouring her lips like I'll never see her again. The air in our lungs thins so I let her go, and she goes back to her seat, touching her lips. I close my eyes. "Nora's friend showed up a day early," I say in one breath. "Very unexpected and not appreciated."

Julie giggles. "Okay, that's not a big deal. What's wrong with that?"

I study her face. Her full lips turn up into a naïve smile and the corners of her eyes crinkle at me and my foolishness. I have to tell her; I know I do. There's no getting around walking into the cabin and Heather opening her big ass mouth. "Have you met

Nora's friend, Heather?" I ask her, hoping for the best.

Julie nods. "Oh yeah, she's...pretty perfect."

No, you *are perfect*.

"Oliver, are you sure you're okay? I'm sure Nora didn't mean to upset you."

My Julie.

Here goes nothing.

"Heather is my ex," I blurt out, watching the happiness fade from Julie's face. I can tell exactly what's running through her mind—the endless questions and self-esteem blows that come and go from her eyes make me sad. The shades of emotions turn in her eyes; she realizes that she didn't put it together when I talked about Heather as my ex. I haven't physically seen Heather in months, so I'm not sure what is going to happen.

"I guess the names didn't click with me," she says. "Are you sure it's the same Heather?"

I nod. "Casey just called and told me. She's at the cabin and I'm making her leave. I can't believe Nora would do this to me—to *you*!"

There is a small squeak that escapes from her throat. "I don't think Nora would have known. She wouldn't have invited her; something isn't right here. Should I wait here?"

"No, why would you stay behind? I'm with you —I'm not with her." I can tell she wants to say something but my head spins out of control. "I didn't know—how could I have known?" I start to worry out loud, wringing my hands and fiddling with the keys in my lap. "I swear, Julie, if I had known it was her, I wouldn't have said yes. I can't fucking believe this…it's always one thing after another with us, isn't it? First it's me being an asshole, then you hated me and I made you need stitches and then have to beat your ex's ass and now this—it's all coming at me at once now and it's too much."

The silence kills me as her sadness tries to suffocate me. That entire outburst was the biggest mistake I've ever made. The problem is it's way too late to take any of it back now. Julie's head falls forward and she quietly buckles her seat belt.

"I'm sorry," she whispers and looks out the window. "Let's go back now; I'll just hide in the bedroom."

"Oh, Julie," I say, apologetically, "I'm not ashamed of you."

She shakes her head. "I know that, but you're right. This is too much, too fast. I think we should just cool it before someone gets hurt—we *do* have different lives in Rockford." Before I can open my mouth and dispute her, she bites the inside of her cheek and a few tears fall. "I'd like to go back now, please."

I do what she asks, but I'm not happy about it. This girl, this fucking girl, has me so wrapped around her finger that I even want to comfort her when she breaks up with me.

"Ollie!" I hear Heather's mousey voice squeak as I park the Jeep and let myself out. Julie doesn't wait for me, instead slamming her door and marching directly inside the house. I want to run after her, but Heather jumps into my arms and wraps her legs around my torso. She kisses my neck, still squeaking in excitement. "When I got the address from Nora, I just knew I had to come early and see you! I've missed you so much, Ollie Bear."

I tense and I nearly drop her on the ground—her bird legs catch her fall. "I don't know what you're doing here, but you have to leave." I grit my teeth. "Now."

Nora crosses her arms and squints at me. "Wait, *you're* the ex-boyfriend who dumped her for no reason?"

I peel Heather off me and scowl at Nora. "You don't know what you're talking about." My voice gets rough. "Heather, leave." As I'm walking away, I hear them talking in hushed voices but I don't even care to know what they're saying.

I spin around when I reach the front door. "Did I stutter?" I ask. "I said you need to leave."

"Dude, it's nearly nightfall—you don't want her navigating these windy ass roads at night, do you?" Casey says from the far end of the front porch. His eyes are apologetic; he knows this is definitely not cool. "Think about who you're talking about; that girl almost hit a light pole in the middle of the afternoon."

Nora chimes in. "Wait, someone needs to start explaining. Heather, I thought you said your ex was an asshole and cheated on you?"

"*Me?*" My voice rises, and if we actually had

neighbors, I bet they'd be looking out their windows right about now. "*Me*, the asshole? What the hell did you tell her, Heather? Did you tell her *you* slept with your brother-in-law?"

Nora's eyes widen but she says nothing. I nod. "Oh, yeah, that's right. In my bed—in my fucking *bed*, Nora!" By now, everyone in the house has come outside to see what the commotion is...everyone except Julie. I want to know where she is; I bet she's locked herself in our bedroom and perched on the golden chaise with her book and the fireplace going.

I need to go to her.

"So now that you know the actual truth—" I look from Nora to Heather. "—scram."

Heather slowly moves toward me. "Ollie, you haven't spoken to me in three months. How can we try and fix it if you won't talk to me?"

Casey stifles a laugh but Nora hears him anyway. "Oliver, I didn't know...I just met her a few months ago...she never told me your name..." Her voice gets beneath a whisper and I can tell Nora had no idea. Heather is manipulative—I believe Nora.

"I'm going inside," I tell them and turn my back. "Don't follow me."

Heather sniffles. "Oh, so that's it? You're going to throw me away for someone like Julie Remington?" Nora tries to stop her, but it's too late—Heather is getting more hysterical by the second. "She's so pathetic it's unreal, Ollie! No one wants to be around her, she brings everyone down—no! Tell him, Nora!"

Heather slaps Nora's hands away from her. "Tell him what she did! She tried to—"

"I don't care what she did!" I scream at her and turn back around, stomping heavily as I enter the house, leaving Heather whining outside. Nora and Staci enclose her in a semi-circle so she can't follow me.

I have to find Julie.

I take the stairs three at a time. The bedroom door is shut and there's a small light on underneath the doorway, but when I reach it, I stop.

What was Heather talking about? I admit I don't know Julie as much as I should, but that hasn't stopped me from caring for her—or hurting her. I groan and pull out my phone, searching Google for her name. I search through a few sites that give me nothing, but the fourth link I click on makes my knees weak. I have to brace myself against the wall.

ROCKFORD WOMAN CRASHES INTO TELEPHONE POLE — POLICE SUSPECT NO FOUL PLAY

That makes my heart burn, but as I read the news article underneath the headline, I catch my breath. The reporter said that even though the police suspected no foul play, the investigation did look like she had driven into the pole on purpose. I keep reading until my eyes hurt. Every article basically blamed Julie for crashing her car, yet she was never arrested or questioned about anything. I remember her telling me about her brother, Randy—he must have gotten her off the hook with the cops. When I've read enough, I stash my phone back into my pocket and don't bother knocking—I just walk in.

The bedroom is empty.

Frantically scanning the room for her, I notice that even her scent of strawberry shampoo is slowly drifting away. The bathroom door is open and the light is off so she isn't in there, either. I think about the articles I read and panic. My stomach drops and I can't move my feet. I don't know the first place to even look for her around here—she and I haven't dug deep enough into each other for me to know where she'd go in a time like this.

First, I check all the other bedrooms in the house in case she just wanted some time alone—or away from me. Then I check the bathrooms, weight room, and kitchen, and still no Julie. The living room is empty too, but she'd been in here because I smell a faint scent of strawberries. I'm at least getting close.

As I stand in front of the double glass doors leading to the backyard and the woods, my hope falls. It's dark now—almost too dark to see without some sort of light—and if she'd left the house alone, that meant she's out in the woods alone.

"What's wrong?" Casey asks from the doorway behind me. There isn't anyone I want to see less than him right now—I could blame this entire thing on him for making me come up here in the first place.

I sigh. "Julie is gone."

"Gone? Like ran off into the woods?" His voice matches my panic inside. "Dude, let's go find her." I turn to him and my eyes start to well. I take my phone out of my pocket and show him the last website I was looking at. As he reads the article, his face looks like what I imagined mine looked like. "Is that true?" he whispers, horror on his face. "Is that something she would do?"

I shrug. "I don't know, but I'm not going to stand here and wait her out."

"Why don't you just call her?"

I dial Julie's number and it rings several times. I call her three times and she doesn't answer. "She isn't answering; I'm going to look for her."

Casey shrugs. "I'm coming with you." I smile at my best friend. He's leaving Nora behind—a girl he's been chasing for six months—to come with me to help find a girl I've been chasing for six days. He pats me on the back as we leave the house and wade into the darkness of the thick woods, using our phones as flashlights.

About halfway to the clearing that Julie and I sat in yesterday, I can tell Casey wants to talk. "What is it?" I ask him in the darkness, my senses still on the alert in case I see a flash of her honey blonde hair in the trees. "I can tell you have something to say."

He sucks in air. "It's just...I know why we're out here, you know? No one should be out here alone when it's dark like this, but..." He's choosing his words carefully. "Heather caused you so much drama. Are you sure Julie isn't causing just as much?"

I turn to face him. Even in the darkness, I can see

him cower. "No, I don't," I snap and cross my arms over my chest. "I like Julie a lot."

"Are you in love with her?" We hear Heather's voice sift through the trees behind us. "Julie Remington, huh? Are you in love with her like you were in love with me, Ollie?" She comes into view with a wicked smile on her face. Her black hair is the same shade as the night sky. "You are *way* out of her league—even she thinks so."

I narrow my eyes at her. "What do you know about it?"

Heather clicks her tongue. "Plenty enough to know that she doesn't want you if she got into a car with some other guy."

My world stops and any air I have left in my lungs is now completely spent. "What the hell are you talking about?" I grit my teeth and grab her arm, pulling her toward me. She squeals a little in excitement, but I don't care. "You better not be fucking with me."

She scoffs and yanks her arm back. "I'm not lying. She just left with some guy in a dark-colored car."

Brandon.

I take off running, but by the time I make it back to the house and into the driveway, it's empty and Nora stands in the light of the front porch, her face pale and sad. I grab her arms and shake her. "Nora, where's Julie?" I yell louder than I should.

"I thought she was with you?" Her panic matches mine.

145

I let her go and get into the Jeep. I can't think of any plan that'll work, but I start the car anyway.

Let her go, Oliver.

She doesn't want to be with you.

"The hell she doesn't," I say and speed down the driveway, kicking up dozens of rocks behind me. A million things run through my mind as I twist and turn the Jeep down the windy lake roads in the darkness.

What is he doing to her?

Why didn't she come to me?

Why did she leave me?

I plan on asking her those exact questions when I find her.

Wherever she is.

TWELVE
HEATHER

I CAN'T BELIEVE what my new "friend" Nora is telling me as I cradle my phone between my shoulder and ear, throwing several articles of clothing into the Betsey Johnson suitcase open on the hotel room bed. She's invited me to stay with some friends at a cabin. At first, I was bored and only considered it to pass the time. But now that I have the address and know who's cabin it is...I'm showing up early. "Who's up there? I don't want to be the third wheel," I lie. I know who's there: That's Ollie's cabin.

Nora lists off some of the guests and I shake my head. "And who is sleeping together already?"

"Well, Casey and I are together obviously," she says and giggles.

Wow.

"And I know the twins, Harley and Victor, are sleeping with Staci and Amber...but I'm not sure who is sleeping with whom."

I know the friends that Nora is talking about. She dragged them along with her to a party I had a few months ago, right after Ollie left me. "Okay, is that it? I know Staci and Amber."

Nora sounds distant now. "And Julie, do you remember her? I think she's sleeping with this guy named Oliver—he owns the house—and he's Casey's best friend. It sucks that you haven't met Casey yet, but you will."

I laugh a little and all Nora can do is repeat herself again about Ollie's little forest nymph and how amazing it is to see them both so happy.

He is so, so happy.

That used to be me—*I* made him happy.

I mean, Julie Remington is a damn mess.

I found out that she even tried killing herself over some loser boyfriend when she caught him cheating on her.

I admire myself in the mirror as I pass it and apply a fresh coat of sinful red lipstick. "Well, I'm packing now, so I should be there later tonight. I can't wait to meet everyone." I smack my lips together, smoothing the colored wax over the skin.

"So, how are you?" Nora asks me for the thousandth time during this phone call. "You don't talk about your ex a lot…what's his name again?"

"Oh, hey. I have to go—I'm going to finish packing. See you soon." I hang up on her. The truth is that it was actually *me* who did all of the cheating. I slept with a revolving door of men when Ollie had too much business to take care of out of town and he left me home alone and bored. There were some times when he just wasn't giving me what I needed— except money...he always gave me plenty of that. I think about Ollie's friend Casey, and know that he hasn't told his best friend that we slept together too.

Most of the time it doesn't bother me that I quit college after my sophomore year to follow Ollie back to Rockford when his grandfather died. Ollie was always this older, mysterious rich guy that gave me anything I wanted. I found myself addicted to the things he could give me and not the man himself. Still, I *do* miss him.

I smile at myself in the mirror and lick my lips. "After he sees me, I doubt he'll even remember her name."

I wonder if Casey will tell his new girlfriend that we slept together too. Casey is like a loyal puppy, following Ollie around and doing anything to please him. To be fair, our hookup was a drunken mistake that he didn't realize was happening. Ollie and I had just started dating, and during a dorm party—with *a lot* of tequila—I simply forgot to tell Casey that I was taken.

I already took what I wanted from him anyways.

I put my phone into the sparkly pink bag next to my sexy lingerie that I plan on wearing to seduce Ollie. I laugh; Ollie has been footing the bill for my hotel ever since he cut off my credit cards. I sobbed about having nothing without him and that the least he could do was pay for my hotel, and he did. He paid the bill and then never spoke to me again, and while at first it was fun seeing other men in my room, ordering room service, and sauntering with them...

I miss my Ollie Bear.

I carefully zip up the suitcase, making sure I don't scuff my newly painted pink fingernails. My stomach is full of butterflies because I haven't seen Ollie in so long. Three months without any money is too long for me—I have to grovel and beg for his forgiveness, play nice, and just live with the monogamy.

He wants a wife—I'll give him a wife.

He wants monogamy...I can try my best to give him that.

I wear flats because the long drive isn't going to work with stilettos, and I note that it's a smart choice as I pull up to Ollie's cabin at Lake Reed. I smirk to myself as I step out of the car, not bothering with the luggage when I can have one of the men inside the house carry it in for me. I text Nora as I walk toward the front door and she and Casey meet me outside, his face twisted in agony when he realizes it's actually me.

"Hello there." I wink at him and Nora growls under her breath. "I'm here a day early—*surprise*!"

Casey blinks at me. "A day early for what?"

"Oh, this is my friend, Heather." Nora's voice is annoyed. "She wanted to come a day early."

I could laugh for hours at the face Casey makes at me, but he doesn't say anything before shaking his head and disappearing back into the house. Staci and Amber come outside a few minutes later with Casey in tow—he has his phone held up to his ear as the girls squeal around me and dance, hitting their hips together with mine. I've only met these girls one time and they act like we're all best friends. Casey shakes his head and goes back into the house, phone still glued to his ear.

I have to endure Staci going on and on about the guy she's been sleeping with here and Amber looks so dumbfounded to be in my presence that she hardly says anything at all. They drag on forever talking about things I hardly care about as I eyeball Casey and Nora on the front porch. Casey looks physically sick each time I catch his gaze, so I laugh loudly to let him know that I could end his friendship—and relationship—anytime I wanted to.

The gravel on the long driveway starts to crackle and Ollie's Jeep comes barreling down the path.

"Ollie!" I squeal as he finally steps out of the Jeep. Out of the corner of my eye, I see Julie get out of the other side and vanish into the cabin. I notice Ollie is watching her every move, wanting to follow her, but I jump on him before he gets the chance, wrapping my legs around him and squeezing his arms while kissing his neck. "When I got the address from Nora, I just knew I had to come early and see you! I've missed you so much, Ollie Bear!" I lower my voice and whisper in his ear.

I can feel his body tense and I frown as he nearly drops me on the ground at his feet like he's throwing me out with the trash. "I don't know what you're doing here, but you have to leave." Ollie's face turns red. "Now."

Nora says something to him, but I'm too pissed to care.

Ollie plucks me off him and shoots a horrible look at Nora. "You don't know what you're talking about." He turns to me and scowls. "Heather, leave." Ollie walks away and Nora and Staci start whispering, no doubt talking about how much he just embarrassed me in front of everyone. I thought he would at least be a *little* happy to see me after three months of no contact at all. He spins his body around and stares dead straight at me. "Did I stutter? I said you need to leave."

"Dude, it's nearly nightfall—you don't want her navigating these windy ass roads at night, do you?" I hear Casey ask from the far end of the front porch. "Think about who you're talking about, that girl almost hit a light pole in the middle of the afternoon."

Nora chimes in. "Wait, someone needs to start explaining. Heather, I thought you said your ex was an asshole and cheated on you?"

I cross my arms over my chest and click my heel on the ground in impatience. "*Me*?" Ollie's voice rises quickly. "*Me*, be the asshole? What the hell did you tell her, Heather? Did you tell her you slept with your brother-in-law?" Nora's eyes widen and she looks at me for answers. Ollie continues his rant. "Oh, yeah, that's right. In my bed—in my fucking *bed*, Nora! So now that you know the actual truth—" he looks from Nora to me, "—scram."

I move slowly toward him and hold up my hands

in defeat. "Ollie, you haven't spoken to me in three months. How can we try and fix it if you won't talk to me?"

"I'm going inside," he says. "Don't follow me."

I opt for the crocodile tears; it's my go-to move that always makes him weak in the knees. "Oh, so that's it? You're going to throw me way for someone like Julie Remington?" Nora grabs my arms, but I break free from her weak grasp. "She's so pathetic it's unreal, Ollie! No one wants to be around her, she brings everyone down—no! Tell him, Nora!" I slap Nora's hands away from me as she tries to hold me back from running after him. "Tell him what she did! She tried to—"

"I don't care what she did!" he screams at me and turns around; Staci and Amber have joined Nora and they make a circle around me so I can't follow him.

"Don't embarrass yourself any more than you already have." Nora's voice is cold toward me. "I can't believe you would use me like that. How long have you known that Oliver was the one we were staying with here?"

"When you gave me the address," I tell her.

She scoffs, completely unamused. "I think you should leave in the morning."

I wave them off. "Fine. I'm going to take a walk to cool off." But really, I see Julie's shadow in the side yard, heading for the walking trail. Hoping none of them had seen her too, I skip down the grassy hill and walk slowly behind her until we get into a more secluded area. She's humming to herself, her jeans scuffing along the dirt path because they're too long for her short body. I giggle to myself; she is so painfully plain.

I clear my throat so she doesn't scream when she finally notices me. "So, you're sleeping with my boyfriend?" She turns around, definitely not amused. "You're one of dozens, you have to know that. He doesn't actually care about you."

She says nothing and it pisses me off.

"Oh my God, say something! Don't you fight for yourself?"

Julie shakes her head. "I've been through too much fighting and this isn't my fight to have. I won't do this with you."

I laugh. "You're right, it isn't. Ollie is mine."

"Oliver," she whispers.

I cock my head and furrow my eyebrows. "Excuse me?"

"His name is Oliver." Her voice is a little stronger now.

A smile breaks out on my face. "Is that so? Well, little girl, maybe you should call a cab and head back home. I'm here now and I'm not going to let you whore yourself around my house anymore."

"I'm waiting on a ride already," she says. "I called a friend."

"A friend?" I laugh and put my hands on my hips. "I'm surprised you have any left."

I see headlights inching down a wider path and a few employees of the Lake Reed Inn wave at Julie from a golf cart, but they frown at me. "My friends from the hotel. Can you ask Nora to bring home my things and I'll come and get them from her? I texted her and let her know I was leaving."

I shake my head. "I'm not your messenger."

"Okay," she says, nearly in tears. "See you later, Heather."

"That's it?" I say. She races toward the cart. "You're not even going to fight for him?" I catch a glimpse of her face as the cart drives away, and I can see the heartbreak on her pale face. "Oh, well," I say to the darkness. I'm making my way back to the house when I hear Ollie and Casey on the next trail, looking for Julie.

The way Ollie talks about her makes me angry; I never once heard him say anything nice about me to anyone else. I'm instantly jealous, but see my opportunity. Sneaking over to their trail and coming up behind them, I stand where I can be seen. "Are you in love with her?" I ask Ollie, the lights from their phones reaching me as they turn around. "Julie Remington, huh? Are you in love with her like you were in love with *me*, Ollie?" I paste a wicked smile on my face. "You are *way* out of her league—even she thinks so."

Ollie sneers at me. "What do you know about it?"

I click my tongue. "Plenty enough to know that she doesn't want you if she got into a car with some other guy."

"What the hell are you talking about?" He crashes through the thick bushes and runs over to me, grab-

155

bing my arm. I squeal with delight. "You better not be fucking with me."

I yank my arm back from him. "I'm not lying. She just left with some guy in a dark-colored car." I watch his face twist in horror as he runs off in a frenzy.

Casey stays behind with me, no doubt to try and hook up with me in these creepy woods. "Why are you such a bitch to him?"

"Why are you such a jerk to him?" I shoot back. "We had sex, remember?"

He chokes. "He can *never* find out about that."

I refresh my wicked smile and stare him down. "He won't as long as you help me get him back."

Because he's mine.

My Ollie.

THIRTEEN
OLIVER

THE ENTIRE THREE hours back into Rockford was nothing more than a dark, lifeless blur, and I don't even care that I can't remember how I even got back here. If Julie knew I was driving like this, she'd be furious. I sniff and clear my throat—who am I kidding?

She left me.

I seethed the entire way back, imagining what Brandon was doing to her, and when I think about it now, my jaw hurts from the tension of the different scenarios going through my mind.

What was she thinking?

I'm hurt that she didn't come to me for comfort, but I'm a stranger to her—why would she? My knuckles are white as I grip the steering wheel and let the darkness of the roads wash over me. My stomach drops when I enter the outskirts of Rockford because I have no idea what I'm going to do from here. This girl has me so jacked up, I don't know which way is up anymore. I pull into an empty parking lot and steady my hands as I dial her number again.

The phone rings five times before her voicemail picks up and I hear her voice, making my knees weak. "Dammit!" I yell, but I wait for the instant I can start talking to her voicemail, so ready to say everything inside my head but finding nothing to say at the same time.

"Hey, this is Julie."

A pain in my chest burns through my flesh, heating the front of the Jeep as the hole in my heart gets bigger. The sound of her voice has triggered something inside of me; the more I listen to her, the more out of control I become.

"Well, you know who this is, since you're the one who called me."

I don't want to, but I smile.

"So, leave a message and I promise I will call you back."

Beep.

"Julie, this is Oliver. You remember me, right? Tall, dark hair, and...can you just call me back? Please, I have to know that you're okay. You can't just leave in the middle of the night and make me wonder where you went. Not to mention who you went with—"

Beep.

The message is too long, so I take a deep breath before it gives me my second chance. "Julie," is all I can get out of my mouth as I sit in the darkness and lose myself in it. After pushing the end call button, I throw the phone on the seat next to me and tap my fingers on the steering wheel.

Where could she be?

I don't know where she lived with Brandon and I doubt her brother or nephew would appreciate me knocking on their door in the middle of the night to tell them I lost her. "Fuck." I shake my head, lowering it into my hands. "What is happening to me?" Just one week ago, I was perfectly fine with sleeping with random women and not knowing their phone numbers—or last names. Heather had broken my insides up so badly that no one wanted to fight to put them back together.

No one except Julie.

I miss her so much already.

I can't smell her strawberry shampoo anymore and that deepens my anger. Tears form in the corners of my eyes as I lay my head back onto the headrest. I want to close my eyes, but I think about going home, back to my apartment. My eyelids are too heavy to get there safely. Every time I close my eyes, I think about Brandon taking Julie's clothes off—

Ring.

Julie's number flashes across the screen and I damn near drop the phone after grabbing it from the seat. I quickly hit the answer button and listen but she says nothing. "Julie?" My voice cracks; I hope I don't hear anything disturbing on her end. "Are you okay?"

She breathes into the phone. "I'm okay."

An immense wave of relief washes over me and I want to reach out and touch her. I don't care where I need to drive—I am going to get her and bring her back home. "Where are you? I can come get you. I'm in Rockford."

I hear her breathe in sharply and then blow it back out slowly, like she's preparing to rip off a Band-Aid from my arm. "You should go home and get some sleep, then, because I'm not there."

"Where are you, then?" I demand. The echo of my voice in the car rings in my ears. "What has he done to you?"

"Who?" Her voice is small as if she doesn't want to wake someone.

I scoff. "I know you left with Brandon."

"No, I didn't…who told you that? Madrie and her husband—you know, the workers from the Inn that I met earlier today? They picked me up in their utility cart down one of the walking trails earlier. I'm still at the lake."

Heather is going to regret lying to me.

"Okay, then I'm coming back to get you." I start the car. "I'll be there at dawn." I don't bother putting my seat belt back on—the sooner I leave, the sooner I can get her back where she belongs.

Here. Next to me.

I hear someone talking in the background and let out a frustrated grunt because she's distracted. "No, you should go home and get some sleep, Oliver. Please?"

I let the silence fill the Jeep. Finally, even though my throat is raw, I ask her, "Why did you leave me?"

"I told you it wasn't going to work, remember? I knew you wouldn't let it go, so I left without you knowing. I'm sorry for worrying you." I picture her full lips frowning. "I have to go, okay?"

"No, don't go," I plead with her. "Just promise me that I can see you tomorrow."

I hear her sigh. "Oliver, I have to go."

"Promise me. I'll go home and sleep and drive back up tomorrow, pick you up, and bring you back to Rockford, okay? Promise me, Julie." The demand in my voice even scares me, but she doesn't seem to miss a stride. She knows how to handle me at my worst.

"Okay, I promise. I'll see you tomorrow, okay?"

My heart stops and I feel like I'm being stabbed in the chest with a rusty knife dipped in acid. "Julie?"

She's already hung up on me. I cry the rest of the drive to my apartment. There's a huge hole in my body and it hurts bad. I lock the door behind me and take a look around. Everything is the same as when I left it, but *I'm* not the same.

I've changed. She's *changed me.*

I want more; I need more.

Julie is my match in every single way.

My Julie.

Once I collapse on the bed, I realize Julie isn't the only thing I miss. I miss sleeping next to her. This bed seems way too big and empty, so I shove as many pillows as I can find on the other side. I groan into my pillow and throw another one over my head to drown out the darkness and silence. "Julie, what are you doing to me?" I whisper. "I don't want to go through this again."

I close my eyes and try to force myself to sleep without her. I hold my breath and wait, listening for her soft breathing, but instead all that meets my ears is someone's deep, familiar voice calling my name.

————

"HEY, BOY, COME OVER HERE," the voice says. "Come look at this bird." I follow the voice and see a man in a blue shirt, crouching on the ground. He's low enough next to an open window that he won't scare the bird off its perch a few feet away outside.

Dad.

"Holy shit," I say out loud and rub my eyes. "You're dead."

He laughs and pats me on the back really hard. "Nice language, boy. Look." He points out a window and there's a fat bluebird singing on the branch closest to us. "It's important to stop and appreciate things like this, kid."

"Dad?" I say, confused. "What are you doing here?"

He half-smiles and I recognize my features in his. "You brought me here, dummy. Think about it."

"Okay, so..." I look in a mirror and see my adult self. "This is too weird. You're dead."

My dad scoffs. "That's rude, son. Keep saying that and I'll leave."

I grab his arm. "Don't leave. Not again."

His hair falls into his face and I shake my head at the resemblance once he brushes it back from his eyes. "So, you're in a bit of a situation, aren't you?"

"How do you know?"

He eyeballs me over his wire-rimmed glasses. "I know things."

"I can't tell her how I feel," I blurt out. "I know you want me to and that's what you would do, but I just can't. Not after what Heather did to me." He nods in silence as he eyes me, moving his head from side to side while I give him more excuses. "And not to mention that we literally have known each other for a week and it's nearly impossible to have strong feelings for someone after such a short period of time."

He keeps nodding and listening to me until I'm finished. "You know who you sound like?" I shake my head. "Your grandfather. He wasn't one for much affection either."

My face falls. "I'm not him," I say. "He was coldhearted and raw."

"And you're not?"

I snap at him. "Of course not, or I wouldn't have been so willing to marry Heather, or like Julie as much as I do."

He clears his throat and places his hand on my shoulder, pushing me down into a chair so I'll shut up and listen to him. "I'm only going to say this once, son: You are your grandfather. You may not want to admit it, but he kept people at a distance too. I'm not saying what Heather did to you was right—hell, your mother did the same thing to me—but what I'm saying is, are you going to let yourself get in the way of your own happiness? Tell her how *you feel or don't, but you'll definitely regret it someday if you choose not to."*

"Dad?" I look up at him and see my own eyes. "Why didn't you ever tell me Mom cheated on you?"

He shrugs. "I stayed with her because I loved her— don't mistake that for weakness."

"I don't love Julie," I say.

"Don't you?" He smiles at me. "Get some rest, kid— you have a long drive back tomorrow and you're going to have some time to think about important things."

"I love you, Dad." My voice shakes. "I never got to tell you that—"

He waves me off. "It's in the past, kid. I'm just proud of the man you turned out to be, despite the person that had to finish raising you. You're a good kid."

———

HE'S GONE before I can beg him to stay. I would've stayed in that dream with him forever if I was allowed to, but the brightness of the morning sun seeps through my closed eyelids, waking me. I roll over and expect Julie to be there. I missed her there, snuggled up next to my body, trying to keep warm from the cool lake air. By now, at the cabin, the fireplace would have sizzled out and I'd have tucked her body into mine and held her there.

I hear the front door to the apartment open and softly shut. My heart skips a beat. I know it isn't Julie, but I hop up and burst into the hallway anyway, nearly giving Ms. Atchley a heart attack when she sees me. "Oh, Jesus, boy!" She gasps and clutches her chest. "When did you get back?"

I know my face falls because her eyes soften like I'm a hurt baby bird. "I came back on a fluke; I'll be leaving again shortly, Ms. Atchley." My voice is cold. "Are you here to feed the fish?"

She keeps eyeing me and nods her head slowly. "I do it in the mornings and around my dinnertime. Why did you travel the long way back for just one night?"

There isn't much I can get past Ms. Atchley, even though she's about two feet shorter than I am and walks with the brightest pink walking cane I could find her for Christmas last year. When she walks around the city by herself, people can see her better and not run her over. She limps toward me and tugs on my hand, leading me to the breakfast bar and sitting me on one of the stools, her eyes never leaving mine. "Tell me all about it, sweetheart."

I cradle my head in my hands and lose my tongue. "I lost Julie, I lost her," I keep repeating as she rubs my back and I cry once again. My grandfather's probably rolling in his grave. "She doesn't want me anymore and she's right—our lives together are too complicated, even in the week I've known her."

Ms. Atchley gasps and then shakes her head. "You're crying over a girl you met a week ago?"

"I know, right?" I laugh through my tears. "You would really like her though, Ms. Atchley, you would. She's really sweet and kind and would probably like doing all the old lady things you do."

She chuckles. "Old lady things? Like what? Please, elaborate."

I frown at her. "I didn't mean any disrespect, I'm sorry."

The old woman hands me a tissue and hobbles her way to the fish tank in the living room, where she uncaps the food and sprinkles some into the water. I watch the bright-colored fish swim toward the top and greet her, nibbling some food and going back to its mundane little life. "What is her name? Julie, you say?"

I nod. "Julie Remington."

She smiles at me. "You must love this girl if you care this much."

"Why do people keep saying that?" I wipe my face off with my sleeve. "I'm not in love with her."

Mrs. Atchley laughs in my face.

In. My. Face.

"Oh, boy, I have been around for a very long time, somewhere close to seventy." She rolls her eyes. "And in my life I have learned a lot. Some things were common sense and some things were hard to learn, but love isn't something that you just know how to do. Love is something that grows and blossoms, and some people aren't even blessed with knowing love until it's too late." She sits down next to me and pats my leg comfortingly. "What do you love about her?"

I scoff. "Again with the 'love' word."

She growls at me in disapproval. "Humor me. What do you love about the girl?"

I think about this for a moment. I never really thought about the word "love" with Julie—I just knew after I stopped fighting it so much that I just had to have her. I feel like I'm addicted to her, like no one else matters and really, no one else *does* matter but her. Still, I try and answer Ms. Atchley's question without embarrassing myself too much. Before I can, though, she pats my leg again and stands up to leave.

"Think about it and be truthful to yourself, boy. The only one that can destroy you, is you. Let me know when I might walk in on something I don't want to see." She winks at me and leaves me alone before I can even mutter the words "thank you" to her.

Be truthful to myself.

I know I'm not in love with Julie—*truth*.

I do love some things that she does—*truth*.

I love the way her honey blonde hair falls down her shoulders in waves of thin strands, tickling her collarbone and inviting me to touch her.

I love how she says my actual name and not some silly ass nickname people made up for me.

I love the way she can be so quiet but her presence still demands attention.

I love the patience she has with me and the way her small hand tucks into mine. I love that she lets me touch her whenever I want—or at least *used* to.

I love how she doesn't care what I can give her or

what I do for her—she wants to spend time with me because of me, not my money.

I love how slow she makes life seem. She quiets the storm around me and I don't have to be someone I don't want to be with her.

I love her smile. And her laugh. And her lips.

I shake my head and head back to the bedroom, confused and very sick to my stomach. I feel like someone has just gut punched me a million times and it's hard to even change my clothes. I brush hair out of my eyes and look in the mirror, frowning at myself.

My father and Mrs. Atchley are right.

I *am* in love with her.

And I honestly don't know how I feel about that.

FOURTEEN
JULIE

I HEAR hushed voices talking in the room next to me at the hotel: Madrie and her husband. They let me stay in one of the rooms for free for the night. They didn't seem surprised when I phoned them last night; they even offered to pick me up and help me almost immediately.

I almost cried when I talked to Oliver late last night, but I held my own and kept it in, even when he said my name with all of that hurt wrapped around it. I had to hang up on him before I cracked. This entire week has been so unreal that it hurts my brain to even *think* about what has happened. I slept with someone I hardly know—let's start with that. My parents weren't the greatest people, but I just know my Aunt Shelley is rolling over in her grave knowing that I did something like that. I mean, that isn't me.

"You want breakfast?" I hear Madrie's husband, Paul, ask me from outside my closed door. They've given me one of the lower-class rooms, which isn't even lower class at all with the biggest flat-screen TV I have ever seen, the expensive furniture, and oh yeah...

The bed.

The. Bed.

I hardly wanted to get up and I'm sure that if Oliver were here and he had it his way, we *wouldn't* get up. It was just that comfortable. *We* were just that comfortable. Paul knocks when I don't answer him, but doesn't try to come in. "Miss Julie? Breakfast?"

I don't want to keep him waiting and be rude, so I pad across the floor and open the door to greet him with a fake "good morning" smile. I extend my hands and take the tray from him and he nods before walking back down the hallway and out of sight.

I leave the door open as I turn to put the tray down. "Waffles and strawberries, huh?" I hear Brandon say, and I nearly drop the tray as I whirl around to make sure it isn't him, but of course, he leans in the doorframe of my room.

"What are you doing here?" I squeak and put the tray down on a table. I really miss Oliver now; my stomach starts to drop and I scold myself for not staying put at the cabin with people I'm safe with.

Brandon holds up his hands in surrender. "I come in peace. I've been staying here since your boyfriend sent me on my way."

"Why?" I slowly ask.

"For you, of course." He doesn't move, trying to calm me down before I freak out. "Come on, Jules, just hear me out, okay? Look." He places his hands in his pockets. "I come in peace, really." My stomach grumbles and I really, really wish Oliver were here already. Brandon tries to nonchalantly look around me into the room to see if Oliver is in there, but gives up when I leap toward him and start to close the door in his face. "Wait." He pushes the door back toward me a little bit. "Can we just talk?" The look in his eye is so intense that I can't refuse him, so I stomp toward the bed and don't say another word as he comes into the room. He shuts the door behind him with a deafening click.

I reach for the coffee Paul brought me.

French vanilla cappuccino.

Brandon looks nervous. "So, where's your boyfriend?"

I scoff into my cup. "He's not my boyfriend."

He nods in relief and throws me a sly smile. "He sure fought for you like he was—maybe someone should tell him that."

I find myself annoyed as I glare at him. "His name is Oliver and I'm not really sure why you even care."

Brandon laughs. "Yeah, I know who he is. Oliver Jackson. You might want to get checked out when you get back to the city." I want to slap his face off, but in all truth, he is right. Oliver is a bit of a playboy —Nora has told me stories about him before this whole trip even happened. I wonder how she knows him, but that isn't really relevant to me now.

I watch as Brandon joins me on the bed, sitting

dangerously close to me, but I don't think quickly enough to move. "I miss you, Jules. I miss our life together. I miss living with you and waking up with you—"

"You should have thought about that before jumping into bed with Rachel." I snort. "Didn't seem like you missed me too much then."

He takes my hand. "I messed up, okay? I was an idiot then, but I'm better now. I want to be better. You remember what we used to be like, right? We were good in the beginning. We can find our way back there. I can be a better person for you."

I can't handle the pressure he's putting on me. It sounds like he thinks I'm stupid, like I actually think things can be different. Maybe a month ago I would have gone running back to him, but *I'm* a different person now. Oliver has shown me that I don't have to be scared to be next to someone. Someone could want to be around me without hurting me. I'd like to say I'm more mature, refined, and just absolutely against anything Brandon stands for.

I still don't hate him.

But I don't love him, either.

"You should go," I whisper as he gets closer to me and takes my hands from my lap. "Oliver is coming to get me." The way his chestnut hair slicks back toward his neck sickens me. I take a quick look at what our time apart has done to him; his skin is pale and his eyes don't have the gold flecks in the muddy brown irises anymore. Instead, he's been replaced by a shell of a person—someone I don't even recognize.

Brandon smiles at me and touches my cheek. "Well, I'm here now—doesn't that count for anything?" He kisses the tip of my nose. "I thought you said he isn't your boyfriend...sure sounds like something a boyfriend would do. I would know."

"H-He's not," I stutter. "P-Please just go."

Brandon presses his lips to mine and for a moment, it feels good and familiar, like time has stood still and nothing had ever changed between us or gone sour. Before I can squeeze a thought out of my head to stop him, there's a knock on the door and it opens. Paul, Madrie, and Oliver stand in the doorway, but by the time the door had opened, Brandon had pulled away and now sits next to me with a huge grin on his face. Oliver looks sick as he storms into the room, glaring at the two of us. He looks like he's ready to kill Brandon.

"I drove three hours for this?" he snaps at me. "For you to show me *this*?" The panic in his voice saddens me, and I see tears forming in the corners of his eyes as they dart back and forth, first toward Brandon and then toward me.

I say nothing.

"Julie," he demands. "Answer me."

My heart breaks down almost instantly. I try to get a grip on my breathing, but I start to hyperventilate and Madrie pushes past Oliver to get to me. "Everyone, get out," she barks to all the men in the room. "She's not well enough to hear this fighting."

Brandon smirks. "Kissing me will do that to any girl."

Oliver whirls around to look at him, his skin so red I think he'll burst. "You need to fucking leave before I do something I can be put on trial for, you understand?"

"She wants me here, right, Jules?"

"Trust me, she doesn't. Like I said, leave."

Paul chimes in. "I think both of you should leave before I call the police, okay?"

The world closes in on me as Madrie pats my back and I take a deep breath in and let it out. "Everyone just shut up!" I scream at the top of my lungs. "*Everyone* needs to leave." When they all look at me in confusion, I scream, "Now!" Paul and Madrie scurry out of the room first.

Brandon and Oliver look at each other and have a silent standoff, waiting for me to turn my back so they can brawl again. "Oliver, you stay," I say. "Brandon, you leave." Brandon opens his mouth to refuse, but I glare at him so hard that I think I see fear in his eyes and he quickly leaves Oliver and me in the room, alone.

"Julie?" Oliver says in the smallest voice he could muster. "Are you okay?"

I nod. "I'm fine. What the hell is your problem?"

He cocks his head; he's taken aback by my sudden boldness. "My prob—what the hell do you mean, my problem? You're the one who ran away and you're the one in a hotel room with your ex, waiting for me to pick you up. So, my problem—" His voice grows sad as he walks to me. I hold my palm out against his chest to warn him to keep his distance. "—is *you*."

I scoff and stick my bottom lip out in a small pout. "Me? Hardly."

"Ugh!" he screams into the air. "Let's just go home."

I cross my arms. "I don't want to go back to the cabin. I want to go back to Rockford."

"I mean home, to Rockford."

"I live in an opposite world from you." I swallow, but my throat is dry and my voice cracks. "I think I should just call my brother; he can come pick me up. I'm sure he would love to know that Brandon trailed me here."

Oliver isn't having it. "No, I'm already here. I came back for you—what else can I do to get you to trust me?"

I slowly take his hand in mine and his eyes soften, but I know he isn't going to like what I have to say. "Can you just take me home? To *my* home?" He nods and squeezes my hand, tugging on it gently so I would follow him out of the room. Brandon's eyes light up when he sees me, but when he notices Oliver holding my hand and leading me away, they narrow with anger. "You're leaving with *him*?" he growls. "I can't believe this, Jules. You hardly know him! What about me?"

Oliver stops and tugs me behind him. "What about you? You hurt her in so many more ways than one. Did you think I'd let her leave with you?" I grip the back of his shirt tightly. The warmth of his anger reaches my fingertips but it doesn't scare me.

I gasp a little as Brandon moves toward us, his eyes full of desperation and stretching his neck so he can try and see me. "Jules, please, can I just drive you home? I'll take you wherever you want to go. I just want to get you alone for a little bit."

I instantly feel scared, and I can immediately feel Oliver's body tense and his temper rise. "Get the hell away from her," he says in a weird tone. "Don't make me kick your ass again."

Brandon scoffs. "Dude, try it. I'll fight for her too."

I expect Oliver to keep it going, but to my surprise, he laughs. He reaches back and finds my hand clutching his shirt. He tugs it free and laces our fingers together, giving my hand a squeeze to let me know I am safe.

I feel *safe.*

"I'm not fighting for *her*," Oliver says smoothly to his brand-new nemesis. "I'm fighting for *us*." He pulls me past Brandon, whose jaw is open wide with shock; he knows he's just been severely defeated. I can see him quickly trying to find the words to redeem himself, but Oliver has already pulled me out of the lobby and placed me in the front seat of his Jeep before Brandon can even pull himself together. I watch him run out the front doors after us as we speed out of the parking lot. Brandon throws his hands up, no doubt cursing to the chilly lake wind.

I can feel Oliver seething next to me as he slows

down a little once we're far enough away from the hotel and Brandon. His hand finds mine and he pulls it into his lap, caressing my fingers with his thumb but saying nothing to me. He gently pulls my fingers to his lips and kisses them before slowing the Jeep down enough that he can look over at me, his eyes dark and full of sadness. "Are you okay?" he finally asks, and I try my hardest not to melt inside. "I'm sorry I acted like that back there—he just pisses me off so bad."

I smile at him without realizing what I'm doing. "It's okay. I'm actually thankful that you showed up." I figure I'd better not tell him that Brandon kissed me, mainly because I don't want him seeing red and running the car off the road with us still inside of it. I can tell that the selfishness of me leaving and giving no explanation has taken a toll on him. Maybe he *tried* to sleep last night like he promised, but his tired eyes tell a different story. "Oliver, I—"

He cuts me off but doesn't let go of my hand. "You don't have to explain," he says in a soft voice and looks over at me briefly. "I just want you to be happy."

My heart skips a few beats.

"I just want you to know that it's nothing you've done, okay?" I say to him, but I know it doesn't matter. I've ripped his heart into shreds for no good reason.

Okay, maybe *one* good reason.

We don't belong together.

"Let me ask you something," he says to me when we're nearing the first hour of our trip back to Rockford. "What could I have done differently to keep you? What can I change about myself to make you want to stay with me?"

My stomach sinks onto the floorboard and I clear my throat to stall for a moment so I can think of something to say. "Oliver, we're just too different, okay? Neither one of us is in a good place in life to be what the other really needs, you know? Brandon messed me up and Heather messed you up—that doesn't make what we have right." I look into his eyes and wipe a small tear from my cheek. "I never want you to change, not for me or anyone else."

He smiles. "But we *do* have something, right? I'm not going to stop chasing you," he says to me with no regret in his voice, "you know that, right? I mean, you and me, Julie, we just…fit."

My voice shakes as I search for the words to say to him. "Oliver, I'm not ready for what you want. I'm not ready to be that for someone."

"I disagree." I feel the car come to a stop and he turns his body to look directly into my eyes as the late morning light filters in through the car windows. "I think you're just scared." He keeps going before I can argue. "And that's okay. I'm scared too."

I can help you carry your things.

His voice from that very first day we met echoes through my head, bouncing off the walls of my skull and taunting me. I don't like the way he made me feel then, just that one short week ago, and I don't like the way he makes me feel now. Once we start seeing buildings and actual neighborhoods, my heart sinks a little. I know that our sad car ride will end, he'll drop me off at home, and I'll never see him again.

He'll forget about me.

I watch him weave through the streets until we get to my brother's house and he slowly parks, making a point to drag the inevitable out. I can hear his labored breathing; he's trying to think of something to make me stay and I think deep down, I am waiting for that too. He opens his mouth, then closes it, opens it again, and sighs a little too loudly. "I don't want you to leave me," he whispers. "Why won't you just stay?"

My eyes are like magnets to the floor. "Oliver—"

He holds up his hands. "I know, I know. I'm sorry. Can I at least walk you to the door?"

I nod in silence and let myself out of the car. He jumps out and runs around the car, sliding his arm around my waist as we walk to the front door of the house. I see someone look out the front window and realize it's probably Clyde trying to sneak a peek at us. "Shouldn't he be in school?" Oliver asks me as we get to the door, his arm still around me.

"He's gifted…he goes to boarding school ten months out of the year." I hope Clyde isn't snooping so much that he's listening on the other side of the door.

Oliver doesn't speak when he lets go of my waist. His arms drop to his sides, like he's unable to decide what exactly he wants to do with them. "I guess this is goodbye," he says. "Although it's the shittiest goodbye in the history of goodbyes."

I giggle. "It doesn't have to be a total goodbye."

His eye light up like a Christmas tree. "Yeah? But I thought you said—"

Before I can control myself, I stand on my tiptoes and press my lips against his cheek, nearly missing his mouth. He wants to touch me, I can feel it, but he refrains and lets me lower myself back down to look up at him with wide eyes. "I know what I said. Just give me some time, okay?"

I don't wait for him to answer before I check the doorknob to make sure it's unlocked and slip through the front door, shutting it behind me. I collapse on the floor, weak and unsure about every single thing in life at that moment.

"I'm in love with you, Julie." I hear his desperation from the other side of the door.

Crap.

FIFTEEN
OLIVER

"I'M in love with you, Julie." I could hear the desperation in my voice echo in the cracked walls of my mind. I told her I loved her after she shut the door in my face, and even if there was a slight chance that she even heard me, she didn't open the door again to let me know.

That was three weeks ago.

Three weeks without her, three weeks of tearing my apartment apart and working out a ridiculous amount every day just to try and forget about her. No amount of physical exertion ever made me completely forget about how her jean shorts hugged her sides or how she smiled when she used a straw, biting the end and leaving her imprint in it. I can't believe I let myself fall in love with someone; I knew love would do this to me again. I knew if I let myself love again, it would blow up in my face. That's why I have rules. That's why I needed to *follow* the damn rules.

She didn't call. She didn't email. She didn't text.

But I'm *still* totally in love with her.

My phone rang off the hook that first week we came back, and between Casey and Heather, I stopped even looking at it when it started to buzz constantly. Okay, that's a total lie…I had to look.

Every.

Single.

Damn.

Time.

Hoping that once, just once, it was her, but it never was. So, here I sit, in my dark apartment on a Thursday—wait, no, Friday—night, the late August air drying out the corners of my eyes. My days blend together—who cares what day it is? I want to hate her so badly, throw myself into bed with dozens of other women whose names I don't care to remember, but that rule has already been broken. There's no going back from here.

I miss her lips and her thighs, the way she giggles when I say something completely moronic, and the way she studies me when she thinks I'm not looking.

I'm *always* looking.

My phone rings on the table in front of me.

Casey.

"Screw you," I say. "I hate you."

"No you don't, dude," I hear him say from the other side of my apartment door. "Come on, Ollie, open the door." I shake my head like he's in the room with me. "Ollie, open the door." I hear keys jingle. I forgot I'd given him a key last year when Heather and I went to Hawaii. He lets himself in and I don't even bother to look behind me to make sure he's alone—I don't even care. Whomever he'd dare bring into my room of depression should suffer the consequences like he's about to. "Dude, you stink. When was the last time you showered?"

I sniff the air. "Who cares? It's not like I have anyone to smell good for anymore."

Casey sits down next to me and I can feel his sad eyes examine me closely for any bumps and bruises I might have from punching any walls around the apartment. "*You* should care. What the hell is wrong with you?"

I hold my hand up for him to stop and shut the hell up. "Just go, okay? I don't feel like talking to anyone right now. Especially not someone responsible for me meeting her."

He snorts. "She's just a girl, Ollie."

Rage builds inside of me. She isn't just any girl. She is *the* girl.

My Julie.

"Dammit, Casey, get the hell out of here," I roar, throwing several sofa pillows at him. He dodges them all. "I said I don't feel like talking to anyone right now."

He frowns and shakes his head. "Okay, then just listen to what I have to say, then you can throw me out. If you care about her so much, why are you sitting in your apartment, not showering or eating or sleeping—" He looks around and notices the empty energy drink cans littered around. "—or even being a human being? Go find her, go talk to her, and figure it out."

I close my eyes, hoping he'll just go away. "She obviously doesn't want to talk to me or she would have called me by now. It's been three weeks."

Casey sighs. "Dude, just call her." He picks up my phone, finds Julie's number, and hits send before I can open my eyes and stop him. He throws the phone at me and I don't want to hear her hit the ignore button, but I hold the phone up to my ear and wait anyway. I hadn't planned to leave a voicemail, I know that much. I won't whine and beg for her—unless she wants me to.

I take the phone from my ear and nearly touch the end button when I hear her voice. "Oliver?"

"Ju-Julie?" My throat is so dry I think I'm going to choke on her name before I can spit it all out. "I'm sorry, Casey called you on my phone...I didn't know—"

I hear her giggle and nearly lose my shit right there. "It's okay, I'm glad you called. How are you?"

How am *I*?

I want to stand outside your house and hope to catch a glimpse of you somehow. I want to touch you one more time, even if it's just our fingertips. I want to kiss you and hold onto you so tightly that you can't run from me again. I want to make you mine again, I damn sure don't want you to leave me.

"Oliver?"

"I'm here," I say and shake the fuzziness from my head. "I'm here, Julie. What did you say?"

She sighs. I can see her full lips frowning inside my mind. "Are you okay?"

"No, he's not okay," Casey says, making sure she can hear him loud and very clear. "You fucked him up, big time."

She stays silent as I punch Casey hard on his shoulder and he cries out in pain. "Julie, I'm sorry he called and bothered you."

"Oliver, *you* will never be bothering me."

My entire body melts onto the floor in front of me. I've desperately needed to hear that for three weeks. I could bawl my eyes out like a damn baby, but I keep myself composed and clear my throat. Casey looks over at me still wincing in pain. "I miss you, Julie," I blurt out.

"I miss you too."

"Can I see you?" I ask, positioning my body away from Casey, who has turned on the flat-screen and started playing video games. I throw a pillow at him to turn down the sound, but he hardly notices anything but the car he's racing on the television. "Julie? Can I see you?" I ask again, and this time, I hear a man's voice in the background and she covers the receiver for a moment.

She uncovers the phone and says, "Of course, I want to see you, too. When?"

"Now?" I laugh like an idiot and then smell myself. I need a shower before seeing her—I look like death warmed over a thousand times and I smell like it too. "How about tonight? I can pick you up and make dinner for you?" I can hear her smile into the phone.

"That would be nice; do you remember how to get here?"

I've only been pining over you for nearly three weeks, girl, did you think I haven't driven by your house a million times? "I think so," I lie. "I can manage to find it again."

"Can you pick me up around six? Clyde is leaving for school soon and I want to spend as much time with him as I can." I have to concentrate on her voice. My entire fucking body is vibrating with excitement. I can't believe all I needed to do was pick up the damn phone and call her. This is my chance—my chance to get it right.

I cough up the dry air that has been bouncing around in my lungs before I even realize I hadn't taken a single new breath. "Six o'clock. I will definitely see you then." I wish I could say more, but my damn body won't function with all the adrenaline running through it. "Thank you, Julie."

There's her laugh again. "For what?"

Casey sticks his tongue out at me and laughs. "You're such a pussy, dude."

I mouth a "screw you" to him and shake my head. "For seeing me, thank you."

"I would never want to *not* see you, Oliver," Julie says to me and puts my entire world back into place —the pieces of my broken life that she shattered rise up and hover over me, finding their way back to their partners. For the first time in three long-ass weeks, I feel free from myself. Free to feel something again.

I don't want to hang up on her because I want it to be real, and it won't be unless I can hear her voice. It's noon; I have to wait six hours before seeing her. I'm not sure I can do it, but I've gone three weeks without so much as a bread crumb, so six hours is nothing to me. I jump up and zip around the apartment for a few minutes, holding my grumbling stomach and wondering if I'll be able to hold something down. I want Julie here with me so I can show her that we belong together more than she is trying to deny it, and maybe—just maybe—she'll see it my way.

Casey isn't any help as he chomps on potato chips in the living room, getting crumbs everywhere as I start in the kitchen, cleaning up my three-week dirty mess of dishes and pizza boxes. After cleaning every room in the apartment from top to bottom, only three hours have passed and I'm left in silence once more with more time on my hands than I wanted.

"Dude, go shower. I'll finish cleaning up in here and head out." Casey shakes his head.

I need to shower badly, so I mope into the bathroom and start the water, spacing out as I watch the fast stream hit the shower walls.

God, I miss her so damn much.

How can it be possible to love someone this much?

My entire body hurts from thinking about her every second of every damn day. I stopped being angry with her long ago; I know it's my fault that she left. I just don't know how to fix it when I don't even know what I did wrong...

The hot water feels good on my skin and I make it a point to slowly enjoy the heat, washing parts of my body several times just so that when I finally get out, I've wasted half an hour and I'm that much closer to seeing her. My heart flutters when I look at the clock and see that it's almost four because I wasn't sure that I had anything in the fridge to even cook for her. Panic fills my stomach when I realize that I don't even know how to cook beyond a high school home economics level.

There are several takeout menus in one of the kitchen drawers, so I find one with options and order a meal for a small army over the phone. Satisfied with what I chose, I bite the inner flesh of my cheek and try to calm my nerves. "It's not like she's a stranger," I tell myself as I walk toward the bedroom. I open drawers and throw a pair of jeans and a black sweater on the bed, followed by other essentials. Then I drop my towel, standing naked in the middle of the room.

I hear her voice in my head. *Well, just you is pretty intimidating.*

It's nearly five when I'm finally dressed and groomed. I comb my floppy dark hair back toward my neck and stare at myself in the mirror. I really hope this is enough to make her stay, but I can't make any promises to myself. The doorbell rings and the delivery guy hands me two huge brown bags full of food and I give him a twenty-dollar tip for his trouble of carrying them all the way to the sixteenth floor, even on the elevator. I make it a point to put all the food into containers that make it look like I actually prepared the meal myself, stashing the bags and takeout containers in the hall closet. I notice the clock.

It's almost six.

My Julie.

My mind races the entire drive to her house.

What will she be wearing?

Will she hug or kiss me?

Will she be happy to see me?

What can I do to make her stay?

It's getting dark outside when I pull up, but her brother's huge suburban mini mansion is lit up inside like it's on fire. The curtains in the living room shift and I know someone is peeking outside as I pull up. Once I'm outside of the Jeep, I fiddle with my keys and walk up and down the driveway several times.

"I knew you were a loser," I hear someone say behind me the last time I walk quickly back to the car. "Couldn't you have refrained from hurting Julie before figuring that out for yourself?"

Clyde.

He makes a sour face at me and acts like he's standing guard so I can't pass him on the walkway. He's scrawny, but through his thick glasses I can see the fire in his eyes. "I bet you didn't even finish high school—do you even have a job?"

I smile at him and nervously tug at my sweater.

"Maybe you're right, Clyde." His mouth wrinkles like he's trying not to throw up. "I should have just left her here that day, huh? Maybe I should have just brought her on home when she wanted me to, then she wouldn't be sad right now."

He looks a little sad. "I didn't say that."

"But you sure wanted to."

The red-haired kid looks sick enough now that I take a few short steps backward. "Clyde?" I hear a male voice call for him. A man my height with the same honey blonde hair as Julie's comes into view and frowns at me. "Oh, you must be Ollie."

"Oliver," I correct him politely and extend my hand for him to shake, trying to show him that I'm a nice guy. "I'm here to pick up Julie—you must be her brother Randy?"

He nods but says nothing. He sure as hell doesn't take my hand, either.

I slowly retract my hand. "Okay, well, nice to meet you."

Randy scoffs and then shakes his head at me in disappointment. "All you jerk-offs think it's okay to just rip her to pieces, don't you? Like she's a doormat for you to shake your shit all over and then leave her to put it all back together herself?"

I hardly know what to say to the man. He's at least a decade older than me, but you could only tell because of the few wrinkles lining his otherwise smooth face. But he has no idea what the hell he's talking about and that pisses me off.

"I think you've been misinformed," I say through

my gritted teeth. "She left me in pieces, not the other way around." I can tell that even if he believes it, he's going to treat me like the loser he's convinced I am.

Randy shakes his head. "I don't think so." He steps closer to me, pointing his finger directly at my chest. "I think you're a worthless little rich boy who finds pleasure in seeing how far he can push someone until they break under his spell."

"What?" I roar and move closer to him this time. He doesn't back down from where I'm about to pounce. "Watch your damn mouth."

"Can we not have a showdown on the front lawn?" Julie says next to us and puts her arms in between our bodies, gently pushing us apart. "Randy, I will be fine. Oliver, let's go." She tugs on my arm and pulls me away from her brother, who looks like he was about to pounce on me at any moment. Julie pushes me into the Jeep and buckles her seat belt before looking at me in wonder of what's coming next.

I breathe deeply and study her. She's *different*. Her hair is longer and shinier, and I want to bury my face into it. Her eyes are brighter, and her lips are glossier. "Hi," she says and her sunshine fills my head like the very first day we met. "It's been a while."

I nod and start the Jeep, speeding off into the dusky night air. "Yeah, it's been two weeks, six days, and nine hours, *actually*." I keep my gaze on the road, but I can feel her body radiating nervousness and confusion. "I'm sorry…let me calm down about your brother first and then we can talk. I don't want to be a jerk to you because I'm upset."

Julie smiles. "There's the Oliver I remember."

My temples are on fire and no amount of rubbing them is making this situation any better. I actually think about turning the Jeep around and taking her straight back home, but there's a twinkle in her eye, just for a moment, and I see the girl I remember from when we first met.

My Julie.

SIXTEEN
OLIVER

THE RIDE to my apartment is bursting with silence because the two of us are trying to figure out how to talk to the other again. I haven't seen this girl for three weeks and it's killing my insides to be so close to her now and not be able to touch her. Julie did allow me to open her door for her and lets me graze the small of her back as we walk into the building and Bernie, the night security guard, smirks at me and nods.

She lightly sniffs the air when I let her into the apartment. A smile creeps across her face as she looks at me and then back toward the source of the aroma. "Is that garlic lasagna from Mara Bello's?" She giggles. "How did you know that is my favorite?"

I blush. Fire rushes through my cheeks and numbs the tender skin. "How did you know?" I smile and tap her nose lightly with my index finger. She blushes a little and nibbles on her bottom lip. "I was trying to pretend like I knew how to cook."

"I'm not worth the trouble, really." Julie huffs and sniffs the lasagna again, licking the inside of her lips just enough for me to see. I feel a jolt of electricity run through me; I am suddenly standing as close as I can get to her, our breaths mixing, and I finger the tassel of her blouse and look into her eyes. "You are worth it to me," I tell her and watch her bright eyes. "Why have you been avoiding me the past three weeks?"

Julie clears her throat. "Because I don't trust myself with you."

"Do I scare you?"

She shakes her head. "Of course not. I just know I'm not ready for anything serious and it was getting pretty serious between us—I'm sure you can agree on that."

"So, what I want doesn't matter?" My voice is gritty and hurt; she isn't playing fair. I have to make myself calm down before I kill my chances ten seconds into seeing her again. "You get to decide for both of us?"

"I don't want to fight." She holds her ground. "I just want to—"

"—I want to kiss you." The low growl in my throat reaches my lips and I devour her mouth with mine, slowly kissing her; my tongue plays with her bottom lip. Julie doesn't put her arms around me or even lean into the kiss, but she isn't pulling away, either. My thumb caresses the outside corner of her mouth as I suck the rest of her lip between mine. Through my ragged breath, I press our foreheads together and say, "You don't know how badly I've missed you."

"Oliver, I have to take this slow if we do this at all." Julie's breath is thick but I feel her strain herself on her toes so she can reach my lips with hers again and we hold each other, locked together like magnets. "I'm too afraid to give myself completely to you again."

"Okay, okay." I let out the rest of the hot air and pull my body from hers. I have to put myself at arm's length from her on purpose. "If you need to take it slow, we're taking it slow. As long as I get to do it with you, I don't care how long it takes."

She raises her eyebrows in intrigue. She knows me better than that, which doesn't make it any easier to earn back her trust. "Are you sure? I'm not convinced you have the capability of slowing things down."

Somehow I fake a warm smile toward her and take my index finger, crossing my heart over my sweater. "I swear, I will try my best to take it slow." The smell of lasagna is filling my nose now and my stomach rumbles. I take her hand and sit her down at the long, oak dining room table and leave to bring in the food to serve her. Once the wine glasses are full and we fill our plates with the garlic goodness, she moves her plate closer to me. Her leg touches mine underneath the table, sending shivers up my spine. "What have you been doing these past few weeks?" she asks me, mouth full of food and laughter. I take a moment to mentally prepare myself for an actual conversation with her. I knew she would ask me questions, but I never thought about what my answers would be. There are hundreds of things I could say to her; I can't seem to find the right words without looking weak.

I never broke my rules before you.

Now I don't know which way is up.

I can't sleep. I can't eat. I can't do anything but think about you.

I am so completely unraveled because of you.

"You don't want to know." I snort and refill both of our glasses with wine. "Trust me, you don't."

Her small hand finds my arm and squeezes. I nearly spill the wine all over the table in front of me. "I want to know, Oliver."

I uncork another bottle and stare at her. I know why I do whatever she asks of me: That's what love does to a man who breaks the rules. "I hardly moved from the couch and I haunted my phone, hoping you'd call."

Her tongue smacks against her teeth. "I'm sorry you went through that." She collects the plates and stands up. She rushes toward the kitchen and I grab the wine, stalking after her. "Oliver, let me have a moment alone, okay?"

I shake my head and drink from the bottle. I'm not letting her do this to me again. I'm going to stand my ground and demand that she listens. "I've done that—you've had three weeks alone."

She sighs and starts rinsing the plates. Her collar-bone is softly poking out from beneath her milky skin. I have to bite my cheek before I sink my teeth into her flesh. "I haven't exactly had a spectacular three weeks either, you know. It's not like I was out partying or having fun…I was in a bad place for a few days."

The rich chocolate dessert that the restaurant sent with the food sits on the counter, begging for me to open it and feed some to her. I look at her lips and my insides twist together. She licks them slowly and it takes everything I have not to take her right here in the kitchen. She takes the bottle from my hand and takes a hearty few chugs. "I enrolled in some courses at the community college downtown," she says. "Randy is helping me with tuition and I'm actually excited to start."

She watches me open the dessert and run a fork through the smooth cake. "That's really great. I could help you with that too—you know that, right?"

She says nothing when I raise the fork to her mouth. A dark smile paints my face. Her lips part and she lets me put the sweet inside. Her lips devouring the fork and I pull it back toward me with greed. "I don't need you to help me." Her voice is raspy. I can hear her faint breath turn ragged—it *slays* me.

A bit of chocolate sticks on the corner of her bottom lip and I kiss it. My tongue gently flicks her skin and she moves her head to kiss me back. "Stay the night," I say into her kiss. "Stay here with me." She knows I'm right. I know she knows that *we* are right.

Before I can stop myself, I pull her body closer to mine and place my lips on hers again. The burning feeling between us intensifies and she breathes against me with a gentle force. "Oliver," she pants and pushes me away, "this isn't going slow."

"I don't know how to go slow with you," I say, trying to catch my breath. "I don't know what the fuck to do here."

I want her.

I need her.

I *deserve* her.

"Stay, please." I hold up my hands in defeat. "I'll try harder to keep my hands to myself."

She eyeballs me but finally gives in. Her ocean eyes soften as she loses the war with her heart. "I really don't believe you, but I'll stay."

I grin like a schoolboy at her and she laughs at my fake innocence. I have absolutely every intention of getting to touch her whenever I get the chance. And I will do absolutely anything to get her back. She yawns, her lips calling to me. She stretches her body so her chest nearly bumps mine, and I nearly grab her tight and pick her up, run to the bedroom, and shut the door behind me.

Cool it, Oliver. You're going to mess this shit up again.

"My pajamas are in the bottom-right dresser drawer," I say to her. Our eyes meet and the room fades away. "You'll probably die a little inside because my pajama pants and old t-shirts share a space."

She winces in a small amount of obsessive

compulsive pain. "I appreciate that, Oliver, thank you." I get a chill down my spine when she says my name. It sounds like she says it for the last time, every time. "We're adults—we can sleep in the same bed. You don't have to sleep on the sofa."

I want to scream: *You're confusing the hell out of me!*

"I think it's better if I stay out here…I don't want you feeling smothered by me." I pray she won't keep it going. I give her a look that hopefully spells out my need to end this part of the conversation. I swear to all that is or ever has been holy to me, a wicked smile appears on her face and she looks up at me.

"If that's what you want," she says. I point to where the bedroom is and she leaves to change.

"Holy shit," I breathe out loudly. I rest my head on the sofa pillow. I can still feel her lips on mine and they tremble as I try to close my eyes. I can't stand the feeling of her being so close to me; I have to see her just in case she leaves me again. I jump up and walk toward the bedroom door. I don't care that I'm about to undo an entire night of trying to get back where I wanted us to be.

"Julie?" She doesn't answer me but I hear her inside the room, shuffling her small feet around. I wonder if she's naked—it drives me crazy enough that I place my hand on the door and *almost* walk in. I can't help myself. I'm so fucking addicted to this girl, no matter how hard I try not to be. I try the door handle and she opens it from the other side at the exact same time.

She has laughter in her eyes, and I see that she

has already undressed and stands in front of me in a pair of my boxer shorts and an old blue pocket t-shirt.

To hell with the damn rules.

"Oh, sorry." I blush. "I was just coming to make sure you found what you needed. It looks like you're comfortable…I mean, you found them."

"I found them." She giggles and curtsies. "Unless you think I wear men's underwear underneath my clothes."

I raise my eyebrow at her and catch my smirk before she does. "I've already seen what's under your clothes—" She gasps and blushes a little. "—and it isn't anything close to that."

"Oh my God," she gasps again and slaps me on the shoulder, playfully. "You're making me blush." I lean toward her and part her lips with mine, locking us together. She sucks on my bottom lip and smiles into the kiss. Her sunshine fills my head again and I can't think straight. "I knew you weren't gonna listen to me about keeping your hands to yourself," she says but can't help but smile and let me kiss her jawline. My hands gently encircle her waist to hold her in place. She lets me taste the flesh on her neck; the salt of her skin tickles my tongue.

"Tell me something no one else knows about you," I say to her and kiss the curve of her neck. She purrs at my touch. "I want to know everything about you, Julie."

"You first." She licks her dry lips. "I-I can't think right now."

My smile makes my teeth nick her collarbone a little. I can feel what I do to her; it's almost impossible for her to control her shaking legs. "What's your favorite ice cream?" She laughs and it vibrates my teeth as I bite down on her skin. "I'm serious. Mine is chocolate chip."

"I never thought about it." She breathes and moans. "I guess your favorite can be mine too."

What's yours is mine. I remember our first night at the cabin; she demanded more space for her clothes and I demanded all of her attention. Little did I know then that I would be breaking the very first rule that was so important to me.

She's carefree and breezy right now, nowhere near the stressed mess she was a few weeks ago. I find myself attracted to her more aggressively as I move in closer to her. I push the rest of her hair away from her neck, flicking my tongue on the soft spots. "I have to go back into the living room before I take you on this bed, Julie." I groan, trying to hide the growing erection now pressed against her.

"Sleep with me in here." She coaxes me and lies back onto the bed. My boxers hug her curves like butter. "You can behave yourself somewhat, right?"

I won't be able to. I know I won't be able to.

"Why are you torturing me?" I whisper and frown. I look down at her body, casting a shadow over her. "I can't do it. I can't sleep in here without being able to touch you."

"*Try.*" Julie nods and studies my eyes. I never know what she's really thinking about, and that scares me. She sweetly smiles at me and pats the empty spot next to her on the bed. "I'm not going to kick you out of your own bed." Her eyes narrow at me in warning.

"Yes ma'am," I mumble and finally give in. I jump into the open space over her body as she giggles. I turn the lamp off and the darkness consumes us, making it hard to concentrate.

Then it hits me. "Give me another week."

"Hmm?" Her sleepy voice moans next to me.

"Another week. Let me have one more week with you. Let me show you what life with me could be like." She turns to face me. I can still see the fear in her eyes even in the darkened room. "Let's go tomorrow night…stay at the cabin for another week. When do your classes start?"

She yawns and her lips tremble. "In just over a week."

"That's a yes, then?" I smile at her in the darkness. I don't care if she can't see me. I know that she feels what I feel. It's like she has a part of herself inside of me.

I expect her to decline my offer, but to my surprise she leans toward me. She kisses my lips and nods. "That sounds perfect."

Perfect.

———

"OH, LET'S STOP HERE!" I hear Julie squeak. There's a child behind me laughing, hysterically. "I have to pee so bad, Oliver—pull over at that gas station! Please, please!"

I feel my arms yank a steering wheel to the right and pull the Jeep into the gas station parking lot. As I look over at Julie and laugh, the child continues snorting but Julie looks completely horrified. "I told you going to the lake this close to the end was a bad idea," I say to her and she grumbles at me. She opens her car door and as she gets out, I notice her growing pregnant stomach again.

"Dad?" I hear the child say as she runs into the store and disappears. "How much longer?"

I hesitate looking into the rearview mirror. I don't know why, but I know that once I look at him, there'll be no going back. I force myself to glance up, and the boy looks exactly like I did when I was a kid.

Dark hair. Freckles. Goofy smile.

He has her eyes.

"Yeah, kid, we are. Your mom just can't help it; she likes public bathrooms so much that she wants to visit them all as soon as she can." I wink at him from the mirror and he snorts. He thinks I'm hilarious and that fills me with radiating pride. His laugh sends a warm feeling through my chest that explodes inside me; I can't even process any unwanted emotions because I'm so happy.

"Can I swim in the lake without my life jacket this year?"

I shake my head. "Probably not, buddy. Your mom doesn't need any more stress right now, okay? That would scare her a lot, but next year I promise you'll get to and I'll be the one to take you out there."

He looks sad but gets over it quickly and looks back up at me; I can see her innocence woven through his smile. "Dad, how many fish do you think are in the lake?"

I laugh at his question. "Probably a million."

He gasps out loud. "A million? That's a lot, right, Dad?"

I nod and try not to cry. "That's a lot, son."

Julie comes back into view with a coffee for me and chocolate milk for her and the boy. She shoots me another warning look and says, "I was also craving chocolate milk."

I say nothing but I smile at her and grab her hand to kiss her fingers. I feel her body relax. "We're almost there," I tell her and pull back onto the road.

She smiles. "We're almost there."

SEVENTEEN
JULIE

SUNLIGHT.

I untangle myself from Oliver's arms and gently place them back onto the bed next to him. I make it out of his grasp without making a sound. It's after eight already and my stomach growls so loud I think it's going to wake him up; the lasagna has already been digested and I need more food. Like, *now*.

His lean body is relaxed as he sleeps soundly next to me—his shirt is somewhere on the floor. He'd peeled it from his body sometime during the night. His hard chest drew my attention first, followed by the bulging sheet where his lower torso began—the sheet only covers him up to the start of his V-shape beneath his hard stomach.

Wait, is he sleeping naked?

I have to get out of here before I can't help myself anymore.

The bedroom door shuts quietly behind me, but getting to the kitchen is a hard task. I make so much noise tripping over things in the hallway; I swear I keep waiting for Oliver's shaggy dark head to peek out of the bedroom to investigate.

I find my phone on the counter where the three empty bottles of wine sit. I shake my head at the reminders of our drunken conversations last night. I pick them up and toss them into the recycling bin. Nora has been texting me all night. She knew I was coming to his house and she didn't like it.

NORA

> Remember the break-up rules I told you about.

> The first and most important rule is... what, Julie?

> Never let them into your heart again, that's rule number one.

She's right. These are rules that I can't afford to break again. I want to trust her advice, I really do. She spoke to me after the cabin fiasco—she begged me to believe her that she didn't know about Heather's games. I believe her when she says that—I *want* to believe that someone couldn't be that manipulative.

Except Heather. She's way past the psycho level of manipulative.

I sigh and put my phone down. I open the cabinets and fridge, but the only edible things I can find are some eggs, milk, and pancake mix. When I find the utensils I need, I start to feel something weird. *I feel like I belong here.* I shake the thought from my head quickly.

I start to scramble the eggs as I move my body to a seductive song in my head. My hips sway side to side with grace because I feel so alive and free. I see an open bag of chocolate chips on the counter so I pop a few in my mouth, then into the pancake batter, while I cook the small breakfast and dance around the cold kitchen.

Nora is going to be so upset with me when she finds out I couldn't even get through one face-to-face with him before breaking the first rule.

Oliver walks into the kitchen and raises his eyebrows at what he sees; he scares the *crap* out of me in the process. His tight blue boxer briefs tug and accentuate everything they are supposed to as he saunters toward me. His warm, lean body brushes past mine to start the coffee in the machine. I have to take a deep breath and blow it out gently, my eyes closed as I let it free. Oliver pushes hair behind my ear and kisses my forehead. My eyes pop back open and I can feel myself blush.

"Good morning, sunshine." He smiles and shakes his tousled hair to the side of his head. "How did you sleep?"

"Fine," I quickly say and flash a brief smile. "What's with the nickname?"

Oliver doesn't miss a beat. "You fill my head with sunshine."

"Oh, okay," I gurgle unexpectedly. "I scraped together a breakfast."

"Eggs and chocolate chip pancakes?" His voice is filled with delight but then his lips turn into a frown. "Wait a second." His palm finds the curve of my hip and squeezes. I can feel the burn where his skin touches mine; it burns me to my very core. While he presses against me, he makes my body lean back into the counter. He leans over and opens the freezer door with no effort. He takes out a carton of chocolate chip ice cream and his electric green eyes are glued onto mine. "Now it's perfect."

I take the tub from him and set it on the counter. I have to catch my breath before I pass out and ruin the moment. Hot air is stuck in the back of my throat, aching to be released. The room spins and I don't know if my feet are even on the floor anymore. I can hear a drawer open and silverware clinking together as he lowers his gaze to mine. "Hey, you still with me?" his silky voice says and I shiver. He's just gliding right past those walls I've spent the last three weeks rebuilding, isn't he? "Close your eyes, sunshine."

I do what he asks of me without hesitation. I can feel every tremble his body makes each time he touches my skin. He stays silent as he pulls my hips into his and slides one arm behind my back. Steadying me with his free hand, he parts my lips with a cold mass of ice cream.

I nearly lose control of my entire body, mind and soul.

My eyes flick open and he takes a bite for himself, grinning at me around the spoon.

Oh. My. God. I can't take much more of this…

I let him feed me another bite, and as the cold travels down my throat, I can't stop my body from leaning into him and meeting his lips halfway into a kiss. Our lips are sticky as he takes control of mine but I don't care—it's amazing either way.

"Sorry," he says and parts from me. "I know we're taking it slow."

"I can't control myself either," I say to him. "How are we gonna do this, Oliver?" I realize how relaxed he's gotten when I say this; it looks like a huge weight has been lifted off his shoulders and floated away into the North Rockford sky. His face crinkles into a thoughtful mess and he pulls himself away from me in frustration. "Did I do something wrong?" I ask him, placing eggs and pancakes on the plates.

Oliver shakes his head and rubs his square jawline. "I'm just confused…I thought you needed to take it slow, but you clearly aren't worried about that anymore." He smiles and slides his arm behind my waist, keeping a tight grip on me. "I mean, I'm not complaining about being able to kiss you, but it's just…really confusing."

"I know, I'm sorry." There is so much remorse in my voice that it bounces off the walls and doubles back to me. "I keep trying to tell you it won't work, but you keep sucking me back in with how adorable you are." I watch his smile grow bigger. His perfectly lined, white teeth blind me. "Stop smiling, it's not funny!" I slap his arm playfully. He catches me and squeezes me into a bear hug, nuzzling my hair with his nose. "Oliver, it isn't funny!"

He laughs and lets me go. Separating from my body, he keeps looking at the plates on the counter. "Let's eat this wonderful breakfast together, okay? Let's just eat and not worry about other shit right now." I watch as he places the two plates side by side on the breakfast bar, patting the seat next to him.

"After breakfast you should take me home so I can get ready to leave tonight." His face brightens; he's completely surprised and smiles wide. "Did you think I'd forgotten?" I laugh when he takes my hand and kisses my palm. He's nearly jumping for joy.

"I thought you were scared or you changed your mind," he says in excitement. "We talked about a lot of shit last night; I didn't scare you away?"

I shake my head. My hair falls around my face with the force of my disagreement. "No way. I like talking to you. I hardly think wanting to open a bar with Casey is a bad thing, right?" I wink at him without meaning to.

"Julie..." I can feel that he's about to ruin everything. "What we had was...*magic*. It's been hell without you, you know that."

"I told you I would give you another week." I think about Clyde leaving for school soon and frown. "Let's just worry about ourselves for a week, okay? A week of selfishness."

That's the biggest smile I've ever seen on his face.

Randy will be furious with me for spending another week at the cabin, but I don't care enough to let it stop me from going. He'll always want to tell me what to do and how to feel; I don't think he would ever try to physically stop me from leaving, though. He hates Oliver, but he isn't going to make a scene and that I am thankful for.

When we're dressed, Oliver leads me back out into the elevator and pushes the button for us to go down. He's changed into jeans; his soft gray pullover peeks out from beneath his black motorcycle jacket. I wait a few seconds before he catches me looking. He leans over and caresses my lips with his thumb, then parts them with his. The kiss is so deep that it makes my head spin, so I can't get off the elevator without wobbling a little bit.

"Are you nervous about going with me?" he asks once we get on the freeway. "If you have any second thoughts, I won't be upset."

I snort. "Yes, you will."

"Okay, you're right, I will." He laughs and gets off the freeway, slowing down once we get into the neighborhoods. "But I *will* understand. I don't want you to be uncomfortable." We pull up to the pool house and he parks. Randy should be at work and Clyde texted me to ask if he could stay at a friend's house. So, the house is hopefully empty and no one is peering down on us like spies.

I lean over to his side of the car and kiss him. He runs his hand down my side and squeezes, making electric jolts run though my legs. I gasp loudly. "I better get inside," I say and open my door. Stepping out, I almost run toward the house. "Pick me up at three?" I say, and he nods before pulling off in the Jeep.

I shut the door to the pool house behind me. I blow out whatever air was in my lungs and double over; I'm trying to catch my breath and stop my head from spinning. I know I only have a small amount of time to pack. I race upstairs and open a suitcase, throwing items inside. I manage to run a hairbrush through my tangled mess of hair, thanks to Oliver and his death grip on it when he kisses me. I take a fresh pair of jeans and a red tank top into the bathroom and dress myself. I add fresh makeup to my face, but none of it takes away the panic in my eyes. I am going up there alone with him. I shake my head and try to fix my mind onto something else.

I should tell someone where I'm going.

I hear someone behind me. "Can I ask where are you planning on going with all of that?"

Randy.

I turn to face him but he already knows. "Oliver and I are going back to the cabin up at Lake Reed for another week."

"What about your classes?" He crosses his arms over his chest. "I thought you had some starting this week."

I shake my head. "No, they start in ten days. Are you checking up on me?"

He shakes his head and sits down in my purple armchair. He crosses his legs and stares at me as if he has more to say. "I'm just checking up on your head, not your actions." He frowns and looks at the suitcases on the bed. "I thought you told me that Oliver left you?"

"That's right," I say, unsure of what my voice sounds like to him. "Why?"

"Well…" He draws out his words while I try to figure out what his end game is. "Mr. Jackson told me different."

"Oh, he did, did he?" I scoff. "Well, I'm not sure he would be so willing to tell a cop the truth about anything."

Randy sighs; he looks up at me with sadness in his eyes. "You want to know what I think?"

"No."

"Too bad, I have every right to tell you." He doesn't wait for me to respond. "I think that after what Brandon did to you, no matter who comes along, you'll push them away before they can hurt you. Why would Oliver come back if he didn't love you?"

Oliver has pulled up right on time. I don't answer Randy as I gather my things, leaving him behind. Oliver is already making his way toward the pool house door when I throw it open and hand him my stuff.

"Let's go," I mutter and he looks confused. "I don't want to talk about it, let's just go." I shut the front door before he can even sneak a peek inside. He doesn't press it and places my suitcases in the back of the Jeep—with grace, this time—and lets me get into the car by myself. He joins me and allows me a little silence as we weave our way back toward the freeway for the second time in two days.

He opens his mouth but I beat him to it. "My brother hates you—he thinks you left me at the cabin alone and you were just playing with my head."

"I know."

My jaw drops. "You do?"

He nods. The car pulls off onto a smaller highway and we begin our journey together. "He told me last night. It's okay though, I get it." He takes my hand, smiling. "I don't care what he thinks about me...it only matters what *you* think about me."

I smile. "Well, I do think rather highly of you."

"I think rather highly of myself too, so we have that in common." He laughs. His grip tightens on my hand. My stomach grumbles and I feel sick—the motions of the car are sending me waves of nausea. I try to breathe in and out slowly to make it stop. I manage to get through an hour before I just have to stop and throw up. "Can we stop at the next gas station?" I ask him and a goofy grin spreads across his face.

"What?" I demand, my arms crossed over my chest. "Is that funny or something?"

He shakes his head. "Nope."

I don't bother looking at him as I rush out of the Jeep. In the gas station, I ask the clerk where the bathroom is and barely make it inside. It seems like forever until I'm able to pick myself back up and check my clothes for vomit. I wash my face and rinse out my mouth. The walk back to the Jeep is dreadful; it gets worse when I see his face twisted in laughter.

"Are you okay?" he asks, making sure not to look into my eyes.

"I feel better, and we're almost there."

Oliver nearly chokes. "We're almost there."

———

"Julie?"

Brandon's voice booms through our small, studio apartment. Before he even opens the door, I can feel the fear stir in my stomach. I sit on the bed with several college brochures littered in front of me. I quickly try to hide them before he comes in the door, but he sees them almost instantly.

"I thought you threw those away?"

My eyes don't meet his when he speaks to me. "I did, but then my brother picked up more and peddled them off on me."

Brandon's eyes are dark for a few seconds. He hates my brother and the feeling is mutual for Randy too. He takes a minute to remember that he came bursting into the apartment to tell me something important.

"We got the apartment, the one on Godwin Place."

I leap off the bed and he catches me. We spin in place as he finds my lips and kisses me. "See, I told you good things were coming to us. I got that job at the law firm and now we get this apartment." His chest swells with pride. "We should celebrate."

"Yes! I'll get that bottle of wine my brother got me for

my birthday." I squeal, grab the bottle from the fridge, and pop the cork toward him. "We don't have any wine glasses; we can use coffee mugs if you want." He starts to laugh. He holds out his hands for the mug.

"That's perfect," he says. He watches me pour the wine into two coffee mugs, then I hand him one and we clink them together. "This is to us. We've stuck together through a lot of bad times before things got better for us. I love you, Jules. I can't wait to spend the rest of my life with you."

We both drink the wine and revel in the moment.

"So, now that we have all of this good karma—will you marry me, yet?"

I knew that's where he was going to take this.

"Brandon, I'm still not ready," I say. He takes my hand into his, squeezing it a little too hard. I'm only twenty; I'm not ready to take that leap yet. I'm really not ready to take that leap with him, either.

"Just promise me that you won't ever leave me and I can wait for you, Jules. You're mine, you'll always be mine. Always."

Always.

EIGHTEEN
OLIVER

THE CABIN.

A month ago, it felt different to see it. Last time I was frustrated because I wanted her. Now, I'm frustrated because I'm trying so hard to keep her. I can feel hope everywhere in the air as I pull up to the house.

It feels like I'm coming home with her.

"You go inside and I'll bring everything in." I kiss her hand. "I have a surprise for you." She squeals with excitement.

The cabin's caretaker wasn't answering my phone calls, so I resorted to a more humiliating option: I begged for some help from the Lake Reed Inn. I hope that Madrie and Paul did everything I asked for. I managed to contact them before picking Julie up, and somehow I persuaded the two of them to help get the cabin ready again. After Madrie cursed at me in another language, Paul agreed and I felt comfortable asking for another favor: to convert my grandfather's study into a library for her.

Golden chaise and all.

I smile as she disappears into the house. I wonder if she'll be drawn to her space and come back to thank me. Once I get all the luggage into the foyer, I hear her shuffling around upstairs. Her light footsteps beckon me toward our bedroom. "Hey, you." She smiles when I walk into the room and she lights a fireplace match, throwing it into the opening. "It's a little chilly in here—is this okay?"

"Of course it is." My hands wave in the air. "What's mine is yours, you know that. You don't have to ask me for anything; I'll give you whatever you want."

Julie giggles. "That's a little…*much*."

"Nothing is too much when it comes to you. I want to make you happy."

Her eyes look like crystal blue gems. I want to reach out and touch her skin so bad it shakes my fingers. "It's almost fall; the leaves will be changing soon." There's magic in her voice. I think about her snuggled up in her chaise, book in hand and raging fire in the fireplace as the snow falls outside and covers the forest in white.

You gotta stop doing this. Calm down and be a normal person.

"We should come back when the snow falls," I say, and she gets lost in thought. She walks around the living room and smiles. Her smile creeps across her lips in slow motion; she bites her cheek when she catches me staring at her.

"Groceries?" My voice cracks and I try to keep my cool. Food shopping wasn't one of the items on Paul and Madrie's task list; I wanted Julie and I to do that together. It's my way of reliving our first day together, pathetic as it was. Julie wants roses and romance, so I'm going to give her what she wants. I grab her hand and throw her over my shoulder. This time she's squealing with delight as opposed to last time when she kicked me in my abs.

"Oliver Jackson!" She laughs and swats my ass. "Put me down!"

"No. Freaking. Way." I dodge her flailing arms and duck through the front door. I jog to the Jeep and I can feel her thighs bounce beneath my hands. The nearest grocery store is ten miles away, but she didn't seem to mind. She rolls down the window and holds her hand outside, surfing the windy waves with her petite fingers. I can feel her calmness as she twirls her hair around her index finger and looks over at me. She smiles like she knows something I don't.

We hold hands as we walk into the small grocery store in town; I smile at the way she giggles and tugs at my hair. We shop and start filling the cart to the brim with junk food and essentials we think we might need. It's so much happier than our last grocery trip together, for sure. I see a few guys checking her out as we pass them and I get pissed off at their glances. My arm snakes around her; I stake my claim silently.

My Julie.

"Beer?" I hear Julie say to me and smile. "Or wine?"

I raise my eyebrows and shrug. "Both? We should be prepared for anything—can never have too much alcohol."

She rolls her eyes at me and places the case of beer and a few bottles of wine into the cart. Then she nibbles on her index finger, deep in thought. "Oh! I want to bake cookies for you." She pulls me down the aisle with baking materials and loads the cart up even more.

"I didn't know you liked to bake," I say. I blush because I know damn well that I had a dream about her baking and sucking the batter off her fingers.

Her body is always next to mine as we walk; she makes it a point to be right beside me—never in front or behind me—when we make our way to the cash registers. We start putting items on the revolving belt and the girl behind the cash register locks her eyes on my body, blushing when I catch her. Julie doesn't notice and that kind of bothers me a bit...I want her to be jealous.

She's so oblivious to men checking her out that it's almost comical: the way she flips her hair and teases us and doesn't even realize. I pay for the groceries and head to the Jeep. I keep hearing a phone ringing somewhere nearby. Julie looks sick to her stomach as she rummages through her bag, looking for something.

"Is that *your* phone ringing?" I try to see the screen as she pulls it out. "Is something wrong?"

Julie looks at the phone and shakes her head. "No, nothing. It's just a wrong number that keeps calling. They'll take a hint eventually."

I don't believe her, but I'm not going to press the issue. I let her lie to me as she stows the phone back in her bag. She doesn't speak as we drive back, but helps me bring the bags inside. She starts fluttering around the kitchen, putting things away with rhythm. Like she's swaying to a song the same as in my kitchen before. I like that she feels free with me; I like that I make her feel safe and wanted.

Because I really, really want her.

No one else has made me even *want* to break the rules.

She is *the one* for me.

She holds up a package of macaroni and cheese. When she shakes the box, her tongue peeks out; it slides across her pouty bottom lip, causing my legs to go weak.

"Mac and cheese for lunch?" She winks at me. Her long eyelashes sway with her seductive wink; I almost fucking lose control. I'm not even sure how the hell I have been able to contain myself since I laid eyes on her. I grumble, "that's fine," and race out of the kitchen. I can't be in here with her right now. I know she knows what the hell she's doing to me.

I lock myself in the master bathroom to catch my breath. "Jesus, dude, get a grip on yourself," I whisper to myself. I sit on the edge of the Jacuzzi tub and think about her.

I can't fucking help it. And I sure as hell can't stop it.

She knocks on the door and I nearly fall backward into the tub. "Yeah?" I gruff and hold myself up, my muscles coming to my rescue. The door opens slowly and Julie peeks her head inside. I forget that I am supposed to keep my hands to myself; I throw myself at her, pulling her closely into my body. Her honey hair tickles my nose when I bury my face into it; the sweet strawberry scent of her shampoo gives me a head rush. I tuck her into my arms and kiss her pink lips before she can protest.

"Oliver?" I snap out of my daydream. She's standing in the doorway, looking at me with amusement because of my glassy-eyed gaze. "Are you okay?"

I choke. I can't answer her even if I wanted to. She walks gracefully over to the mirror. Watching her own eyes in the reflection, she frowns. She doesn't like what she sees and that bothers me. No, that *infuriates* me. Fuck the rules. I've already thrown the first rule of love—that I created myself—out the window. All I can do now is open my heart to her and not break any more of my own damn rules.

"Mac and cheese is done, but can you help me with the cookies?"

Cookies. In the kitchen. She licks the batter off her finger.

I squirm. "Yeah, I think I can do that."

She knows something weird is going on with me.

I try my best to let it go and act normal. I let her lead me back down the stairs and into the kitchen. She has ingredients lined across the countertops, neatly. And all of my insides nearly drop to the floor when I see what she's gesturing toward.

The. Bowl.

A silver, stainless-steel mixing bowl in the middle of the counter.

"Hey, don't just stand there." She giggles. "Lend me a hand."

I do what she asks; I'm afraid to disappoint her. I weakly smile down at her as I approach her side. I can't fucking believe this is happening right now. She giggles again, hands me a wooden spoon and mouths the word, "Stir," at me.

This is my dream coming true.

I watch her dip her finger in the cookie batter. She puts her finger in her mouth, slowly licking it off, and moans so loud I think my head is going to fucking roll off. "That is so *perfect*." She purrs and snuggles her body next to mine. Her curves fit into my side like a puzzle piece.

I slam the bowl down on the counter. "I can't take this shit anymore."

Julie frowns. She's confused, as if she doesn't know what the hell she's doing to my brain. I'm sure that she knows each time she pulls me into a different direction. "What's the matter?" she quietly asks me as if I were going to yell at her. Her finger is still sliding across her lips; I start to reach out and replace her finger with mine.

"Nothing," I grumble. I force myself to stop and pick the bowl back up. I continue to stir the batter like she asks. She prepares the cookie sheet and then takes the bowl from me, putting spoonfuls of the gooey goodness on the sheet in rows like an art piece.

"Are you hungry?" she asks me and breaks the haze in my head. There she is: There's the sunshine that she fills my entire body with. She reaches into the fridge and grabs two beers. I take one from her and follow her to the table. I let her serve me and we eat in silence. She finally puts her fork down and stares directly at me. "I don't like this."

I put my fork down and look into her darkened eyes. "I don't like it either."

"Is this what life with Oliver Jackson is going to be like?"

I blink several times. Trying to figure out what the hell she means by that, I clear my throat. I take a long drink of my second beer, swishing it around my mouth to bide me some time. I don't want to put my foot in my damn mouth. Not this time. "What do you want from me?" I ask her, making sure I watch the tone of voice I give her.

"I don't know, I guess." I barely hear her. She crosses her legs. "I thought this would be a fresh start for us. We could really see each other for who we are, you know? And how we wanted to be together."

"I *want* to be with you, Julie, you know that."

She sighs. "Yeah, but why?"

I'm in love with you, dammit.

I scoff. "Do you really need reasons? Or are you

224

scared?" She stays silent. I don't think that she even knows what she wants. I lean into her and take her hand. "Just let it go, okay? Let go whatever is holding you back. Just let yourself be happy with me. I promise you I have no bad intentions and I'm not trying to hurt you."

"I never thought that," she says.

I click my tongue. "Yeah, you have."

She sits up straight and uncrosses her legs. She glides over the three feet between us and sits in my lap, facing me. I allow myself to place my hands on her back but nowhere else. "I'm sorry I am so confusing." She buries her face in my neck. I hold her for a long time; there isn't anything she can say or do to make me let her go. "I know the hot and cold is getting old for you."

"Not enough for me to ever leave you," I say and smile. I gently push her shoulders back so I can see her beautiful face. She is the most beautiful disaster I have ever seen. "I'm not going anywhere, okay?"

She brushes her leg against my dick on purpose. As she holds out her hand for me to take, her sultry laugh completely floors me. "Yes, you are." Her voice is bubbly and light, reaching into my soul and tickling my intrigue. "Come with me, please."

"Where are we going?"

She giggles. "To the south end of the property."

"Julie…" As much as I want to grab her and take off toward the rock pool…"It's nightfall already and it's about half a mile down the trail. It's not safe." She pouts and stands in front of me. The roundness of her breasts nearly smacks my face. "Fine, let me get some things."

When I give in, she squeals with delight. She bends down and kisses my cheek. I find a small zipper bag and throw in some flashlights, bottles of water, some beer, and a few snacks just in case she lets me work up an appetite. She had raced upstairs to grab some towels and when she comes back into the room, she's biting her bottom lip. I can tell she's trying to get out of it.

"Ready?" I ask her, and don't wait for an answer before I tug on her hand and pull her out of the house. We walk toward the middle walking trail at the end of the backyard.

I leave her alone with her thoughts, mainly because I am on high alert for any animal larger than me. Even I can't take down a bear with only my hands. As we walk slowly and carefully in the darkness, nothing is illuminated unless it's by our flashlights.

It takes the better part of twenty minutes to get to the rock pool. At first I think the lights from the house are ricocheting into the clearing. I'd forgotten that Heather had outdoor lighting installed to make it look like stars in the night sky above us. I click off the flashlight and look at Julie. She's already begun the low self-esteem binge she's famous for by hunching so far down into her sweater I can't see one curve on her body.

I start to take off my boots and socks, hoping she'll get the hint and join me. The natural bubbles in the rock pool let off light steam. The warm mist tickles the bare skin of my feet as it laps onto the rim of the pool. "Do you want to go back to the house?" I ask her.

She shakes her head. Her pale skin glows with the soft lights. I can tell she's debating her answer. Her decision weaves in and out of her glassy eyes. "No, go ahead. I'm just taking it all in…did you do all of this?" Her fingers swirl in the air at the lights above us.

Take it, Oliver. Take the credit: Don't mention Heather.

"Yes," I lie.

"It's gorgeous." There's a twinkle in her eyes; I can tell she's happy. Her broad smile grows.

"Yeah, it kind of is." I agree with her, taking off my shirt. Her eyes glisten as she looks my body up and down. I like when she looks at me like that—I like that she makes me feel like I'm the only person on the planet. Like she only has eyes for me. I sure as hell only have eyes for her. I smirk toward her and laugh, "Like what you see?"

She laughs. "Oh, God, this again?"

She gasps as I step out of my pants. I keep my boxer briefs on, not that it matters. I get into the rock pool slowly and feel the heat, making my whole body relax. "You *have* to come in here, it's amazing." My words link together as I drift backward. I let the water consume me. "But it's up to you."

Fear flashes across her face. I am going to leave it all up to her—this was her "make it or break it" moment. She either wants to be with me or she doesn't.

I'm leaving it up to her.

Don't let me down, Julie.

Don't let me down.

NINETEEN
BRANDON

MY FINGERS DIAL her number for like the hundredth time today.

I let it ring six damn times.

Voicemail.

"Hey, this is Julie."

I listen to her sweet little voice tell me that she promises to call me back. I know deep down that she is lying. "Jules, call me back. I have left dozens of messages over the past few weeks. I want to see you."

She better not be ignoring my fucking calls to be with that rich pretty boy. Her brother is probably brainwashing her into hating me again, like he tried so many times before. I'm sure he just loved the perfect gentleman that Oliver is toward Julie. He probably has Randy eating out of his hands by now.

I can't stop thinking about her. I want her back so bad it's killing me. I need her, because without her in my life I don't feel like my feet are on the ground.

That sparkle she had in high school, the light that attracted me to her, making me obsessed—that's all gone now. That jerk doesn't know her like I do. He doesn't know what she's capable of doing for you and he never, ever will find out if I can help it.

I dial her number again and it goes straight to voicemail this time. I don't leave one before slamming my phone down on the table next to me. I found out where she was before, I can do it again. My fingers find the phone and buzz across it, texting anyone I can think of to help me. I come across Nate's number and hesitate at first but click on it anyway.

> Need to find Julie, she's in danger.
> Can you help me?

Now Nate will think Julie is in trouble and want to help me like a friend should. There isn't much I can do now except wait around for someone to answer me. I kick off my shoes and relax on the new mattress I bought a few weeks ago. I thought maybe getting a new place to sleep that hadn't been tainted with my mess would bring her home. Or at least tantalize her enough to step foot in this apartment again.

I want what is mine.

She *is mine.*

My phone goes off next to me. I snatch it from the bed, hungrily searching for a name.

RACHEL

Want to hang out?

I smile into the empty bedroom. I start to feel guilty for finding joy in her persistence. It hadn't been long since Rachel and I had sex—only a few days or so. Still, I want to be with Julie. I want to touch her, be inside of her, and remind her that she is mine. It isn't like she is coming home right this *moment*...I can have one last hurrah with Rachel if I want.

Come over.

I didn't plan on Rachel getting to the house so soon. I had changed the sheets on the bed and felt like I should put another one on top, just to be safe. Plugging my phone into its charger, I jog to the door and open it. Rachel jumps into my arms and plants her wet lips on mine. My hands find the door and slam it shut, then claw at the short dress she wears. I rip it off of her from the back, my hands following her moans like a map. My mind wanders to Julie, naked and waiting for me. We used to take lavender bubble baths together; the memories of her start to flood my brain. Rachel's moans aren't doing it for me this time, but thinking of Julie in the bathtub is really turning me on. I think about her soft blonde hair pulled up on her head and her pink, pouty lips smiling at me.

My phone goes off in the bedroom. I push Rachel

off of me and go to it, picking it up with hungry eyes. Rachel pads into the bedroom, her bare feet hitting the hardwood floor. Her footsteps sound close enough to sandpaper to make me cringe.

NATE

Word of advice: Just leave her alone.

I smash my fingers on the phone to answer.

Not going to happen. She belongs with me, you know that.

It takes Nate a few minutes to text me back. Rachel paws at me from behind, craving my attention because I had rejected her.

She's with him again. Let it go.

I throw the phone on the bed and scream my head off. The walls bounce my anger back at me and burn my ears. Rachel covers hers with her hair and frowns. I can hear the fear in her voice when she can finally speak without yelling over my scream. "What is wrong with you?"

Should I stay and have sex with Rachel or should I try and find Julie?

I turn around and grab her hand. I lift her up so she can wrap her fake-tanned legs around me; she scratches her fake nails down my shoulder blades. I push her against the wall and force myself between her legs, pushing and pressing, no intentions of stopping. When her dress has fallen off completely, I throw her onto the bed and undress myself. I manage to hold her in place as I launch myself into her and don't look back.

Rachel's wild strawberry-blonde hair is everywhere on the bed sheet once I finish and let her go. That's another thing I have to get rid of before Julie comes home. Her narrow eyes look at me from the bed; she knows that I no longer have a need for her to stay.

"Can't I just stay the night just one time?" she whines. I stand up and pull on my jeans, careful not to look directly at her. "Don't you want to cuddle or something? I'm not okay with these booty calls anymore."

"I couldn't care less if you're okay," I scoff and don't bother looking back at her—I meant what I said. I don't care about her any more than I would care about my mailman at this moment.

I am okay, I feel good, it feels good to me, and that's all I give a shit about until I can get Julie back here with me.

I don't care how bad or good I was, but I snicker because I know the sex was good for her.

I don't care if I was too rough or it hurt her.

She is nothing to me anymore.

———

"Julie!" I yell for her up the stairs. She must be cleaning the bedroom, something she liked to do when I wasn't in

NICKY SHANKS

the house. I know she throws my things away when she thinks I won't find out. I plan on telling her that she needs to clean this living room; it's getting filthy around here.

"Julie, come down here!" I yell again. There isn't a sing-song tone to my voice as much as annoyance. I hear her light footsteps skip toward me. She pads down the stairs, her face stained with tears and mascara. I roll my eyes. "God, can't you get some waterproof makeup or something? I can't take you in public when you cry all the time and people can see it."

She wipes her eyes but that makes it worse. "Sorry."

"We need to talk," I say and pull her into the living room. I sit her down on the sofa and sit across from her on the coffee table. "I know you saw me with Rachel last night."

She nods. "I did."

"And? How do you feel about that?"

I smile at the horror on her face. "You really want to know?"

"Of course I do. Do you think I want you to see that? Do you think I want to hurt you intentionally?"

"No, I guess not." I relax and I find myself reaching for her. I touch her face and feel sorry for hurting her when I always swear I won't. Her smile widens as I touch her skin. The fragile little butterfly I caught in high school will always be loyal to me. "I know what I can do to make it up to you...let's stay in together tonight."

By the way her face lights up, you would think I offered her the moon. "Really? We haven't spent a night in together for so long!" She squeaks and jumps up. She sits on my lap, smiling. Her eyes lower and she whispers, "I can try to be better."

I can't help but pull her closer to my chest and hold her there; what have I done to her? This isn't the strong, independent cheerleader I fell in love with. The first time I touched her fingertips, I thought she was it for me. She isn't the same Julie that would fight with all she has for something she believes in.

I've taken that from her.

Her breathing levels and I know she's comforted by the fact that I've reached out to her. I know I can't repair years of damage with just one squeeze, so I hold on a little longer. I try to be something I know I'm not anymore.

I squeeze her anyway. Tight.

"I don't want to ever let you go," I say. "I do love you, you know that, right? I have always loved you and I will always love you."

"I know," she says into my shirt.

She doesn't say it back.

I blink a few tears from my eyes. My hand runs down her back. "Hey, do you remember that bottle of wine we opened when we found out about this apartment?"

"Of course I do." She bats her eyelashes at me; that hot liquid feeling rises up in my throat, the one that she used to give me when I first laid eyes on her.

"I know we don't have that, but maybe we can open that bottle of tequila that my boss gave me for Christmas." I smile and watch her get excited to be getting so much attention from me. That makes me feel powerful and in control.

"You haven't opened that with Rachel?"

"Of course not, baby, that's ours." I can see the shyness of her eyelashes grazing her cheeks. "You go get it and I'll find a scary movie so we can get drunk and yell at the stupid people who die first." I swat her ass as she jumps up to do what I ask of her. I don't click the TV on to find a movie to watch. Instead, I sit in the empty room and cry like a baby.

I'm going to lose her.

I'm going to lose her because I can't be normal.

I want too much, I take too much.

I'm going to lose her because I am who I am.

She brings the drink back with no glasses. I watch her pop the top off the tequila and drink straight from the bottle. Her nose crinkles a little from the bitter taste but otherwise she swallows it down like a champ. Her small hands shake as she gives the bottle to me. "I was always jealous that you never needed a chaser," I say and take the bottle from her. Her body sways to a song in her head. She does this a lot—I catch her dancing to her own tune when she thinks she's alone.

"Come here." I pull her between my legs. I tip the bottle to her lips and the amber liquid sloshes down her throat. It's a bigger amount than she drank before, but I want to get her so drunk that she doesn't remember anything.

I've figured out a way to always keep her coming back.

I let her continue to tip the bottle into her mouth as I pretend to drink from it too. She's almost guzzling it now, her body going limp from how much she's consuming. I know I have to stop her before she gets sick—or worse.

"Hey!" *She pouts and gives me a sloppy, wet kiss on the lips.* "You took my bottle."

I chuckle and put the bottle behind me. "I'm cutting you off; you're already sloshed."

"I'm a lightweight." *She giggles and wraps her arms around my neck. The old feelings tumble in the pit of my stomach and I can still see her as the quick-witted, bad ass senior cheerleader she used to be.* "I used to be able to drink so much more—remember that bonfire in the West Plains fields that we had after we won State? I got so drunk that we had to sleep in the backseat of your car in the cold."

I laugh with her and rub my chin. I'm unsure if I want her to bring up all of these old memories; it reminds me of the person I used to be before I completely messed everything up. "I remember. I also remember you trying to steal my car because you were pissed at me for cutting you off, which is what I'm doing now."

I let her relax into me. She hugs me tight with her chin on my shoulder. I can feel her heartbeat chasing after mine; I get a pain in my chest that warns me to make sure and keep her at arm's length.

"We should get married." *I look into her eyes for confirmation. She should be just drunk enough to go through with it. Not that I would admit to her my plan...*

"I told you that I'm not ready." *Her voice is flat and annoyed.* "Give me one good reason."

"Because I am in love with you."

I see the corners of her mouth turn up into a drunken smile.

I think she's actually going to go through with it.

TWENTY
JULIE

I FREEZE.

My feet won't move, or *can't* move, I'm not quite sure.

Oliver waits for me to join him in the rock pool. I can see the question in his eyes. The twinkling embers above us shower the ground with little specks of light; they remind me that I'm not doing a very good job of stalling him.

He wants me.

I can feel it in the very air I am breathing.

"Julie?" Oliver softly calls to me from the pool. "It's okay if you don't want to…we can head back up to the house." I see the sadness in his eyes as he stands up. He is ready to climb back out to make me comfortable. The water drips from his biceps and down his hard stomach, igniting something inside of me.

"Wait," I blurt out. "I'm…here I come."

I slowly take off my clothes, all except undergarments (I thankfully wore a set of matching black lace bra and panties to be spontaneous), and stand in front of his hungry eyes. My thighs rub together as I shuffle my feet toward him. I start dipping my toes into the warm water. The bubbles tickle my toes as he reaches for me to help me in. I take his hand and slide the rest of my body in and relax against him.

Oliver nuzzles into my hair. "Goddamn, I've missed you." He breathes so deep I think he might pass out. "Do you know what you do to me?" He doesn't wait for me to answer. "You completely fucking *slay* me." I let him run his hands down my sides and squeeze my hips. The warm water around us bubbles and dances around our bodies. I thank God secretly that I shaved my legs a few days ago; they're still semi-smooth enough that he doesn't flinch when I wrap my legs around his torso, pressing my body into his. Oliver looks right into my soul, the kind of look that you just know you can't escape from. It will find you even in the darkest corners of your mind.

"I heard what you said to me," I blurt out. "What you said to me on the other side of the door at my house."

Oliver tilts his head to the side and pretends to be confused. The boyish grin spreading across his face taunts me. "You'll have to be more specific. I say a lot of things to a lot of people, especially to pretty girls like you."

I narrow my eyes at him. I'm not joking and it's

annoying that he's treating it like a joke now. "You know what I'm talking about."

He laughs and it makes me angry. "Baby, I have no *idea* what you're talking about."

Okay. Two can play at this petty little game. "Oh, never mind then. It must have been someone else I'm thinking of, I'm sorry."

He's not laughing anymore. "That actually brings me to a question that I have for you." His rough hands cup my ass and pull me flush against him. "Is there anyone else besides me? No other men fighting for your love that I need to know about?"

"No one else that I know of," I quickly say and avert my eyes toward the side of the pool. "But if someone shows up, you'll be the first to know."

He doesn't let it go. "There's no one else for me either; there hasn't been since I met you. I can't be with anyone but you."

"Oliver—"

He holds up his hand. "Julie, please don't explain. I just wanted you to know."

I don't know what has come over me, but I kiss him.

I mean, kiss him like I'm never going to see him again.

I can hear his soft grunts through our breathing. I feel him holding back a little; I nibble on his bottom lip to ease his worry. He thinks that I'm going to run from him and I want him to enjoy this for what it is. He crinkles his forehead in frustration. As he pulls away from me, his brown eyes search for answers.

"What the hell was that?" he says, trying to catch his breath. "That was...*surprising*." My index finger finds its way toward his lips; I hold it there to shush him. "Why do you like teasing me so much?" he says and smiles, tugging at the ends of my hair.

I giggle. "Why do *you* like it so much?"

"I think you mean, why do I *love* it so much?" He parts my lips with his and kisses me again. He takes what he wants from me in the gentlest way. His tall body nearly swallows me whole. "The answer is really simple, if you really think about it."

I raise my eyebrow. "Oh, yeah? And what's the answer?"

"You drive me fucking crazy, that's the answer." There is a hungry growl in his throat as he separates our bodies. The force pushes me to the other side of the rock pool. "We should start heading back to the house soon." He leaps out of the pool and holds his hand out for me. I sit still at the edge of the pool with a dumb look on my face. I take his hand anyway and let him pull me up but when he does, one of the straps on my bra breaks. Everything—I mean every-thing—falls out.

Oliver laughs and hands me his shirt, wrapping me inside of it. "You're lucky I don't make you walk back naked—please don't hide your body from me." He stops in front of me, bending over and looking back with a childish look on his face. "Piggy back ride?"

I jump on his back and he carries me the entire way back down the trail. It's pretty hard since it's almost complete darkness all around us except for my flashlight. But he doesn't let me down until we're safely in the house and behind closed doors. It's nearly midnight and I yawn against my will, trying to hide it. He snaps his fingers toward me and points to the staircase. "Go to bed, young lady." He pats my butt as I walk past him.

I jump and smile at him. "You're lucky I like you a little bit."

A snicker escapes his mouth. "Oh, I think you like me more than just a little bit."

I watch him light the fireplace when we walk into our bedroom. So many good feelings come rushing in from seeing the same furniture and bed sheets as before. I let him cradle my body as we lie in the darkness, waiting for sleep. I can smell the woodsy and rainy scent of his skin; I breathe it in deep because I have missed it. His fingers reach down to my leg, touching the scar where I'd cut myself a few weeks ago.

"It's healed," he whispers into my ear and kisses the top of it. "That's a great battle wound story."

"Battle wound?" I shriek. "More like surprise attack."

We laugh together until we fall asleep. I listen to his faint snoring behind me as I stare off into the darkness for a few minutes, trying to clear my head. I know there is absolutely no going back now; I have gone way too far to turn back and leave him cold again. Still, I have this gnawing feeling in my stomach that it isn't going to last. Something is always going to try to keep us apart. I should just run back home to my brother and let him tell me "I told you so" forty times before hugging me like a child.

He'll always see me as a child.

———

I GET into Randy's car and don't say a single word. I buckle my seat belt and he sneaks a peek through his dark-tinted side windows, making sure that Brandon isn't looking to see where I'm going. I want to laugh because Brandon doesn't care where I'm going or who I'm going with. Brandon only cares about himself.

"Well…" Randy moves his glasses back up his nose. He looks ahead instead of at me because he knows I don't want to hear his criticism right now. I mean, I never really want to hear it, but he never cares what I want. I guess it's because he's fifteen years older than me and he's been married before—to Clyde's mother—but she left after Clyde was born. "I'll have someone look into his life; maybe I can find something that will scare him enough he'll just disappear."

I sigh. "Can we just go to your house? I'd like to sleep."

Randy scoffs and makes a left-hand turn. "Sleep? Julie, you let men walk all over you. It's horrifying and completely mad."

I stare him down. "I know, right? Funny how that happens to me."

"Oh for God's sake, I don't mean me." Randy shakes his head. We pull into the wealthy suburb of Rockford that

he lives in. "You know what I meant. Although, if you ever tell me that this little asshole ever laid a finger on you other than a loving one, we won't be still talking about this. I will throw him in jail."

As he drones on, I make it look like I'm interested in what he's saying. I don't need him to know what Brandon has actually done to me; I just need him to know that it got bad enough to me to walk away. If he wants the entire truth, he'll have to wait for the novel and buy it like everyone else.

The mini-mansion he calls home is dark and quiet. It's February so Clyde won't be home for another few months. It'll just be Randy and I—until I decide to go back to my old life with Brandon like an idiot.

"You go ahead inside and I'll be along shortly. I want to go back to the office and check some things out," Randy says and pulls into his driveway. "You know the drill: Make yourself at home. You can have the pool house for as long as you want."

I want to tell him not to bother, that I'll just be going back to my home in the morning. He's already sped off and opened the garage for me to enter. It's eerie inside, so I turn on every light I encounter and make my way toward the kitchen.

I make a sandwich and grab a pint of chocolate chip ice cream, toting it all toward the pool house. Once I hit the backyard, I don't have enough hands to turn on the outdoor lights. I have to navigate my way in the darkness and I'm proud of myself for making it without making a mess at my feet.

I try turning on the TV and nothing interests me so I turn it back off.

I try reading a few books on the shelves but I have read them all already. This isn't the first time I've slept in this pool house.

I eat the sandwich and half of the pint of ice cream. I start to feel sick to my stomach because I'm too full and stressed out. It's nearly midnight and I haven't seen Randy come home yet. I get even sicker when I think about Rachel and Brandon in the bed that I sleep in. Thoughts of their sex sweat getting on my pillow makes something inside me click. It's not enough for me anymore to daydream about what our life could be...Well, what it could be if he'd just fall back in love with me.

I fall asleep sometime during my fit of anger. I wake up with a splitting headache and nine messages on my phone.

Message one through six are from Brandon.

BRANDON

Hey, you can come back now.

It's been over an hour since I told you to come back home, where are you, Jules?

It's after ten, get your ass home!

Julie. Get. Home. Now.

You better not be dead or I will be so pissed.

If you don't call me in the next ten minutes, you'll regret it.

Message seven and eight are from Nora.

NORA

Brandon is blowing up my phone
looking for you.

Julie? Are you okay? Where are you?

And message nine from Brandon makes it all come crashing down.

BRANDON

You better not be cheating on me.

I stomp across the yard to the main house. I pad through the house and find a set of keys on the counter to Randy's BMW. I get inside, start it, and sit in silence. It seems like I sit here alone for hours. I want Randy to find me—I want him to come running out and physically remove me from the car. I want him to stop me from driving back to confront Brandon; I've gotten a sudden surge of courage. I want to hurt him like he has hurt me.

I drive off instead.

Everyone's voices swirl in my mind.

Brandon: "You better not be cheating on me."

Nora: "I told you that he was bad news, Julie."

Randy: "When are you ever going to learn?"

I feel the car lurch forward, hit something hard, and stop. My head hits the steering wheel so hard that it knocks me out for a few minutes. I don't come to until I hear people screaming. I can hear myself crying. I try to move my head to look around, but it makes me cry out in pain. An older man steps over to me and says, "Don't move, honey, we called an ambulance. You were in an accident."

"Did I kill anyone?" I mumble and then cough. Something is pressing on my lungs. "Please tell me I didn't hurt anyone."

The old man shakes his head. "Almost yourself, but that's all. Try and relax, the ambulance is on its way. You've lost a lot of blood there, sweetheart."

I almost killed myself.

The world goes black and the screams drown out my heartbeat.

TWENTY-ONE
JULIE

IT WASN'T the darkness that kept me up at night these past few weeks. It wasn't the uncertainty of what Oliver might be doing. Or who he was doing it with. I never really worried about him coming back to me, I guess. I sort of just assumed he always would. I feel like our lives are glued together whether we like it or not.

I smile. Daylight is now coming through the open curtains of the room. I can feel Oliver's warmth behind me as he shifts his weight, and his grip loosens. Our first night back at the cabin—the place where it all began—and I made it so complicated and full of drama that I am really ashamed of myself.

"Good morning, sunshine." His voice is raspy. He buries his nose in my hair. I wonder why he likes to do that so much. It's...different.

Sensual.

Brandon liked to grab and pull, take what he wanted. Sometimes with so much aggression that it hurt a little; I was a little scared to even go to sleep at the same time with him. Oliver likes to nuzzle and paw; he likes to be gentle and sweet with me. Every little amazing thing he does for me cancels out one bad thing that Brandon has done.

I slowly roll over to face him. I notice that his eyes are still closed but he's smiling. The sunlight catches his face just right and he looks fuzzy; his five o'clock shadow has now turned into a ten o'clock thick patch of dark hair. As he yawns and stretches, he playfully tugs my body to his. I feel like the Earth has stopped moving just for the two of us and I never want it to start again.

"Good morning to you." I giggle as he kisses my fingers. He opens his eyes to take his first look of me of the day. I take the time to study him.

Bright emerald eyes.

Dangerously square jawline.

Thick, warm lips.

Big, rough hands.

Shaggy, dark chocolate hair.

He yawns again and looks at the oversized wall clock. He shakes his head. "We slept in, it's almost ten." He nods toward the clock. "We can be lazy; we could just call it a day and stay in bed. I think that sounds like an excellent idea."

"It's vacation, we *are* allowed." I giggle. He shakes out his tousled dark hair and runs his thick fingers through it. "But, I can't stay in bed with you all day. You won't be able to keep your hands to yourself."

Oliver smiles. "I like being here with you. Is that such a crime?"

I jump out of the bed—out of his reaching grasp —and flick my hip to the side. "You like being here with me, huh? How much, exactly?"

His interest piques as he climbs out of bed from the other side, slowly. He's wearing nothing but a pair of boxer briefs; he must've gotten hot during the night and taken off the rest of his clothes. I can see his ripped body creeping around the bed to get to me. I back up into the bathroom slowly, not really thinking of a strategy or an escape route.

"You know I love being here with you," he says.

I'm fully in the bathroom now and he owns the doorway. I'm stuck inside the room. There's no way out, even if I wanted one. I stand my ground and dig my heels in. I pout and stare directly into his eyes. "Prove it."

I don't even get to take a single breath before he reaches me. He picks me up and throws me on the bathroom sink, pressing his body in between my legs. He locks his warm lips with mine, taking control of my...*everything*. Body and soul, he has taken them both from me. I just hand them to him like I was only guarding them. His lips feel so nice and familiar, I find myself leaning into his kiss with each passing millisecond.

I try not to think of the ways I can avoid it like I used to do with Brandon. I meet each of his twists and turns perfectly. His hands slide down my sides and rest at my hips. I want him so bad I can't stop my brain from whirring around the thought. It excites me that I excite him. I can feel the desire radiating from him, but he pulls away from me and kisses my forehead. He leaves me sitting on the counter and turns on the shower. I watch him take off his boxer briefs and give me a glimpse of his ass before stepping in and shutting the door behind him.

"What was that?" I gasp into the air. "Why did you stop—what's wrong?"

He laughs and peeks his head around the shower door. "It's called blue balls, sunshine. It's about time I gave them to you since you've been giving them to me for weeks."

I touch my lips; they're still vibrating from his rough kiss. I can still feel him there, his tongue on mine and the taste of last night's beer now back in my mouth. I jump off the cabinet and storm out of the bathroom.

I change into some jeans and a fresh t-shirt, ready to explore the other rooms of the house. I'm still really pissed at him, but this house is so big that my anger fades every time I discover something new. I've already seen the four bedrooms, so I skipped those. There are four bathrooms with lush tubs and showers, one with heated floors and a bidet. I think about the night I had to pee and barged into the bathroom while he showered. I'll never admit to him that I didn't know about the other bathrooms.

The last room I step into is the most magical place I have ever laid eyes on. Books on shelves from the floor to the ceiling, a light blue suede sofa on one side, and the golden chaise from the bedroom on the other.

"Oh, good. You found it," I hear Oliver say behind me. He slips my hand into his. "This is for you. I thought you might want a place you can get away from me when I piss you off or you just want to be alone. A place of your own inside the cabin."

I don't even know what to say to him. I feel embarrassed for acting like a baby but this is so incredible. I squeeze his hand before letting go so I can examine all of the books and choose where to start. "When did you do this?" I run my fingers down a row of leather-backed first editions.

"Madrie and Paul did it before we got here," he confesses. "It's my grandfather's old study, so it wasn't that hard to change around." He could have taken the credit, but his honesty makes me smile. "They were more than happy to help me doing something nice for you after I begged and pleaded my life away." I can't help myself as I turn swiftly on my heel and throw myself into his arms. They tighten around me. I thank him by crying all over his shirt and he even has to place his hands on my hips and help hold me up.

"I'm glad you like it." He smiles down at me. He keeps my body close to his as I turn back to the mountains of books around me, and I wonder how many there actually are sitting up there, calling my name for me to crack them open and read their insides.

"THANK YOU, OLIVER." I walk over to another shelf with old fairy tale books on it. "This is too much, even for me."

Oliver waves me off with one hand. The other hand hooks onto my jeans belt loop and tugs me backward into his grip. "Nothing is too much for you. I will always do anything I possibly can to make you happy. Does this make you happy?"

I nod. "So, *so* happy."

He smiles and looks proud of himself. He obviously doesn't always get something completely right. "Well, then, I'll leave you alone for a while so you can lose yourself in another world." He mocks me by wiggling his fingers and acting like a magician saying abracadabra. I don't even care or notice him leave. I open my first book and read the first few chapters of *The Wizard of Oz*. I set the book down and walk over to one of the bookcases by the window. I pick up another book, a tattered orange-colored hardback, and open it. There's a man's handwriting, short and scratchy. As I start reading a few pages, I realize it's someone's personal notebook. I instantly shut it and blush, but there's no one around. I'm not about to read someone else's personal thoughts. What if it's Oliver's? No, this book is too old. I look around the room as if someone might be watching me. I take the book back to my chaise, slowly opening it again and reading the first page.

September 8, 1991

Veronica is back. I'm not quite sure what is wrong with me; my father thinks I am too soft because I cannot fight her influence. I am completely in love with her. I tell him this, but he doesn't care.

My father does not know what love is.

I let her back in my life only because she has come to me, telling me she is pregnant. Is the baby mine? I don't know. I am not sure that I care. I will love that baby to the ends of the Earth just because it is a part of her. And even if it is not a part of me by blood, I will do everything I can to make sure that child has what it needs.

Until my father cuts me off when he finds out, of course.

He hates that Veronica is a waitress at the Inn. I love her just the same. She has cheated on me several times. I love her just the same. She tells me her hopes and dreams and I want to make them come true. I have never, ever, in my whole twenty-five years of life loved anyone more than my Veronica.

Until the moment she told me she was pregnant.

Is it possible to love someone when you haven't met yet?

I will never admit it, but I am secretly hoping for a boy.

Blood does not mean family.

Love means family.

I READ A FEW MORE PAGES, biting my fingernails. I really hope I don't uncover any juicy family secrets. This book has to be from Oliver's father, Colin; I gathered that much just from reading the first few pages. I hear someone knocking lightly at the door and I panic; I hide the book underneath *The Wizard of Oz*. Oliver sticks his head inside and smiles at me. He whispers, "Are you hungry?"

My throat is so dry I can't even begin to say anything. I nod and paint a sweet smile on my face. I try to hide the fact that I uncovered a family secret that Oliver might not even know about. I curse myself the entire walk downstairs. He's prepared a cute little brunch with peanut butter and jelly sand-wiches, grapes, and strawberries. For a moment, he distracts me by pulling out my chair for me and tucking me in under the table. He pours a glass of champagne into a flute in front of me. I watch his lean body sit down in his own seat and he grins. "Fancy, right?" The laughter in his eyes almost makes me spit out the champagne. He refills the glass as I sit it back down with no judgment.

"I love peanut butter and jelly." I wiggle my nose at him. He leans up and kisses the tip of it. "How could you possibly have known?"

Oliver scoffs and winks at me. His gestures hit the bullseye every single time lately. "Everyone likes it, it's part of everyone's childhood."

Is it possible to love someone when you haven't met yet?

I will never admit it, but I am secretly hoping for a boy.

I shift my weight in the chair and get nervous. Oliver is good at seeing right through me; it's going to be nearly impossible to keep this from him. I try to small talk with him for the better part of an hour but he knows something is up with me. I watch him search his mind for the right question to ask. So I don't get offended and storm off, I'm sure. "Are you chomping at the bit to get back to your library?" He sheepishly glances over at me. I can feel the pride it brings him to have put that together for me.

"I really do love the library, thank you," I say around my third glass of champagne. The room is getting a little fuzzier. I finish the fourth glass and bite my lip in embarrassment. I don't think he even notices in the middle of his fourth beer, though. That makes me feel a little better. "I think I will go back in for a while, if that's okay with you."

He nods and waves his hand toward the doorway of the kitchen. "Go, please. I want you to enjoy that library as much as you can while we are here." His eyes darken as his voice thickens. "And when we come back for other visits too." The hope in his eyes fills the room and I can feel myself thinking about the future and how much he believes in it.

I don't say anything when I stand up and kiss his cheek. I nearly skip out of the room and leave him behind me, speechless. I feel like I am never going to reach the library again; I'm out of breath from running back here. I shut the door behind me and launch myself back at the orange journal from Colin.

I open the book and go back to where I left off. I read a few more pages before I have to shut it again. Some of the entries are light and happy, some of them are far from that. I feel bad for Colin for the way Veronica was treating him. I also feel love for him for taking care of her when he wasn't sure if Oliver was his son or not. I force myself to open the journal again and scan through a few more entries, coming across one that starts to make my eyes water.

December 25, 1991

We are having a boy! Merry Christmas to us!

I am in such shock and amazement; this is all I have ever wanted.

And I want this with Veronica. She asked me

the most horrific question this morning. Even
after I greeted her with Christmas presents
and breakfast in bed. She asked me if I would
adopt the baby if he wasn't mine.

Oliver is mine, I tell her. He is mine no matter
what.

She believes me, I know she does. That is why
she laughed at me. She didn't want me to only
claim Oliver, she wanted me to take care of
him alone. I ask what she means but I
already know the answer, she wants to leave
me. She tells me that she doesn't want to be a
mother. She tells me that if I don't take care
of the baby, she will leave him with strangers.

She said the word adoption but that means
leaving him with strangers.

Oliver deserves so much more than that.

Oliver deserves the world. He deserves to laugh
and play and be free and loved by me and by
Veronica but she doesn't believe that. She tells
me that she doesn't want to be with me but
yet she keeps showing me signs of love. She
holds my hand, she kisses me, she tells me
things that she doesn't tell anyone else.

So, why won't she just stay?

Why is she fighting it so much?

I don't know how to make her believe that I am in love with her.

But it's killing me to keep trying.

I cry so much that I have to put the book back down. I hide it just in case I can't see Oliver come in through my tears. I feel so bad about what I am doing to him; this is the same thing his mother did to Colin. I want to read more but I decide that I should put it away for now. I sneak a peek at the next entry before I do. I have to satisfy my curiosity and then I promise myself I'll return it to the shelf and never look at it again.

January 1, 1992

I caught her again last night.

I wish she would stop doing this to me.

She tells me she loves me and then lets me down.

Time after time.

I can feel Oliver kicking inside of her when we fight and then things calm down. He doesn't like the turmoil she brings either. What am I going to do? I can't have him be born into this. I want so much better for him.

My beautiful son.

I haven't met you yet but I promise you I love you already.

I promise you life and love, I promise you safety.

I promise you more than this, more than she gives me. This is all she will ever be able to give to you. I wish she didn't hate us both, son, but I can't control her. No matter how much I wish I could. I am done even trying.

Once you are born, I will welcome you with open arms.

It will be us against the world, Oliver Frank-ford Jackson.

You and your Dad.

All we need is each other.

All we need is love.

I force myself to close the book before my tears smear the ink. I wish Oliver's father was still alive. I have a feeling I would have liked him a lot. Maybe that's how Oliver is such a soft-handed man most of the time, being raised by someone like Colin.

Oliver hadn't talked about his parents before, unless you counted him telling me that his grandfather was a jerk and then he died. I never knew Oliver's mother's name; he never spoke of her at all except that he has no clue where she is or if she's even alive.

I sit in my chaise, so devastated that it's hard for me to breathe. I pray that he doesn't interrupt me until I am better. I hear him talking on the phone somewhere in the house. I'm able to get myself together and figure out a game plan, ready to make a break for the bedroom if I have to. I don't want him to ask me a million questions about why tears are rolling down my cheeks. I think about Colin and how sad his life must have been before Oliver was born. All he ever wanted was to be loved—cherished by the one person he wanted the most.

I have to get over myself and start being better for Oliver.

I have to allow myself to be loved by the one man that loves me.

Triple crap times infinity.

Screw the rules, I wasn't meant to follow them anyway.

TWENTY-TWO
OLIVER

SHE HAS BEEN in her library nearly all day. I stand outside the closed door and wonder what she's reading; I think about how cute she probably looks all cuddled up on her favorite chaise. I almost knock three different times but keep myself from disturbing her. I know that I won't be able to do it for long.

I made dozens of phone calls already this morning. Just because I don't have a job doesn't mean I don't work: I spend my morning checking on investments and making my grandfather's money work for me.

She waits until I'm about to knock again before she opens the door. "Come in." She motions for me to sit with her. There isn't space for us both so she stands up, gently pushes me down onto the chaise, and then places her body in my lap. She curls up with her legs against my chest. I can feel her sadness through my shirt, it's almost deafening.

"What's wrong, sunshine?" I say softly to her and

stroke her hair. "Do you not like the books here? I can get you different ones if you want." She shakes her head and places her ear over my heart. She listens to my heartbeat, which is getting faster by the millisecond. I can feel her fingers gripping my shirt. Something is wrong with her. "Tell me what's on your mind," I demand, sitting her upright to face me. "I can't fix it if you don't tell me."

Instead of bursting into tears and telling me her problems, she turns her lips from a frown into a smile. She gives me a quick kiss on the lips. "I'm having a good time up here already."

"I'm happy to hear that," I say and pull her into me. I tuck her beneath my chin. "What have you been reading in here all afternoon?"

Her breath hitches; she shifts her weight on my lap. "Just some old books, mainly fairy tales."

I smile. "Fairy tales, huh? Sounds pretty good, maybe you can read to me. I like a good fairy tale."

"I'm a little tired of reading today, maybe tomorrow?" I thank God that she says no. I can't sit here and watch her lips move inches from me and not devour them. I hate to break the bad news to her that we have to leave a little earlier than we planned; there are some things I have to drive back into North Rockford and put my signature on.

Like a house.

With red shutters and a backyard and a garden.

Ten minutes from the campus where she signed up for classes.

I need to build her a library.

"I have to drive back to Rockford on Thursday, is it okay if we leave a little earlier than expected?" I listen for a change in her breathing. She continues to play with my shirt. She nuzzles her body into mine, her breathing stays steady, and the air around us doesn't change. "Julie, are you sure you're okay?"

Her body bounces up; she is ready for anything. "I'm sad that we have to leave early, but I understand. Did you want me to make you something for dinner?"

I know I have a twinkle in my damn eye. "Only if you want to." I try not to seem too excited that she is willing to take care of me. But my damn insides twist and turn at the thought of her in the kitchen, wearing nothing but an apron—

She grabs my hand and squeezes it. Then she leads me toward the kitchen and I notice that nightfall has already started surrounding the windows. It's enclosing us in the duskiness of the start of evening. I watch her flutter around the kitchen. She has no idea where anything is, yet she does know at the same time.

Julie finds a bag of spinach and starts washing the pieces. She lays them on the counter to dry. I watch her carefully select what type of blade she needs to cut it and it is like watching a ballerina practice for the ballet. She blushes when she notices me staring at her. I look away to make sure she doesn't get too distracted and cut herself again in my presence. "Can I do that for you?" I nearly launch myself toward the knife in her hand.

She stops chopping and glares at me. Her electric blue eyes burn into my flesh. "You think I will slash myself again? I'm not accident-prone, Oliver."

"You are too perfect to slash up." I try to take the knife again. "I don't want you hurting any part of your beautiful body." I kiss her neck and make a third attempt.

"I can handle this; you can grab some veggies from the fridge and start washing them for me."

Anything for you, Julie.

My Julie.

I wash off several different vegetables and lay them out in front of me. I hand them to her one by one; she chops them quickly and adds them to the massive wooden salad bowl. I slide my arms around her a few times. I drop some of the items into the bowl to "help" but she swats my hands away every time. She turns to boil eggs and I sit up on the counter to watch her dance to a song in her mind. This is the second time I have seen this; I like when she feels comfortable enough to sway her hips like that.

I lick my lips and take my phone from my pocket. Finding a slow song, I jump down and take her hands in mine. I lead her around the kitchen. She giggles against my neck as I whisk her petite body around the floor.

"Don't tell anyone I can dance." I twirl her around and dip her low. "It might ruin my reputation and I might need to cash in on that someday."

Julie rolls her eyes. I swing her back up and bow

in front of her, thanking her for letting me dance her around the kitchen. "Is there anything you aren't good at?" Her eyes are innocent and pure of any dark thoughts.

I clear my throat and hide my worried face from her. "Apparently there are a few things. Like holding myself back from you, that's one that is too hard to even think about."

She finishes mixing the salad and hands me empty salad bowls. She takes the larger one to the table and waves me over to join her. I feel like a zombie, it is hard to tell what I can and can't do when it comes to her.

I groan and get two glasses of ice water, drinking mine in one gulp. I get back up for more and think about what awkward thing I could say to her next. She digs into her salad, enjoying it, and my mouth waters as she licks the dressing from her lips.

"I want to talk to you about something I found today," she says and then blushes. I can tell it isn't something pleasant.

"Okay." I put my fork down before even digging into the food. "What did you find?"

Julie frowns. I know she knows I don't want the salad. "Oh, well—it was nothing really, just an old book from a long time ago."

"Oh, yeah? My grandfather liked to collect old shit." I take a small bite of the salad to appease her. Once I notice her shoulders relax, I shovel more of the atrocity into my mouth. I pray I will be able to sneak back down in the middle of the night for a turkey sandwich. I eat the salad because I love her; I love the way her eyes watch me as I pretend to love it.

"So, two more days up here…" She pauses and I can see her choosing her words inside of her mind carefully. "What should we do? I do feel like being totally lazy."

I chuckle and run my thumb over her fingers sitting on top of the table. "We don't have to do anything, we can just be lazy. That's what vacations are for. As long as we spend some time together up here, I'm good."

"I thought you were going to show me what it's like to be with the great Oliver Jackson." She giggles. I somewhat think she's a little serious. "Are we going to just sit around and be lazy the rest of our lives? We would get bored with each other."

I ignore the scream building in my throat. "I will do whatever you want to do with the rest of our lives —I belong to you now."

Julie blushes. I thought I was a little too intense, but I hardly care. I'm not into hiding my feelings anymore; that's what breaking the rules will get you. Thank God I only broke one rule, even though it's the one that will ruin me. "Oh, well—for right now, I think I would love to take a bubble bath in that enormous bathtub upstairs. I have wanted to dip my toes in it since I laid eyes on it."

"In our bathroom? It is pretty relaxing *and* it's big

enough for two." I wink at her. She shakes her head, her eyes laughing at me. "I think I can scrounge up some bubble bath in this house somewhere. Why don't you let me do the dishes while you get ready for the bath?"

I wait a few seconds for her reply but she doesn't have one. To my surprise, she stands up and touches my arm, disappearing from the room. I throw the dishes into the sink and leave them there, untouched. I look everywhere I can for bubble bath. I finally open a hallway closet with toiletries. Behind some shampoo bottles and soap containers sits a bottle of lavender-scented bubble bath. I snatch it up and hoof it toward the bedroom. I really fucking hope she hasn't started without me.

The door is open and the fireplace is lit. She sits on the bed facing me in nothing but a pair of matching black lace panties and bra. I am completely mesmerized by her; I don't want to touch her in fear that it is all just a dream.

"Is this okay?" she whispers. I can barely hear her over the crackle of the fireplace. I don't have to hear her because her eyes say it all. I force myself into the room and take three long steps toward her. With no hesitation, her body is pinned beneath mine as I take her lips. The magic that sparks around us as I kick my shoes off and unzip my jeans is so intense that I can feel my bones vibrating.

"Did you find any bubble bath?" she moans into my mouth.

I nod. "Dresser." That's all I can manage. The air is so thick with want that I can barely breathe. I just want to lose myself inside of her—forget anything that has ever happened to either one of us and just be happy together.

I feel her peel her body away from mine and let herself down. She grabs the bottle of bubbles and then takes my hand, leading us both into the bath-room. "I'll run the bath, take off your clothes," she demands. When she bends over to start the bathtub, it literally takes every fiber of my being not to take her right here. I undress and immediately blush at my hardness. "You know I want you; I won't be able to hold back much longer."

She doesn't miss a beat. "After you, Mr. Jackson."

I get into the tub first. I sink into the hot water, helping her in the process. I don't want her to slip and fall or break any of her perfect limbs. She sits on my lap facing away from me. "Oh, should I go across the tub?" She giggles.

I put my face into her strawberry-scented hair; I quickly shake my head no. "Stay where you are, don't you dare move. I like when you touch me."

She lets out soft air from her lungs. I watch her trace some bubbles with her fingers in the water. We sit in silence until I just can't take it anymore. "Tell me something no one else knows about you."

"This again?"

"I told you, I want to know everything." I take her hand into mine; I pull it out of the water to snake my fingers around hers. "Please, Julie," I whisper into her ear. Her back tenses against my chest.

"I am twenty-two?"

I scoff. "I am twenty-five. Not to mention I already knew that—and it's not a secret."

"Oh, it has to be a secret?" She gulps.

I know what I want from her but I'm too afraid to ask. I want to know how Julie…*became* Julie.

"I grew up in San Diego. I moved around a lot when I was a teenager. I told you about my parents, what else is there?"

I hear my phone ringing from the other room but I don't care.

I want more.

I always want more with her.

"Um, let's see. Randy is my half-brother, we share the same father. He grew up with his mother in Rockford." She looks at me as if I would indicate when to stop. "What else do you want to know?" I reach for her and gently drag her back toward me, placing her back on my lap.

The phone rings again in the other room.

"Do you want to get that?" She starts to move from my lap. The water laps around her body, letting me see things that drive me crazy.

"No," I instantly say and pull her back. "Whoever it is, they can wait."

She nods and twirls back around to face me. Her skin slides against mine like hot butter; I nearly lose every ounce of control I have left. She holds my head in her hands and looks directly into my eyes. It's like she'll see something in there that she hasn't seen before. Something that no one else can see.

"What about you?" She looks sad.

"My mother skipped town when I was young. My father died when I was fourteen in a car accident. And you know about my grandfather." I have no emotion. "My grandfather got stuck with me after my Dad died and then he passed. So here I am, alone with no family."

Tears roll down her cheeks. "You're not alone."

I wipe the hot liquid from her face. "I know that now because I have you, don't I? It all happened a long time ago. I'm over it now, so why are you crying?"

"It's just sad."

"Julie—" My phone starts ringing again. I feel her hand underneath the water, sliding up my leg and stopping at the inner edge of my thigh. She grips my erection—*hard*—and looks back into my eyes. The sadness has turned into curiosity as she moves her hand slowly, back and forth. She climbs up and lowers herself onto me, never losing eye contact. I don't even care about a condom this time—she is on and ready to go.

I let out a loud, satisfied moan when she slides onto me. It's been weeks since I felt her like this. Her thighs grip the outer meat of my legs. "God, you feel so damn good," I whisper into her hair; I grip her tight and try hard not to let go.

She moans quietly. I swear to God I hear her whisper my name. I lift her closer to me and lose myself inside of her, the emotions of the past three weeks cracking my insides. She holds onto me so tight I know there will be marks. She doesn't care about being quiet this time; there isn't anyone in the house to hear us like before. My breath quickens as I wrap her legs around my waist and let her bite down hard on my bottom lip.

Then, she does it.

She screams my name.

A guttural, primal, gut-wrenching, nail-biting, call the cops scream.

My Julie.

Her long, wet honey hair is matted around us. The water starts to cool; our lips are raw and pink from being attached so long. My legs are too weak to even think about using them. Julie kisses the corner of my mouth and I feel drunk. I run my fingers through her hair and try to catch my breath. Her forehead finds mine and I close my eyes and smile. "What are you doing to me?"

She giggles and relaxes onto me. "Do you not know what we just did?"

I roll my eyes but smile. "You're sexy but sarcasm doesn't become you."

My phone rings for the fourth time.

"Are you sure you don't need to get it?" She splashes water at me.

"After what we just did, I'm not sure of anything." She shakes her head. "Okay, fine, I'll go get it." The air outside of the bathtub is cold, so I wrap a towel around my lower half. I look back to wink at her, then run to re-light the fireplace before I do anything else. "So fucking cold," I say as my teeth chatter. I pull on some gray sweatpants and then dig around my bag to find my phone.

"It's in the pocket of your jeans," I hear Julie say from the bathroom.

I check the pocket of my jeans and sure enough, there it is.

How does she do that?

I look at the phone and Casey has been the one blowing it up. I roll my eyes and am in the middle of dropping it back onto the bed when he calls again. I hit the ignore button but he calls once more.

"God, what?" I roar as I answer it.

There are sirens in the background so I can hardly hear anything he's saying. He walks to find a place where he can talk. When it's quiet, I can hear the fear in his voice. "Where are you?"

"You know I'm at the lake, why?"

"You two need to come back to town. Now."

"Casey, I'm hanging up," I say, but can't bring myself to do it. "What's wrong with you?"

Silence.

"Casey!" I yell into the phone.

"Brandon attacked Nora and she's in the hospital. He's looking for Julie."

The energy drains from my body. I start to panic, but then realize that we are three hours away and we have time to leave. "When?" I choke out.

"I'm not sure how long ago it was—I just heard from her."

I hang up the phone and look around the room.

I am frozen and I don't know what my next move is going to be, but I know one thing.

Brandon isn't going to hurt Julie.

I'll kill him first.

TWENTY-THREE
JULIE

"WHAT IS IT?" I ask Oliver when he comes back into the bathroom. His entire body has lost all color. For a minute, I really think he's going to tell me that he'd just seen a ghost in the bedroom. "Oliver?"

"Get out," he says in a harsh voice. "Julie, come on, you have to get out." He reaches into the tub, pulling the plug, and the water starts to drain around me. It leaves me naked and cold. He walks over to fetch me a towel and wraps it around my shivering body. He helps me out so I don't slip and break any bones.

Something is clearly bothering him but he doesn't say a word to me as I follow him back into the bedroom. I watch him get dressed in his jeans and burgundy pocket t-shirt; he puts his socks and boots on and then starts rummaging through my things to find me clothes to wear.

"I can dress myself," I say in a cold voice. "What is going on?"

Finally, he takes a deep breath and looks *at* me instead of *through* me. "Brandon just attacked Nora, she's in the hospital."

I nearly collapse onto the floor. His arms catch me just in time. "What? Why? Is she okay?"

"He's looking for you." Oliver goes to the bedroom window, looking out in suspicion. "I don't know any other details. Look, we have to get out of here. We aren't safe here and he might have a weapon, okay? So let's just get dressed, leave our shit and I'll have Madrie and Paul bring it back to Rockford when Brandon is caught."

Nothing he just said to me registers in my mind. I think about Nora and how this is all my fault. Brandon wouldn't have attacked her if it wasn't for me. I want to ask so many questions but I know Oliver is right; if Brandon is capable of hurting someone so badly they needed to go to the hospital, we need to get out of here.

Without protest, I shove on the jeans and sweatshirt he pulls out for me; I tug on my shoes and watch his eyes shift toward the bedroom door like he is waiting for something to pop out and yell "Boo!"

"Stay here." He starts to leave the room.

"Don't you dare!" I hiss, grabbing his arm. "I need you here with me."

He smiles wider than I have ever seen. I have stroked his ego, even in a tragic and hard-pressed moment like this. His smile brings me comfort and I don't feel the fear as much. "I will never let anything happen to you, I'll kill him first."

"No one is killing anyone!" I hiss again. "We are leaving!"

I think about Colin's journal. I can't leave without it. "I want to stop into the library and grab a few books to take back with me, okay?"

Oliver shakes his head. "No way, we have to go."

"It will just take a few minutes. You can go stand guard at the front door and make sure we are clear to leave, okay?" I kiss his cheek. I'm trying to calm him down so he can at least focus to drive, but in this moment he looks like a zombie. "Just go downstairs, okay? I will be right behind you."

"Two minutes." He holds up two fingers. He leads me into the hallway and we part ways at the closed door of the library. My hand is so shaky that it takes a few tries to open the door; the darkness of the room spooks me so badly that I have to force myself to go inside. I turn the lights on and rush toward the bookshelf that had the orange book on it. I take it off the shelf and notice several books that look similar to it, in different colors. I grab two more of them and bolt from the room, not bothering to shut the door behind me. Oliver's eyes relax when he sees me; he has already checked outside and we are clear to rush toward the Jeep.

I put my head into my hands once we are safely on the road. "I am so sorry." I start to sob and rub the salty tears from my eyes. "This is all my fault."

"How?" he asks, keeping his eyes on the road. "How can this possibly be your fault?"

"Brandon kept trying to contact me when I got

back from the cabin the first time," I blurt. I never thought I would tell Oliver. "He tried to see me but Randy and his cop buddies ran him off every time. He even told Randy that he would get me back no matter what it took. I should have known he would take it to this extreme, he never was one for small gestures."

Oliver growls. "He isn't getting you back, you're not his property. He isn't going to take you from me."

"I don't want anything bad to happen to you. Maybe I should just call him and see if we can meet—"

I feel the Jeep swerve onto the side of the road and he angrily puts it into park. "I need you to listen to me carefully because I am only going to say this once more to you, okay?" He doesn't wait for me to say anything. I am able to nod in agreement as he places his hands on my shoulders, turning on the overhead light so he can see my eyes. "You have done nothing wrong here. This isn't your fault; Brandon is messed up in the head. I will never, ever let anyone hurt you or do anything bad to you as long as I live, do you understand me?"

I nod, locking our eyes together. I could get lost in these Hershey bar colored eyes of his; I could forget about the world and gaze at him all day.

"Say you understand me, Julie."

The air that I have captured coming from my lungs makes me sick a little. I push it back down underneath his glare. "I understand."

"Good." He wipes away my tears with the pads

of his thumbs. "Now come over here." He motions for me to slide over toward him on the long seat; he cradles my body beneath his muscular arm. "You should try and sleep, okay? You know it's a long drive." I rest my head on his shoulder and watch the darkness go by us.

"Actually, do you mind if I read a little?" I ask, taking out my phone for light and waving it toward him. "It won't bother you, will it?"

He gives me a weak smile. The car turns back onto the road, putting us back on our journey. "No, sunshine, you go ahead. What are you reading?"

"A journal." I test the waters a little to see if he knows anything about them. He is just as puzzled as I was when I found them. I think quickly about lying, but being vague seems like a better route. "Someone's personal journal."

"Oh, yeah? Any juicy gossip in it?"

"A little. I'll let you know when I finish it." I hope that he leaves it at that. I can tell he wants to concentrate on the road so I take the orange book from the floorboard and tilt it on my lap. I position the phone at a different angle to shine light on Colin's words. I want Oliver to have a hard time seeing what it says. I want this to be my little secret for now; I promised myself I would fill Oliver in later. It makes me a little sick to think that I have any claim over these journals at all; I think that Colin would like me if he were still alive.

I find the place where I stopped reading, sifting through a few more entries before looking over to make sure Oliver isn't reading it too. When I feel safe again, I glue my eyes to the journal. I scan the pages, trying to read the scratchy handwriting.

February 4th, 1992

I let Veronica come and go as she pleases. All I ask her for is that she doesn't shoot up or snort anything while Oliver is still growing inside of her. I ask that she comes home often so I can check up on him and make sure he is still healthy.

My father hired a private doctor for her visits, he is a very discreet man.

I haven't been able to bring myself to decorate the spare room on the third floor into a nursery. Partially because I am too busy with chasing after Veronica and partially because I am scared that Oliver won't make it out alive. When she returned home last night—the fourth night in a row that I begged her to come home—her hair was a matted mess and she looked like she had been sleeping in a trash bin for a week.

I know she is scared about the baby. I am scared too. I am scared that she will leave us and he will never know his mother. He will never see her smile or see her freckles. He will not experience how kind and generous she can be or how smart she really is. She doesn't believe it about herself. I know she hates herself but I thought that the amount of love I have for her would conquer that.

I was wrong.

I know that now.

So I decided that I will now completely let it go. We have three months until Oliver is here. Three short—or long—months, however you choose to look at it.

I just need to remember to breathe sometimes.

I do worry about my son.

If he ever reads this I hope he realizes just one thing.

I will never, ever let anyone hurt you or do anything bad to you as long as I live.

I would kill them first.

I gasp.

Oliver glances over at me. Maybe he just thinks that I am really involved in this book.

I *am* totally involved in this book.

I turn a few more pages and stop.

March 16th, 1992

Veronica actually attended a scheduled ultra-sound this morning! Then she disappeared and I was served with papers at my father's doorstep from the sheriff. I am being summoned to court so that she can hand the baby off to me when he is born.

Oliver.

I am so sorry, son.

March 31st, 1992

Just a few more weeks, son.

Veronica is finding it hard to move now so she is staying in more frequently. Her entire body is apparently on fire, or so she claims.

I believe it's called a withdrawal.

The police requested that we keep her indoors; she was just caught with an unsettling amount of cocaine in her pocket a few days ago. Not to mention the prostitution, which I don't quite understand. I give her more than enough money to do anything she wants with.

My father swears that is the issue: He says I enable her to do these things.

He doesn't understand that I just want my son to be born so we can run away from all of this.

Oliver, I will shield you from this world.

I promise you.

I WANT TO CRY. I know Oliver will ask me what's wrong, so I stop my tears. I glance over at him again—his eyes are tired but still focused. "Do you want me to drive for a while?" I ask and he smiles sweetly and finds my hand on my lap, squeezing it. "No thanks, you go ahead and get some rest, okay? That book must be good—you've been reading the entire drive home."

We're almost in Rockford and I have been reading his father's private thoughts the whole time with him sitting inches away.

"You should call your brother and let him know

you're okay. I'm taking you home with me where I can keep you safe." I don't argue with him. I put the journal away and dial Randy's number, letting it go to voicemail. I leave him a brief message with the information that Oliver just told me. I didn't want to upset him any more than he possibly could be—

Ring.

"It's Casey," Oliver says and answers the phone.

"Yeah?…Okay. No, no, okay, I get it…Can we see her?…Okay, man, we'll come straight there." He hands me his phone to keep. I make a point to brush hands with him so he will smile. "Nora is awake… we can see her. Do you want to stop by the hospital on our way home?"

I nod. I know he can hear my thoughts loud and clear. "Okay, but only for a few minutes, okay? Brandon is still out there." He knows that I'll do what he asks of me—I know he doesn't want to control me. He just wants to keep me safe.

I feel the Jeep lurch toward the freeway and we get off on the first exit. I start seeing signs for Rockford Memorial Hospital on the side of the road. They get bigger as we approach the enormous buildings, a set of three high-rises as tall as the clouds. I think about Nora inside of there, somewhere, hurting because of me.

Oliver's eyes are tired and heavy. He helps me out of the Jeep and takes my hand. We walk into the hospital lobby and he smiles for a moment. "What is it with us and hospitals?" he whispers and winks, which makes me feel a little better; I don't dare laugh at his joke. "She's in room 314. That's on the third floor of the hospital, so let's find an elevator." Once he says this, we hear an elevator ding to our left. Casey pops out, his gaze darkens, and his skin is seeping sadness.

"Oh, hey guys," he says softly. "She's awake if you want to see her."

"Aren't you staying?" I ask, but he can't look either one of us in the eye. Oliver turns to me and motions to get onto the elevator. "You go ahead, I'll be right up, okay? I'll talk to him." I rise up on my tiptoes and kiss his warm lips. I look into his eyes as I lower myself back down and step into the elevator. The doors close and I am alone. Even though it's only for a few minutes, I can feel the silence in my veins. I'm not sure what I will be walking into when I see Nora. I definitely still believe that it's my fault what happened to her. No amount of angry eyes from Mr. Jackson can relieve that.

The doors open and I stand in the elevator, my legs planted firmly on the floor. "Come on, Julie, get out," I whisper to myself. "You have to get out."

I step out so the elevator can go back down to Oliver, but I don't move.

"Can I help you?" a young blonde nurse asks me as she passes.

I shake my head. "I'm going to room 314."

"Oh." Her eyes sadden. "Are you family?"

I clear my throat. "She's my sister."

The young nurse nods toward me. The elevators ding and when Oliver steps out, her eyes glow and suddenly I am invisible to her. "And is this your...*husband*?" She does everything but lick her lips at him. Oliver notices, so he places his arm around my waist and tugs me close to him. He looks down at the girl with dark eyes. "Yes, I'm her husband. Where is room 314?" She huffs and points down the hallway in front of us. Oliver pushes me toward Nora's room. The door is shut but I can see her inside, bandaged up and wounded.

"I'm right here behind you, okay?" Oliver says and squeezes my sides. "I'm not going anywhere... you can just go in and see her and come right back out if you want."

I nod. "Let's do it."

The door creaks so loud when it opens that Nora looks over at it slowly from her gaze at the window. She looks so miserable and her face crinkles in anger when she sees me. "Get out." Her voice is slow and drugged up; she's having trouble focusing her eyes.

"Nora—" Oliver starts to say, but she cuts him off.

"Your deranged ex-boyfriend pushed me down the stairs. I have a broken leg, all because of you!" Her screams get louder as I back up into Oliver's body. "Get the hell out of here! I don't ever want to see you again! I wish I had never met you—this would never have happened to me!"

He whisks me out of the room. We back down the hallway to the elevator. I let him hold me up until we get to the Jeep. He places me inside and buckles me in. I can feel his remorse for making me do that.

"I am so sorry," he whispers as he gets in and looks over at me. "I had no idea—"

I hold up my hand to shut him up. "Let's go home."

I want to go home.

Together.

TWENTY-FOUR
CASEY

I DON'T KNOW what the hell I'm doing here.

I like Nora a lot.

I mean, I really, *really* like her.

That's why I chose to answer Heather's text earlier—she said she wanted to talk about Oliver. She wants to come to some kind of agreement. I just want to put her whole dramatic self behind me so I can focus on Nora, someone who is normal and not full of hot air and lipstick.

So now here I am. Standing outside room 1409 at The Ritz-Carlton, waiting for Heather to open her door.

"Hey, sexy." She peeks from behind the white steel door frame. Her black hair flows around her pale, almost translucent skin. "Come in, I've been waiting for you to get here."

I scoff as I enter the suite. "That's funny, I only got the text fifteen minutes ago and I wasn't even sure I was going to show up."

She slides her arms around me from behind; it makes me jump. "Oh, I knew you would show up. Do you want to have some fun?" She walks around my body, her dangerous eyes fixed on mine.

I shake my head. "I came here to tell you to leave me the hell alone."

Heather rolls her eyes, but her fake eyelashes hardly move. "Leave you alone? But you promised to help me get Ollie back." Her smile turns devilish. "Or did you want me to just tell him about our little affair way back when? I'm sure he would hate you for a very long time."

"You guys had just met each other, you were hardly in love," I growl at her. "You were drunk, I was drunk, and Ollie was drunk, okay? You guys were dating for like two weeks, give me a break. Why do you think he will even care? He can't even stand to look at you after what you've done."

"Do you think he will give *you* a break?" She laughs. "He will hate you and Julie will rip him into a whole new world of soccer mom minivans and school plays with little half-mutant children running around."

I shrug her panicked voice off; I hardly feel sorry for her. "Then so be it. He actually deserves a better person like Julie to be with." Heather's eyes widen in anger. She almost tackles me to the ground. "And maybe he also deserves better friends that won't betray him."

"You don't mean that." She sounds worried. Her fit body stands in between me and the door. "He's been your best friend since grade school. You two have been inseparable…trust me, I have *tried* to get rid of you."

I shake my head. She has a point; I don't want Oliver to hate me. If he finds out I had sex with Heather when they were together, he will *definitely* hate me. I hardly care about what happens to her, though. "I will tell him myself." I watch annoyance grow on her face. "Yeah, I think I'll just do that."

Heather takes out her phone. "I'm going to do it right now."

I snatch her phone and corner her against the wall. "He's moving on with his life after you fucking destroyed it—don't you think you owe it to him to just disappear?"

She gulps. "Disappear?"

I let go of her. "Not like that. I wouldn't hurt you."

Her body stops shaking as she fakes a laugh. "I know that." She puts her long arms around my neck and tugs a little at my hair, making me excited.

"What are you doing, Heather?" I ask but I don't push her off of me. Instead, I let her press her lips onto mine and slash her tongue around my mouth. I have to get her undressed enough to take her to the bedroom in the suite. It feels good to be wanted; Nora has been shafting me for a few days. I am just pissed off enough to not think about what I am doing, letting her grab at my body parts like a hungry animal.

In the suite that Oliver has paid for.

That doesn't stop me as I let her unbuckle my pants. She pulls them down and off of me, and I step out of them and throw her onto the sofa in the small living space. Her eyes are like fire, she wants me so badly, and I'm not sure why the hell I want her. I let her slide a condom—that I swear is scented like banana—onto my hard flesh. I don't know where she got it.

I'm halfway into her when my phone starts ringing and I ignore it. I fully push into her flesh and listen to her horrible moans. I try to drown them out but they just sound so much like a chicken being beheaded that I welcome the ringing phone for the third time.

"I got to get that," I say, out of breath. I pull away from her and listen to her agitated scoffs. I jump up and sift through my pile of clothes for my phone. She is already behind me, plucking the phone from my hands and knocking me to the ground. She places her body on top of mine and continues what we started. Before I even know what's happening, it's over.

What the hell did I just do?

No, what the hell did I just do—*again*?

"You should probably get this." She hands me the phone.

"Nora?" I clear my throat as Heather slaps my ass and licks her lips.

"Casey? Casey—I need help." Her voice is weak. "I already called the cops; they are on their way over here."

"Nora? What the hell happened?" I say loudly

and Heather's interest is piqued. She raises her eyebrows over the glass of red wine she had just poured herself. "Are you okay? Why are you calling the cops?" There is some commotion and I hear police sirens. Nora calls them over to her and then the phone goes silent. I turn to Heather and notice that she doesn't even care. "Nora is in trouble—are you coming?"

She shakes her head. "Um, no. I have better things to do."

"Are you serious?" I yell. "Look, what just happened, *didn't happen*. Do you understand me?" She scoffs. I'm not playing with her right now, and I *need* her to know that. I run over to her and grab her arms, but this time she squeals with delight. Like I'm about to take her on the floor again. "Don't play with me. I will tell Ollie about us, but right now you need to disappear. Don't let me see your face around here for a long time."

"O-okay, you're hurting me." Tears form in her eyes. I can see that I've succeeded in getting my point across enough.

"Good." I throw on my clothes and run out of the room; my head spins from what just happened.

I really, really like Nora.

But I just had sex with her friend.

I had sex with Heather—again.

I broke the number one rule of the brother code: Any girl, past or present, is off limits.

Only idiots do that, idiots who don't get the girl

of their dreams because they mess it up. My phone rings again and I answer before looking at it. "Nora?"

"Casey, it's me." Her voice sounds so good to my ears. "I'm being taken to Rockford Memorial, okay? Can you meet me there?"

"Of course, I'm on my way," I say before even thinking about it. "I'm not too far from there right now."

She coughs and screams in pain. "Please, hurry. Ouch, that fucking hurts! Isn't there anything else you can do besides kill me faster?"

"What happened, Nora?" I get into my car and start it, driving out of the hotel parking lot. I am holding back so much fear I think I'll explode. "Did you get into an accident?"

I hear her scream in pain again. A few people talk around her; I assume they are paramedics trying to help her. "Brandon—he came to my house about an hour ago. I thought he just wanted to talk about Julie. He got angry when I wouldn't tell him where she is. He pushed me down a flight of stairs…I think my leg is broken. Brandon is still looking for her; he ran out of my house and the cops can't find him."

"She's with Oliver, she's safe," I tell her. "I'm going to find that bastard."

Then the phone goes silent.

I race down the slick streets toward the hospital. I dial Oliver's number with the phone in my lap, trying to weave around the other cars on the road. He doesn't answer and I call over and over again—

five or six times—before he finally picks up. "Where are you?" I am barely able to choke out the words.

"You know I'm at the lake, why?"

"You two need to come back to town. Now." I can't think of any other way to say it. I know it will create a panic and someone else could get hurt.

"Casey, I'm hanging up," Oliver says and I try to catch my breath. "What's wrong with you?"

"Casey!" Oliver yells.

"Brandon attacked Nora and she's in the hospital. He's looking for Julie," I blurt out before I can stop myself. I can just see the look on Oliver's face.

"When?" The fear in his voice trickles through the phone.

"I'm not sure how long ago it was—I just heard from her." He hangs up the phone. No doubt grabbing Julie and getting her into the car at that moment.

As I pull up to the hospital emergency entrance, a text comes through on my phone from Heather. I ignore it.

I shouldn't have done that.

I ask the front desk clerk nervously for Nora's room number. "She came here with a broken leg."

The older lady purses her lips. "Are you family?"

"Yes, he is," I hear Heather say to the nurse and then saunter into the lobby area. "He is with me, Petunia. It's okay, thank you."

The nurse nods. She goes about her business as I glare at Heather. "How the hell did you get here so fast? I left before you did."

She shrugs. "Valet car service at the hotel. I tip

them well for extra speed. I just got done talking to my little friend about where her boyfriend was when she needed him the most. Of course, she's up there waiting for you to come and explain yourself. How could you do this to poor little Nora?"

My world melts around me. "You didn't."

Heather clicks her tongue. "Oh, I did. So, she's waiting for you. Good luck! I hope it all works out for you two!"

I race to find Nora in room 314, where they've managed to stabilize her enough with pain medication that she's still a little coherent.

Until she sees my face.

"Is it true?" Her words slur a bit. "What Heather said?"

I lower my head. "It's true. I don't know what the hell is wrong with me. I'm so sorry, Nora. I never meant to hurt you, really—I never meant to hurt you, please, you have to believe me."

I can see confusion in her eyes; it must be the medication. "I don't understand how you could get this past me."

"Me either. I can't believe I slept with her. I'm so sorry, Nora. I like you, I really do—I actually might lo—"

"You *slept* with her? She just said that you had a surprise for me." A bubble forms in my throat and I now I can't breathe. "You *slept with her*?" she asks again, raising herself up in the bed. "This is just great. My best friend's ex-boyfriend nearly kills me and you sleep with my crazy ass psycho former friend. What is this, a freaking reality show? You can leave now."

"But, Nora—"

"*Leave!*" Her scream echoes off the walls. A young blonde nurse comes into the room, giving me dirty looks. I back out of the open door and turn away from her.

Heather is going to pay for this.

TWENTY-FIVE
OLIVER

JULIE SITS NEXT to me in the Jeep, silent and horrified. I think about what Nora said to her. I shake my head; I'm trying to fathom how in the hell she could even bring herself to blame Julie. I once again find myself starting to dislike Nora. She hasn't completely redeemed herself—not in my eyes. I don't believe she's even a good friend to Julie—I haven't heard her say one word about Nora since we've gotten back together.

Are we together?

Were we together?

I have to ask her.

I need to know; it's not the best time, though, so I take her hand and squeeze it. I don't feel her squeeze it back.

She's not here with me; she's locked inside her own mind.

"Let's go inside, okay?" I whisper, but she doesn't move. She doesn't even acknowledge anything I'm saying to her. "Julie? Can you walk?" She doesn't answer me, so I get out of the Jeep. When I reach her window, I can see the tears staining her cheeks in the light of the parking garage.

I have no idea what to do for her. I hate Brandon and Nora both for doing this. Julie didn't ask to live with a crazy person. She didn't ask for him to cheat on her. She didn't ask for him to stalk her and she sure as hell didn't call him up and say, "Hey, if you love me, you'd go push my friend down a flight of stairs."

I open the door and unbuckle her seat belt. Making sure I'm being gentle, I tug her toward my chest and shut the door with my foot. She doesn't nuzzle into my body like normal. Her eyes are cold and distant; it's hard to see them because of the hair hanging in her face.

I walk to one of the elevators in the lobby and step inside. Bernie nods at me with understanding. "She okay, sir?"

I nod. "She'll be fine—it's been a long night."

He looks at me doubtfully, and I return it with a look that tells him to back off and not ask any more questions. When the doors close behind us again, I shift her weight in my arms. I force her against my chest so she can at least get a little comfort in all of this craziness. I can feel her soft breathing; she puts her head over my heart to listen to my heartbeat. I can just imagine how broken it is with her sadness tainting it. I don't care. I don't want her to feel bad for me—I just want to make her happy again. I try to calm myself down to make her feel a little better.

Mrs. Atchley is in the hallway talking to another neighbor. When I come out of the elevator holding this weak, sad girl, she wobbles her way toward me.

"Where are your keys, kid?" I stick my right hip toward her and she shoves her bony hand into my pocket. She has no trouble fishing out my keys and opens the door. "Put her to bed…I'll take it from there."

Mrs. Atchley is another woman that will always have a hold over me. I do what she asks too. Every single time.

Julie isn't asleep, but she isn't awake, either. I lay her on the bed and sit in the chair in the corner. The old woman tends to her, patting her hands. "Child, can you hear me?" She strokes her silky, honey blonde hair. I watch Julie's eyes flick over toward her. "There you are, girl. What happened to her?"

I can feel the old woman's eyes on me, but I don't look up. I'm frozen with despair; I should've known not to take Julie to the hospital. The old woman throws a pillow at me and snaps her fingers. "Buck up, kid, you're needed here. What happened to her?"

Julie clears her throat. "I'm fine, really, thank you. You remind me of my Aunt Shelly before she passed away."

Mrs. Atchley eyeballs me and groans. "That's always nice to hear, that you remind a person of someone they can't forget. Oliver, go get this girl something to eat."

"All he has here are some eggs and a few slices of bread." Julie smiles warmly at me. She's doing the best she can. "I'm fine, really...I just had a little weird moment, but I'm pretty much all better."

The old woman scoffs. "More like an anxiety attack." She turns back to me. "Order her some take-out, then—she needs food. *Protein*, Oliver." Julie starts to protest again. Mrs. Atchley gives her the stink eye and she quiets down. I jump up and kiss Julie on the head, squeeze Mrs. Atchley's frail arm, and leave the room.

I'm headed into the kitchen to get the takeout menus when a wave of darkness washes over me. I have to lock myself in the bathroom. I turn on both faucets in the sink and lower myself onto the floor, putting my head on my knees. I press my back against the wall and cry my eyes out. The bathroom spins around me. It feels like there's no way I can get up and order food, but somehow I push through and do it anyway.

I have to be strong for her if no one else will.

I have to be strong for her because I love her. No one else is going to hurt her as long as I'm around.

I open the door and walk into the kitchen, squaring my shoulders. I'm prepared to do whatever it takes to make Julie happy—I owe her that much. I owe her more than that, actually. When we met, I was a shell of a person. I slept around so much that it had become normal. It was normal to not remember who was in my bed just hours earlier. I didn't like myself and I hated Heather.

Well, that hasn't changed very much, at least: I *still* hate Heather. Probably more now that she's pulling more crazy schemes.

I choose the place Julie loves the most out of the menus and order her favorite garlic lasagna, some side dishes, and a few bottles of wine and then put the phone on the counter. I wonder if it'd be okay for me to go to her. *I need her. I need to feel her.*

I want her.

I want to make her pain go away.

I have to make her pain go away...I can't stop thinking about it.

Mrs. Atchley and Julie are giggling when I come back into the room. "Well, what do we have here?" I look at the two of them. The old lady starts to stand up, but I hold out my hand. "Please, stay, Mrs. Atchley. I've ordered enough for all of us. Please join us for dinner?"

"Yes, please do." Julie wipes her eyes and smiles at the old woman.

I know she'll try and snake her way out of it. "I insist," I say, widening my eyes at her—silently letting her know I need her just as much as Julie does. The old woman nods and hands me her apartment keys. "Go over and get Mikey." She shoos me away.

Mikey is her stinky old bulldog that hates me; I can smell his farts from the hallway. I open her door and he rushes to greet the visitor, but once he notices it's me he starts growling.

"Mikey, come on, man. She's over at my place—

do you want to go over?" He snaps at me, but he understands what I'm saying. He runs from the apartment and trots into my open door. I have to jog behind him as he sniffs around for her and jumps on my bed.

Mr. Smelly Dog Farts is on my bed.

Next to my girlfriend, who is rubbing his belly.

Is *she my girlfriend?*

I still have to ask her that. It weighs heavily on my mind. "Looks like he found another friend." I fake a smile and pat the dog on the head. He nips at me, which makes the two women laugh hysterically.

"Mikey hates this one." Mrs. Atchley points toward me. "But they tolerate each other."

I shake my head. "No, I tolerate *him*. He just plain hates me."

The doorbell rings and I go to get the food. But when I open the door, it isn't a delivery person. It's Casey, and he looks *rough*.

"Just hear me out," he says before I can shut the door in his face. "Look, Ollie, dammit I'm sorry."

"You're sorry that you slept with my girlfriend?" I whisper angrily, looking around to make sure that Julie can't hear what I am saying. In the few seconds that she'd rode up alone to visit Nora back at the hospital, Casey had dropped that bomb on me. I didn't have time to worry about that then because of Julie, but now I want to punch his fucking lights out.

He hangs his head. "There isn't an excuse but trust me, if I'd thought it was a serious thing I wouldn't have." He notices my eyes and holds up his hands in a truce. "That doesn't make it right, but you're my best friend and now Nora hates me—"

"Why does Nora hate you?" Julie says, walking up behind me. I start to shut the door so Casey and I can speak outside; Julie stops me and looks at Casey for an explanation. "Why does she hate you?"

Casey looks sick. "I slept with Heather. Earlier today."

Julie's face is hard to read for a few moments. Finally, her lips curl and she starts laughing. Mrs. Atchley has positioned herself in one of the armchairs in the living room with Mikey. She shakes her head while Casey and I both look at each other in confusion.

"He slept with her when Heather and I were together," I growl at her, but that doesn't get her to stop laughing. "Julie, it's not funny—it's messed up."

"I know, I know." She has to clear her throat and make herself stop giggling. "We're all so fucked up that we belong together."

Now *Casey* is laughing hysterically. "I've never heard you swear. That's *hilarious*."

Julie slides her hand into mine and kisses my cheek. "Let him in…let him eat with us. We can sort through all of this stuff later, right? Screw all the rules."

I am so in love with this girl.

"Right," I choke out. I let Casey enter the apartment. The delivery guy is getting off the elevator with our food so I intercept him just in case Julie wants to invite anyone else to dinner who doesn't belong here.

She *is* right, though. No matter how messed up it is that Casey did that to me, Heather wasn't exactly innocent in all of this.

Casey is in the living room petting Mikey. He chats with Mrs. Atchley as I put the bags down on the counter. I slide my arms around Julie's waist and pull her backward against my chest; I lean down and nuzzle her neck and cheek. "You are so completely amazing that it surprises me sometimes, you know that?" I whisper into her ear. I can feel her smile. "You're stronger than you know. I just want you to remember that I'm here and I'm not going anywhere, okay?"

She nods and continues with the preparations.

"Julie? I lo—"

"Casey, will you set the table for me, please?" Julie cuts me off and kisses my cheek. She looks into my eyes to tell me that now isn't the time for what I was about to say.

Casey comes into the kitchen, feeling the tension. He looks at me with concern but takes the plates and wine glasses to the table. Mrs. Atchley refuses any wine at first, then motions for me to pour it in. "Keep pouring, son, you know I like my Piño." We all laugh together. I fill the glass until it's almost overflowing.

The entire meal is so pleasant that we all forget about our troubles—even if it's just for a while. Julie and Mrs. Atchley have a spectacular time giving Casey and me trouble. The entire meal, Julie has her hand on my leg underneath the table. She takes small bites of the lasagna and smiles over at me each time I can catch her eye.

Once the food is gone and the wine is in our blood, Mrs. Atchley scoops up her dog and says her goodbyes. She thanks us for the company and for keeping an old woman entertained. Casey offers to walk her to her door—maybe trying to save a little face with me. He didn't say much to me at dinner and I was okay with that. I don't want to hear his excuses. Honestly, it doesn't even matter to me anymore.

Once we're alone, Julie starts buzzing between the dining room and the kitchen. She cleans up the dinner mess, and I try to help her but she hands me another glass of wine and tells me to go sit in the living room. I finish the glass and take it into the kitchen where she's finishing up. She turns to face me once she feels my presence. "I'm ready to let it go," she says and lifts her chin. "I'm ready to be free."

"What are you saying?" I put the glass in the sink and brush her hair behind her ear. "Are you saying you want to be with me? No more running, no more acting scared and pushing me away—you're ready to do this?"

"I'm ready to do this," she says into my shirt as she wraps her arms around me. "I'm ready to forget everyone and everything. Forget all that's happened in both of our lives…I'm ready to just start over. And I want to start over with you."

I close my eyes and smile. "It's about time. What made you decide this?"

"I just don't want to be sad anymore...there isn't a reason for it. I know what happened to Nora is awful, but it isn't my fault. She should have never let him into her house or answered his phone calls. And Casey loves you—he made a mistake, but you need to let it go too."

"He slept with Heather while we were together," I tell her. "It's not right, no matter how you look at it."

She shakes her head. "No, it isn't right, but you have to let it go if you want to move on too."

"Fine, I'll let it go. Only on one condition." Her eyebrows raise and I can see that she has her own conditions, but I need to sell her on mine first. "You have to live by my rules."

She giggles. "What rules?"

I take her hand and show her I'm not joking. "The rules I've created for my life. I don't want to be hurt again, not by anyone or anything." I know I blush when she cocks her head and the strands of stray hair caress her cheek. "I live my life by a set of rules, Julie. You made me break the first one, and you could have destroyed me."

"Oliver, you're being dramatic."

I slowly let the air out from my lungs. "All you have to do is agree to the rules. That's the only way our life can be...*perfect*."

It's torture, watching her decide. "What are the rules, then?"

I clear my throat. "There are four. The first rule is

not to let your guard down. I put up so many walls after Heather fucked me up, I didn't want anyone to try and break them down. But you did. You smashed right through them. So I failed my own first rule, but I'm fucking happy I did." I run my finger down her cheek; she smiles at my touch. "The second rule is don't take life for granted—you never know when it'll end. Next, don't let your secrets destroy you."

She holds up her hand. "I don't have any secrets."

"Good, because I don't like secrets. Now would be the time to tell me anything I wouldn't like, or confess something." She shakes her head, so I continue. "And the final rule is: Don't destroy your own happiness. If you can't make yourself happy, you can't make anyone else happy."

The air between us is a little chilly. Once she thinks about the rules, she nods in agreement. "I can agree to those, but there's just one thing I have to show you first." She holds out her hand. "I need your car keys."

"For what?" I fish them out of my pocket and give them to her.

"To obey your 'no secrets' rule. We need to go to the car, but Brandon is still out there—"

I hold my hand out to her. "Let's go."

We trek down to the Jeep and she rummages through it. She pulls several worn and tattered books from the underside of the front seat. She doesn't tell me what they are, just takes my hand again and drags me back upstairs. "Let's get ready for bed and then I'll show you what these are," she says and starts stripping naked in front of me.

She isn't a stranger to my bedroom. She knows where to find a t-shirt to sleep in as I take off my jeans and hop into bed next to her. "Okay, I'm ready."

Julie bites her bottom lip. "Okay, before you freak out—"

"What are they, Julie?" I demand. "Just tell me."

She sighs and pushes an orange book toward me. "Your father's journals. I have four of them but there are dozens back at the cabin."

"Journals? Like diaries?" I open the book. Sure enough, my father's handwriting is kicking me in the face. "How far do these go back?"

She shrugs. "I'm not sure. I started reading them when your mother found out she was pregnant with you."

My face pales. "My mother?"

"Yes, and you probably won't like hearing what he has to say about her. She doesn't seem like she was a very nice woman."

I have to keep these journals away from her.

"She wasn't a nice woman," I mutter and slam the book shut, taking the rest out of her hands. "We should put these away for now."

Julie tilts her head in confusion. "Don't you want to know about her?"

I turn off the lamp beside the bed and lie down with her. "I know about her; my father told me stories. I have some memories of her. Let's just go to sleep, okay?" I want her to stop asking me questions about it; I don't want her to know any more than she needs to.

I told her not to let her secrets destroy her. Destroy *us*.

But she can't know this one.

TWENTY-SIX
HEATHER

THERE IS ABSOLUTELY no doubt in my mind that Oliver will come running back to me. Once he's done with what's-her-name, that is. Honestly, I think this is good for him to get out of his system before we get back together. So he can know, without a doubt, that with me is where he truly belongs.

Julie is so...*dull*.

I wonder if he even buys her nice things like he bought for me. Of course, I had to sell most of those things to afford to continue my lifestyle. It's just a matter of time before I get back into Oliver's pocket —I mean, get back into his *heart*. I laugh and the bed stirs next to me. I forgot that I'm not alone. Before I can come up with a plan to escape, he groans and holds the pillow over his head to block out the sunlight.

Whatever his name is.

Mark...Josh...Brandon. That's right. Brandon.

He literally ran into me down at the hotel bar last

night. He was so freaked out that it was sort of pathetically cute. I was more than desperate to sleep away my frustration over Oliver not returning my calls. Preferably with someone other than Casey—that was getting old.

Poor Nora though, she didn't look well after I'd left her hospital room, and Casey, he's just a walking disaster.

"Oh, man." Brandon rubs his eyes and opens them. He tries to focus with all the fresh sunlight in the room. "My head is pounding."

"Here," I say in a cold voice. I hand him a few aspirin and some water. "Take these and leave."

He sits up slowly and rubs his head. He pops the pills in his mouth and guzzles down the water in two drinks. "I'll leave when I damn well please."

I scoff. "Oh my God, do I need to call security?"

Brandon's smile widens and his hands creep underneath the blanket. He grabs my thigh and squeezes it—*hard*. "If you want me to do what I did to you last night again, just say the word. Your wish is most definitely my command." His hand slides up my thigh and starts moving toward my inner leg. I let him touch me for a few more minutes so I can remember what it feels like, getting my fill and shaking him off as he laughs.

His laugh chills my bones.

"I was pretty drunk last night—what did you say your name was?" He rubs his eyes again. He's pretty good-looking, but he isn't sexy like Ollie. Every single woman I've ever encountered when I was next to him acted jealous; I always laughed in their faces when they even tried to talk to him. He always blamed me for him not being able to make and keep friends, but I was always looking out for his best interest: Me.

I bite my bottom lip. "I'm going to order breakfast —are you staying?"

Brandon nods and groans. He floats back down into the soft, expensive mattress. I roll my eyes and pick up the phone on the bedside table, dialing the number one. I wait three rings before I hang up. Annoyed, I dial another time.

"Good morning, this is the front desk. My name is Alejandro, how may I assist you?"

I sigh loudly into the phone. "Alejandro. This is Heather from room 1409; how many times do I have to ask you people to pick up on at least the second ring?"

He doesn't speak.

"Okay, let's just see if we can get my breakfast order right this morning, shall we?"

"Yes, Miss Heather. What would you like this morning?" His voice is steady. I know he's probably rolling his eyes at me but I don't care.

"Strawberries, pancakes and eggs, some bacon, and maybe a little avocado...can you handle that?" I snip at him. Alejandro reads my order back to me and then I hang up the phone. Brandon slides out of the bed and locks himself in the bathroom. I heard the shower running and I cringe.

Who takes a shower without asking someone in their own home?

I take this opportunity to get dressed and run a brush through my black hair. I apply a little foundation and natural-colored blush to my cheeks, then pinch them to make them a little pinker. I roll on some tinted lip balm and shiver at the thought of Ollie's lips on Julie's. I run my hand down my left leg and frown. I need to shave, but he's in my shower.

The waiter with the food knocks on the door. I don't have any money for a tip, so I search through Brandon's pants for his wallet and find something else instead.

A large wad of rolled-up money.

I find his wallet and open it, taking out all the cash in there too and sifting through for a twenty. Then I put everything back in the way I found it and open the door for the waiter. He brings in the food and lays it out for us, serving me my usual morning mimosa. I hand him the twenty without saying a word so he'll leave.

I hurry up and stuff my face full of pancakes and strawberries; I slide a few pieces of bacon into the bedside table for later. I like to eat in peace where no one can judge me sometimes.

Brandon comes sauntering out of the steamy bathroom, towel around his waist. He sits down across from me, shoveling food onto his plate.

"So, who were you running from last night?" I take a few more strawberries and nibble on them while he eats like a pig. "You said something about doing something bad."

He nods. "I don't know if I did something bad, but I'm leaving town just in case."

I pout a little and whimper as if I really care that he's leaving. "So soon? You couldn't have done anything that bad—you don't seem like a bad person. Not that I'm one to judge anyone right now."

"I'm a bad person, trust me," he mutters, and it kind of creeps me out. "You don't know me, you don't know what I've done to people, and you don't know what I am running from."

"O-okay, well…" I hold my arm toward the front door. "Feel free to mosey on out whenever you feel like it, then."

He snickers into his pancakes. "Oh, I intend to. I just want to fill my stomach first. Is that okay?"

I nod and say nothing. I'm not quite sure if I should call the cops. I would have to explain how I know him and that would be embarrassing. He eats for a few more minutes and then pulls his pants on. He takes out his wallet and I cringe. He opens it and sees the money missing.

"Just give it back to me and I won't hurt you." He's suddenly next to me, looking down into my eyes. "All of it. I'm serious."

I squeak and take the roll of money from my pocket. "I have it all but the twenty I tipped the waiter." I think he's going to snap my neck off, but he sighs and takes the money from my hand and returns to putting on his clothes.

He hurries and dresses, looking around to make sure he's not leaving any traces of himself behind. He stares at me for a moment from across the room. "I'm not going to hurt you—please relax," he stays. "I'm just going to leave, okay? I have a train to catch anyways. I'll bill you for the twenty." He winks and takes one last look around before leaving me alone in the room. I quickly run to the door and use the chain and all the locks, letting out a long breath and clutching my chest.

That was a close one. At least he said he was skipping town. I feel gross enough to shower and finish the bacon in my nightstand, but I realize I'm alone again. Well, at least I'm alive.

I can't very well win Ollie back if I'm dead, can I?

TWENTY-SEVEN
OLIVER

I MAKE it through the entire morning without Julie asking me about those damn journals or my mother again. I know she wants to, though. It's shaking her to her bones, all the questions that she has for me inside that beautiful head of hers.

My father did tell me stories to glamorize my mother, but I always knew the truth. The last time I saw her was when I was five, but I know that she lived in and out of Rockford until my father died and then I lost track.

I truthfully don't know if my mother is alive or dead.

Right after I tell Julie I don't want any more secrets, I pile mine on thick. To be fair, this isn't so much of a secret as it's just something I don't want her finding out. My mother isn't a good person, point blank. But I can't even be honest with her about how I feel, and I'm lying to her.

She paces the floor while talking on her phone.

Her legs call to me. I'm not sure who she's talking to so I don't reach for her. Her eyes dart to mine, as if she's reading my mind, and gives me a warning look. "Nora is asking for us." She sits down next to me, pocketing the phone. "That was her mom."

"*Both* of us?"

She nods and looks over at me, tears in her eyes. "I'm not sure that I want to go. This doesn't feel good."

"If I have to forgive Casey, you have to forgive Nora." I watch her pout her thick lips at me. "You're the one that said you wanted to move on…well, this is part of moving on."

"You're right," she says, and I'm a little surprised. "You're totally right. I should give her the chance to apologize and then just set her free too. I'm not sure she even cared about me at all during our sudden friendship."

I raise my eyebrows. "Sudden friendship? I thought you two were best friends?"

"We went to the same high school. Then a year ago she messaged me online and wanted to hang out. We found a kinship in each other," Julie says to me. "So, then we started hanging out more and she introduced me to Staci and Amber. Then we suddenly were all best friends and I was sucked into this typhoon of mascara and fake nails and designer handbags."

I laugh so hard my gut feels sore. "Must be difficult to be so incredibly beautiful and loved."

"It really is," she jokes and snorts.

I start to reach for her, but she's already moving off the bed. She dresses in her clothes that we came home in last night. "We need to get you some clothes for that closet if you're going to be staying here more." I wink at her and make her blush. "You can even have all of my dresser drawers if you need them."

"Oh," she says, "like move my things here?"

"Only if you want," I quickly say to try and save face. "No pressure."

She sits down in a chair in the corner to put her shoes on. She's careful not to make direct eye contact with me. "Let's just get through this and then we can focus on everything else. Breakfast?" She stands up as if nothing just happened. "I'll make you some eggs while you get dressed and then we can go."

I nod as she leaves me alone in the room. "Dammit!" I hear from the kitchen as I pull a pair of jeans on and a black t-shirt from the chair I'm not sure is even clean. I find her sucking on her index finger and furiously fluffing the scrambled eggs with a fork. When she sees me come into the room, she shows me the finger. "I burnt myself," she says, and I kiss it. "Thank you. The eggs are almost done; sit down." I let her serve me scrambled eggs and toast, then serve herself and sit down.

It's nice to see Julie slowly slide the fluffy yellow eggs into her mouth and savor them. Heather hardly even picked up a piece of bacon around me, but Julie is sitting less than five feet away and she's already eaten two pieces. She hands me the salt and I hand her the pepper; we both smile at each other. I pat her leg underneath the breakfast bar. I feel so at peace right now that I must be dreaming her up entirely in my head.

I want her so damn bad that it hurts.

"What do you want to do after we see Nora?" I ask.

"Oh, we should go to the zoo."

"The zoo? What in the hell for?" I laugh but I can tell I've hurt her feelings. "I've never been to the Rockford Heights Zoo, have you?"

She nods. "I go at least once a month. I like it there—it's peaceful."

"Then to the zoo we will go."

Julie can tell I have no interest in going to see a bunch of animals in cages. Actually, the thought of zoos always depressed me. Like elephants at a circus...you won't catch me at one of those, either. "No, it's okay, I can go another time," she says. "We can go shopping—we *do* need groceries."

I smile and I can tell I'm blushing. Her giggle makes me blush harder. She catches my embarrassment. "We need groceries, huh?"

"Oh, well..." She bites her bottom lip.

"I haven't been to the zoo. I want to go. Agenda solved, ready to go?" I don't give her a chance to answer before I tug on her hand; we leave the plates and food where they are. I want to rush her out before she has time to rethink going to see Nora. I can tell she's worried the entire ride there. Even when we get inside, I have to push her into the elevator before it closes on her.

Nora's door is open and ready for us to walk right in. I do, but Julie doesn't.

"Oliver," Nora says, surprised to see me. "I didn't think you would come, especially not by yourself."

I look around for Julie and see her silhouette outside in the hallway. "Neither did I, but I have someone I really care about hurting because of what you said to her, and I'd like to hear your side of it."

"I'm really sorry, Oliver. I shouldn't have taken what Brandon did out on you guys."

Julie sneaks into the room and hides behind me. "I know, Nora. I forgive you," she says and goes to her friend. As they embrace, I can feel a large balloon expanding in my chest. Pride overcomes me and I sit in the chair next to the door, watching Julie.

Everything she touches turns to gold.

She is absolutely perfect in every single fucking way.

"Oliver?" Julie giggles and snaps me back to reality. "Did you hear what she said?"

I shake my head. "No, sorry."

Nora looks annoyed. "I wanted to apologize to you about Heather. I don't know how she knew that all of this would happen, but she knew."

I suddenly find myself drawn to Julie's eyes. When she looks at me, everything else melts away. I don't give a shit about Nora; I don't give a shit about what she's saying. I think I hear her whisper something to Julie about the rules of breaking up. I need to make her *shut* up so I can take Julie home.

"Don't worry about it," I grunt. "I believe you."

Nora puts her hand over her heart. "Okay, thank you. That means a lot."

I make a weird noise and blink at Julie. "Okay, we're going to let you get some rest, but make sure that you call if you need anything, okay?" Julie looks nervously at me. She knows I'm aching for her; I know she can feel my overwhelming desire from across the room. I wave at Nora as Julie pulls me from the room and it isn't until the elevator doors close that she finds the words she wants to use.

"You're pretty amazing." She smiles wide. "I'm glad that happened."

The doors open and I walk her back to the Jeep in silence. The car lurches forward, heading for the zoo exit on the freeway. I want to take her there. I want her to feel some sort of peace away from all these fucked-up parts in her life. When we park and enter the small zoo, I've calmed down just in time to see her eyes light up. We walk up to a large mesh cage that holds a few small monkeys.

"They don't live a free life, but sometimes that's better than the one they could have had," she says to me, smiling at the monkeys. "Even though they're caged here, they could be prey out there."

I hold my breath. "Do you feel caged with me?"

"Oh no." She smiles and lays her head on my shoulder. "With you I feel freer than I ever have."

My heart leaps out of my chest. I want to hold her

tight. "Julie, there's something I have to tell you." I swallow hard, preparing myself to come clean. She leads me down a long, brick path and we come across a large fenced-in area with several giraffes towering over us. "It's about my mother."

"Hmm?" she says, but she's in another world with herself and these animals. It's like magic, the way she watches these creatures. To her, they're all mythical and she's seeing them for the very first time, every time. She waves and coos at them; she talks to them like they're human beings. When we've looked at our last exhibit of koala bears, her mind and soul seem more at peace than I've ever seen them.

"Ready to go home?" she says in a dreamy state. "I could use a nap."

"Only if you listen to me first when we get there. I have something to tell you." She nods in agreement, but I'm not sure exactly how I'm going to tell her I lied straight to her face. The entire ride home I hope and pray that she'll understand why I don't know, or care, if my mother is alive. My mother never cared about me, that's for sure.

I can remember everything:

The day she left.

The day I found out about cocaine and heroin.

The day I saw my mother cheating on my father.

The day I got the shit beat out of me by her dealer.

I can remember it all.

"YOU'VE BEEN QUIET." My mother's voice wafts to my ears. Her sour perfume burns the inside of my nose and I make a face, plugging my nostrils. "Where have you been hiding, Ollie?"

"Under the stairs, Mommy," I say and point toward the door leading underneath the stairs. It's cracked open and things are littered around on the floor.

She gasps and shushes me. "It's time to go back and hide, okay? Be a good boy and don't go under the stairs anymore—that's Mommy's special place, you know that."

I hold out the needle and other things I found that she loves so much.

She curses and takes them from me, stashing them in her pocket.

"Go now," she says and pushes me. "Go before Mac gets here."

She pushes me again.

Hard.

I nearly hit my face on the corner of the wall. I look back at her and see that man—that dirty man that always comes around. He likes her and always grabs her where Daddy grabs her, but it's not the same. He does it hard and hurts her.

I play in my room but I can hear her screaming. I get up and open her bedroom door and see the dirty man naked with her on the bed. They don't see me as they stop wrestling and start sticking the needle in their arms and then sniffing things on their fingers.

They are so weird.

Why do they do this every single day?

Then he sees me.

He yells and gets up from the bed. I run and hide.

But he finds me.

And he hits me. Hits me a lot.

I bleed and Mommy screams.

She leaves me on the floor where he throws me like a crumpled-up paper bag. I watch her walk outside with him.

She doesn't come back for me.

She doesn't hold me or hug me.

She doesn't kiss my ouchie.

I hope she never comes back.

TWENTY-EIGHT
OLIVER

I HAVE to tell her the secret I've been keeping about my mother. I need her to understand what kind of monster my mother is; I need Julie to be afraid of her, to not trust her.

She's almost asleep and she looks so peaceful. "Julie?" I whisper her name; I really don't want her to hear me. "Are you awake?"

"I'm awake." She yawns, opening her eyes. The ocean blue waves wash over me even in the darkness. "What is it? Are you okay?"

"I lied to you about my mother," I blurt out before I lose my nerve. "When you asked me all those questions, I didn't want you to know. I knew my mother, she lived with us for a while."

She doesn't look surprised. "So, she didn't run off?"

"Yes, she did," I say. "I don't know where she is or even if she's really still alive or dead. I haven't seen the woman in over twenty years."

"Do you *want* her to be alive?"

"That's a hard question." I want to tell her I don't care, but I do. "I don't wish for her to be dead, but I don't want her around either, I guess."

She smiles into the darkness but I can still feel it. "Do you miss her?"

I groan. "I can't miss someone I hardly knew."

We sit up together and she grips my t-shirt. She's come to bed in one of my clean t-shirts; her silky, bare legs glide against mine as she sits on my lap. I run my hands slowly up her back; I tug at the ends of her mess of blonde hair. She steadies me on the bed with her body.

"What do you remember about her?" I can feel her fingertips graze my chest and nothing else matters except her touch.

"I remember she had several men in and out of our house since I could walk. I remember picking up her used needles. I nearly killed myself with them as a toddler because I was curious and not supervised." Her face falls—I guess in her mind my mother wasn't a raging drug addict. "I remember when my father had to take business trips. I would stay with Mrs. Atchley sometimes so he could make sure I got fed and not beat up."

Her mouth forms a small "oh" but she says nothing. "So that's the connection you two have." I can tell she's embarrassed by bringing it up, but I'm not upset with her. "I hadn't gotten that far in the journals." Her voice is small and I can imagine her blushing. "So you've known Mrs. Atchley for over twenty years?"

"Yeah, I pay for her rent in that apartment. She took care of me when I needed it the most. I owe her more than some fancy one-bedroom." I squeeze her arm gently. "We can keep reading the journals if you want, sunshine. I'd like to see them, actually."

She hesitates but takes the orange book from her nightstand anyway. I turn the light on and wait for her to open it. Instead, she stares blankly at the closed journal and waits. "Are you sure you want to relive this pain? I thought we were moving on?"

"Julie, nothing that is in that book is going to make my life worse, okay? I let go of my mother a long, *long* time ago. I was able to have a somewhat normal childhood with my father, so there isn't any more sadness there." I suck in a deep breath and look at her. "Unless you count the fact that he's gone and all I have left is you now."

She smiles. "I'm here for you." She hands me the book. I open it to where she's left a green ribbon marking her place. I shake my head at her and let her crawl into my lap; we start reading together.

April 13th, 1992

Defeated.

I have finally worn Veronica down.

She hasn't been out in weeks. She says she

doesn't miss her old life but I don't believe her. I told her I would do everything I can to take care of her—all she has to do is give it all up for Oliver.

For me too.

She says she will.

She promises me she will.

My father's lawyers tell me that I need to go ahead with the custody hearing. They want a paternity test done. I am not okay with this. I have already decided that Oliver is mine, no matter what any test or difference in DNA there is.

Oliver is my son.

Julie looks over at me to see my reaction. I guess it doesn't surprise me; I'm grateful that he stepped up to take care of me. When I think of how I could've ended up or who could be my father if he isn't, I die a little inside. Who knows if I would even be alive right now if my mother hadn't left? Not that I'll ever tell Julie this, but I tried to find my mother right after my grandfather died. I hired a private investigator, but everything was a dead end.

He couldn't confirm her death *or* her proof of life.

I keep reading through the entries. Julie hops out

of bed and leaves the room. She comes back with the tub of chocolate chip ice cream and one spoon. She smiles sweetly and hands me the first bite. "You look like you need this."

"I have everything I need right here in this bed." I kiss her on the lips, sneaking the spoon from her grasp. I shovel a huge bite into my mouth. She giggles and takes the spoon from me, nibbling on her own small bite as we continue to read on.

May 1, 1992

Just another week or so to go before my son arrives.

Words cannot express how relieved I am to finally meet him...excited too! I wonder if he will have my eyes, or my nose.

Veronica has dropped out of giving me full custody of Oliver, which is sad news. She promises me that she will be better and do good by him. I tell her that I won't go after custody again; she needs to live by my rules. I know what is best for her and my son. As long as she lives under my roof, she has to live by my rules. She actually agreed to all of my terms.

And told me she loved me for the first time in a long time.

I still love her.

I will always, always love her no matter what she does.

I just want to do what's best for my son. Deep down, I know that not fighting for his freedom from her isn't the best thing. I have to be a little selfish too. I want her to get better and the only way she can do that is if I can keep an eye on her and show her what she will be giving up.

I can show her how life can be with me.

Will it be enough?

I will never know that answer.

But I know I cannot wait to meet my wonderful son.

I close the book and put it on my nightstand. I take the ice cream container back into the kitchen where it belongs. I know she realizes I need a moment to myself; she doesn't follow me, but I can feel her love from the other room.

In some ways Julie is just like my mother—not the

bad parts, but she's afraid of feelings and emotions just the same. Am I going through the same things my father went through? Julie feels deeply for me—I can feel it—but she hasn't said the words yet.

Then again, neither have I.

We keep going back to the same thing. We circle around each other like sharks until one of us just lets a little blood out of our hearts; we're ready to attack but we're good at swimming around the issue so we never cut ourselves.

She smiles as I enter the bedroom and lets me lay my head on her stomach. I wrap my body around hers underneath the blankets. "I have something to show you tomorrow, but you have to promise me that you won't get scared and run." I instantly regret showing my hand this early. "It's nothing bad, but it's going to be a little bit of pressure on you."

I feel her run her fingers through my hair; her breathing hitches a little. "Okay. Can I ask what this mysterious thing is?"

I prop myself up on my elbow and look at her. I wanted to surprise her, but she hates it already, I can tell. She doesn't like surprises at all. We've had our fill of those these last few days. "I bought a house and I finalize the paperwork tomorrow. I'll be moving in soon."

Her eyebrows raise. "Oh? Is it in Rockford?" The nervousness in her voice excites me a little. I know she wouldn't want me to move out of town.

"Of course it is. I wouldn't just buy a house and hope you'd come with me." I laugh, hoping to lighten the mood. "I want you to look at it tomorrow and then you can decide."

"Decide what?"

I clear my throat. "Decide if you want to move in with me."

"Oliver—"

I reach up and turn off the bedside light. "Don't decide now. Wait until you see the house."

She stays silent for a long few minutes. I can hear the gears turning in her mind. She's either trying to get out of going to see the house or she's thinking of a way to turn me down gently.

"Did you buy me a house?" Her voice floats through the darkness like a silk ribbon. "I mean, did you buy a house hoping that I would move in with you?"

I smirk. "This apartment is a bachelor pad...you like it here?"

"I like this apartment."

My laughter booms through the room and she swats my shoulder. "Well, I just think I might start needing a bigger space."

She tenses and pushes me off her. My head hits the softness of the mattress beneath us. "Sorry," she says. "I'll be right back." She hops quickly out of bed and rushes to the bathroom. I can hear her turn on the water faucet so I can't hear anything. I'm somewhere in between a light sleep and a dream when she comes back. She tucks her body next to mine, letting me fold her against my chest. I think she might've been crying a little, but I don't want to push it because now we are exactly where I want us to be.

Intertwined.

———

"I'm so sorry for your loss."

I am so tired of hearing that it's sickening. My grandfather wasn't a good man; he was a rich man and there were so many vultures surrounding his casket that it nearly suffocated me to even be in the same room. I hear Heather's prickly laugh and I search for her. I really need her right now. She's busy giggling at another man's jokes and touching his arm. No doubt to show him some affection just in case he has more money than I do.

He doesn't.

Not that it matters now.

She's been gone every single day for a week, always returning home to me with bags of new things and mountains of receipts. I just let her do what she wants because I'm tired.

I'm so fucking tired.

Tired of caring and tired of giving a shit about anything or anyone.

I don't even think I love Heather anymore, let alone like her.

"Oliver!" a man's deep voice calls. I slip into the men's restroom of the funeral home before whoever it is can reach me. I need some air, but I can't get out of the place without someone noticing me. Heather would just blow up if she

knew that I'd skipped out and left her here to deal with all of this.

I open the bathroom door and peek out, making sure the coast is clear. I dodge the sea of suits to make it out the back door of the funeral home. Once I do, the smell of cigarette smoke invades my nose and I cough as someone laughs next to me.

"Casey, what the hell?" I fan the smoke away from my face. "Since when do you smoke?"

"I don't, but I figured why the hell not now?" He coughs and blows out more smoke.

"Classy, man. My grandfather just died of lung cancer, you moron. You know how he got it? Smoking cigars and those nasty things." I stare him down but he doesn't care. He puffs once more and then throws it on the ground. He holds his hands up in surrender, and I shake my head and start to walk away from him. He calls out my name and says something I don't quite understand. I whirl around. "What did you say to me?"

"I said—" Now I can tell he is clearly drunk. "—your grandfather deserved to die. Did you hear me that time?"

"How so?" Even though I hated the man, he didn't deserve to be spoken ill of on his celebration of death day. "You hardly even knew him."

"I knew him well enough to know he was an asshole."

I hold my hands up for him to shut the hell up. "You better stop while you're ahead, Casey. I'm leaving; you should call a cab."

"I know where your mother is," Casey blurts out and then stumbles over his own feet. He falls onto the stairs. "He paid her off to run away, did you know that?"

I don't really care. "How could you possibly know that?"

"My father does his books, remember? He paid her a hundred thousand dollars to leave." He hiccups and I step back, just in case he decides he wants to hurl all over me. "You're not the only one she left behind, Oliver," he says and swigs rum straight from the open bottle in his other hand. "Do you think that you're so special that you're the only one?"

"Casey, what the hell are you talking about?"

He launches himself at me and pushes me to the concrete. He grips a fistful of my hair, trying to slam my head onto the pavement. "Get off of me, asshole!" I scream and a few funeral patrons come down the alleyway to pull him off me. "What is wrong with you?" I spit out blood from the few blows he managed to sneak in. I stand up and Heather comes running out the back door to see what the commotion is.

"I think I need to get home," he mumbles and shoves his way through the crowd. He growls at Heather as he passes her. She looks angrily at me for causing her embarrassment.

Yeah, it's my fault.

Blame the guy with the dead family.

TWENTY-NINE
JULIE

WHAT IS WRONG WITH ME?

I literally have to ninja my way out of the bed four times during the night. All because I need to run to the bathroom; I had to pee so bad. Oliver is still snoozing next to me. He's unaware of my frequent trips to the bathroom; I'm so quick that I'm back in my warm spot just minutes after leaving it. My space never grows cold enough for him to notice I was gone. I decide to try it one more time before daylight really hits us and he's easier to wake. I manage to maneuver my way out again and once I'm done, I feel so hungry I think I might throw up.

We have no edible food in this entire apartment. I am sick to my stomach. I think I'm going to lose whatever I have left in it on the floor.

Oliver looks peaceful and happy in the sunlight. I sigh, not really wanting to disturb him, but I really have no choice. "Hey sleepyhead, do you want to get up and run to the store with me?" I whisper into his ear, careful not to fully wake him. "Or I can go by myself if you let me drive the Jeep."

He mutters something. I swear I hear, "Take the Jeep." I don't ask again; I find the keys and dress quickly, careful not to wake him any further. I just need a break from everything. I need something I can do on my own without someone holding my hand. Or asking if I'm okay every three seconds.

I realize I left everything at the cabin. We left in such a rush that my bag and wallet are still there. "Great," I say out loud and hear feet shuffle behind me. I scream when I turn around; Oliver's tall body is behind me, hovering. "Going somewhere?" His arms are crossed over his chest and there's a broad smile on his lips. "I thought we were going to look at the house today…where are you running off to?"

"I asked you if I could borrow your Jeep to go to the grocery store. You said yes, so I'm going." I shake the keys at him. "I just need some money because mine is all up at the cabin still."

"Paul and Madrie are bringing our stuff back tonight. We can go then and then *I* will pay for them, not you." He stands his ground but I'm not having it.

"Oliver, I want to go alone, okay? I just need some alone time." I say it before my brain can catch up. I realize how that must sound to him. To my surprise, he walks back into the bedroom and comes out with his wallet. He hands it to me and smiles. "I want you back here in no less than an hour. We gotta get to the house…I have to sign the papers before noon."

Finally, an ounce of trust from someone.

"Take care of my baby." He winks at me.

I groan. "I won't hurt the Jeep."

His lean body towers over mine. He leans down to kiss my forehead and pulls me into a tight hug. His lips are brushing the top of my ear and he whispers, "I wasn't talking about the Jeep."

I blush so hard I think my skin is on fire. I kiss his cheek and zoom out of the apartment so fast I probably knocked some pictures off the wall. Mrs. Atchley is coming out of her apartment but I politely wave and enter the stairwell. I don't want to wait to be stuck on the elevator with her.

I just need to remember to breathe sometimes.

The parking garage is stale, like something died in the corner overnight. The air is still and odd. I put the key into the driver's side door of the Jeep, and someone shuffles their feet directly behind me. I roll my eyes, annoyed that Oliver followed me down here.

"Jules."

Brandon.

I panic and drop the keys at my feet, too scared to turn around.

"Jules, please don't be scared. I won't hurt you."

I want to call out for Oliver, but I'm an idiot and told him to stay upstairs. I wonder if I'll ever see him again.

"I need to talk to you, okay? Can you turn around?"

No.

NO!

I feel him grab my arm and my body goes frigid. He spins me around to face him; he looks pale and tired. "I'm leaving town. I just wanted to see you one last time before I go. Don't worry, okay?"

"G-Go away," I stutter and tears form in my eyes. I feel for my phone in my pocket, and I think about dialing Oliver before it's too late.

Even if it's to say goodbye.

I want to tell him that I love him.

"Jules, please, look." Brandon takes a few steps back, his hands up in surrender. He's shaking so hard I think he might take off like a rocket. "I'm not here to hurt you. I just wanted to tell you I'm sorry and to say goodbye. I'm skipping town; I'm sure you've heard about Nora."

I nod but say nothing.

"Okay, well…I think you need to know the truth. I didn't just go looking for trouble, you gotta know that. I don't know what happened…she said some things I didn't like and the next thing I know she's tripping down the stairs."

"That's because you pushed her," I squeak.

The parking garage door opens and Oliver steps through the door. He looks like someone has just hit him with a freight train. He gazes at me, scared and backed up against the Jeep, then at Brandon, who doesn't see him until it's too late. Oliver tackles him to the ground. They both wrestle around on the concrete until Oliver pins Brandon and holds him there.

"Call the cops, Julie!" he yells at me, but I can't move.

"Wait, just wait!" Brandon screams as Oliver starts to punch him. I hear the thuds of Oliver's rough knuckles hitting Brandon's face. I can see the blood from his jaw start to splatter the concrete.

"Give me one good reason why I shouldn't kill you right here," Oliver growls at him.

Brandon looks up at me with sorrow in his eyes. "I don't have one. I'm sorry for fucking up your life, Jules. Dude, please, you can hold onto me, but let me just talk to her, okay?"

"You don't ever get to speak to her again."

"Oliver, let him up," I say, surprised. Oliver looks surprised too, but he does what I ask. He holds onto the back of Brandon's jacket as he brushes himself off. "What is your problem? Why can't you just leave me alone?" I say to him, but he doesn't try to move toward me. His body language isn't vicious like last time; he hangs his head in sadness.

"I know I was a horrible person, both when we were together and afterwards." Oliver looks like steam is going to come out of his ears. We lock eyes and he eases up a little. "I don't have an excuse for that, okay? I just know that I needed to apologize and see you before I leave town and tell you both that I'm sorry for what I've done."

Oliver scoffs. "Nora is the one you should be apologizing to right now, don't you think?"

Brandon shakes his head. "I didn't push Nora— she tripped. It was an accident. I just went over there to ask her to help me. I swear, Jules." He starts to move toward me but Oliver stops him. "You have to believe me. I've never hurt anyone like that before, not something like that. I couldn't. Not that it matters, but the cops are looking for me. Can you just give me a half an hour head start, dude?"

Oliver laughs and lets go of Brandon. He throws him against a pillar to his left. "Two minutes, dickhead. Go."

Brandon takes one last look at me. His steel-colored eyes are cold and lonely. I don't know him anymore, not that I have for a long time. Something inside of him has changed. We forced each other to grow apart. And now, as he locks eyes with mine, I feel bad for him. We hear sirens somewhere and he disappears onto the street.

"What the hell was that? Were you going to call me?" Oliver's voice booms in the garage.

"Call you—wait, what? He had me cornered, how would I have done that?" I yell back.

He shakes his head. He looks around to make sure we're alone. "Do you believe him?"

I look at the ground. "I don't know what I believe."

We stand in silence. He walks over to me and pulls me into a fierce hug. "Are you okay to drive?" He looks down at my face.

"You're still going to let me go alone?" I'm startled by the surprise in my voice. Oliver isn't controlling—he just wants me to be safe. I mean, look what happened when I demanded a taste of that freedom: Brandon.

"I think you're safe. I'm pretty sure he won't be showing his face around here anymore." I don't wait another minute. I kiss him goodbye and pull the Jeep out of the parking garage. I catch myself still looking around for Brandon on the streets around me. When I'm safely out of view, I park the Jeep in an empty parking lot and sob into my hands.

There's a knock on the window and it startles me. I nearly jump out of my skin. A police officer is motioning for me to roll down the window. Her eyes soften when she sees that I'm crying. "Is everything okay here?" She looks around the front of the Jeep, no doubt checking if I'm alone.

I wipe my face and fake a smile. "Yeah—yes, I'm sorry. Did I do something wrong?"

"No, I just saw you sitting in an empty parking lot crying and thought I could help. Are you sure you're okay?"

I nod at her and sniffle. "Just emotional, I guess. I had to pull over and have a good cry."

She smiles. "I know that feeling. Where are you headed?"

"Valkson's Grocery on Ninth," I tell her, hoping she'll go away, but it takes a few more tries. The officer drives off and I make sure to drive carefully to the store. I've already been gone for the better part of twenty minutes; Oliver wants me back soon to go look at his house.

I fill the cart once I get into the store with tons of

food and essentials. I pick up a new toothbrush for myself and Skittles for Oliver. I'm not paying attention to the time as my phone starts buzzing in my pocket.

OLIVER

Where are you?

I put down the shampoo I'm holding to respond.

Valkson's. Be back in fifteen minutes, had a slight delay.

His response is instant.

Are you okay? What happened?

I type a quick *yes* and shove the phone back into my pocket. I look around in case anyone noticed me blushing. I slowly walk through the rest of the aisles, thinking of the past few weeks. My mind is tired just thinking about my life—where I've come from to where I am now.

I was weak. Abused. Neglected. Stepped on. Hated.

I met Oliver and that all changed.

Now he wants me to follow his rules.

I broke through his walls and he broke through mine somehow, walls that I didn't even know I had built. A visit to the hospital for stitches is what it took for us to admit that we even had a connection. A few crazy exes thrown into the mix, a fistful of drama, and some extra incredible nights getting as close to one another as humanly possible and—

Now here we are.

Afraid to tell each other, "I love you."

Well, I'm not afraid anymore. I plan on telling him once I get back to the apartment. I bite the inside of my cheek as I walk down the feminine hygiene aisle. I'm still in an Oliver love daze in my mind, but that doesn't stop me from knocking over a tampon display in the middle of the aisle. One by one, I pick up the boxes and my head starts to ache. I think about the last time I needed a tampon and how horrible it—

Wait. When was the last time I needed them?

I take out my phone and check a few things on my calendar. The aisle starts to spin around me and I can feel the panic start to rise in my throat. I push it back down because now is not the time or place to panic.

I am late.

Like, late—*late*.

Okay, now is a *perfect* time to panic.

THIRTY
OLIVER

NONE OF THIS IS REAL.

Julie isn't real, her love for me isn't real.

My love for her isn't real.

It can't be. Something that makes me feel this good just can't exist.

I'm standing on the edge of something incredible and pure, but I feel like there's always going to be something getting in the way of my happiness.

Then there's Julie.

I am *so* in love with this girl. For a million reasons even I don't understand.

There's too many reasons to even explain why she's the perfect one for me. She's changed me into someone I actually like. Someone I can stand to be alone with. Hell, I may even *love* myself.

…Okay, let's not get too crazy.

She walks in the apartment like she owns the place. She makes simple things feel like they're on fire in my brain. I watch her body dip and bend as she empties the grocery bags. She doesn't even look back at me for confirmation; her presence demands the space she's in without even trying. She moves like she's meant to be here.

She *is* meant to be here.

She was made for me.

"Oliver? Can you help me with the high shelves?" Her voice is strained. I see her stand on her toes to try her best to put boxes away. I smile and slide up behind her; I purposely feel her warm ass on my thighs. I'm glad I put on basketball shorts. I press my body into hers and I swear I can hear her giggle. I place the boxes on the shelf and shut the cabinet, brushing her hair off her neck and kissing her collarbone.

"Oliver, I have to put the rest of these away— you're distracting me." She giggles louder. She turns her body to face me, letting me press my lips to hers. Her mouth tastes like peppermint and it reminds me of Christmas; that's something I haven't thought about in a long time.

I *hate* Christmas.

Christmas was never kind to me. If my father was home from his business trips, he would dress up as Santa Claus. If it was just my mother and me—which it usually was—there would be nothing other than a normal drugged-out day. Maybe if she passed out with a needle sticking out of her arm underneath the mistletoe it would count as festive.

So, I learned to hate Christmas.

As I lose myself in her taste, I swipe my arm

across the kitchen counter. Everything falls off onto the floor and I pick her up, placing her on the now-clear surface. I'm done with trying to control myself around her.

I belong to her.

I am completely hers.

I will do anything and everything she ever asks me to.

"Are you okay?" She breathes rapidly, her heart pounding through her chest. "Are you nervous about looking at that house?"

I forgot about the house. I look at the clock on the microwave and help her down; I smooth out my clothes and kiss her forehead. "No, but we're late—can you finish this later?" I motion around the kitchen. "Or we both could finish what we started later?" I gently pat her ass and wink down at her.

She giggles. "Deal." I grab my shoes and put them on as we leave the apartment; my arm is around her waist the whole trip downstairs and it just feels so damn…

Amazing.

I tuck her into the Jeep and she doesn't even buckle herself in. Instead, she slides over to my side and sits dangerously close to me. She nestles herself between my side and my arm. I don't even bother moving it; I can drive with one arm. I can tell that she's looking forward to seeing this house too.

Suddenly, all of the lies and the drama melts away and it's just us.

Oliver and Julie.

Broken rules and mended hearts.

It feels like we've been together forever, like we've been best friends since the beginning of time. I hardly know anything about the girl; I trust her with everything I have and everything I ever will have. I mean, I've been dreaming about her. The girl's face may have changed in my dream but the concept was always her.

My Julie.

Someone my grandfather would hate.

Someone my father would love.

The house is ten minutes into the suburbs of Rockford, a little closer to Randy's house than I originally wanted. But maybe that will bring her comfort and she'll be more willing to say yes and move in with me. Am I crazy to have this girl move in with me, though? I mean, people have fallen in love and gotten married in less time than we've known each other.

Married.

I sweat a little when I think of the word.

I could see Julie as my wife, cooking me breakfast on Sunday mornings in her cute pajamas as I drink coffee and take in how beautiful she looks even when she's just woken up.

We pull into the driveway of the mini brick mansion. I can see the sparkle in her eyes as she looks at the endless windows and layout of the property. It's in a gated community—a little posh for her liking, I'm sure. She launches herself from the Jeep to start exploring anyways.

"Oliver, this is...too much," she says slowly as her

eyes scan the house from top to bottom. "This is a lot of house for one person."

"Two people," I correct her and look down into her eyes. "Two."

She nods. "Okay, even so…" My heart dances around the manicured green lawn right then. "This is amazing. Huge, but amazing."

I smile. "Wait until you see the inside. There's a private library and a baker's kitchen."

Her eyes gloss over and she can hardly wait for me to open the door. I let her inside to check out the features. With each room we pass, I can see her face light up even more and she looks like a kid in a candy store. She runs her fingertips along the marble countertop in the kitchen like a piano. I imagine her in an apron—*only an apron*—making breakfast after a long night in bed.

"Did you already buy this house?" There's hope in her voice.

I nod. "The realtor will be here soon with the papers. It's all ours."

My Julie.

She clicks her tongue as she steps through the glass doors leading to the bright green grass of the endless backyard. "It looks like the cabin, only brighter." She crosses her arms over her chest. "Maybe we can put a rock pool at the end of this property." She winks at me and it makes me blush. "Only if you want to."

I grab her sides and pull her closer. "Oh, I want to." She lets me kiss her in the backyard. The sunlight beams down on us, inviting us to have a happily ever after.

Someone clears their throat behind us: the realtor, a plump older woman named Pearl. Her curly white hair and the dimples that form in her cheeks when she fake smiles remind me of Mrs. Atchley.

"Mr. Jackson, nice to see you." She holds out her hand for me to shake. "And you must be Miss Remington."

Julie frowns and looks at me. "Julie." She shakes her hand, not letting go until the woman nearly peels her hand away from the girl.

"Julie." Pearl squints her eyes and fake smiles, her white curls dancing around her head. "Well, has Mr. Jackson shown you the house? Do you have any questions or concerns? Anything else I can do for you before you sign the paperwork?"

"None that you can solve, I'm afraid," Julie says and looks at me. "I think Oliver and I should talk a bit more before I agree to anything."

Pearl looks sick to her stomach. "Oh, I thought you two had this figured out already."

I clear my throat. "Can you give us a few minutes, Pearl?"

The woman nods and disappears into the house. I follow Julie inside, watching her pace around the kitchen. She fiddles with the strings of her t-shirt. I can tell she wants to say something but is holding back; the air between us grows weird and tense. Her mouth opens and closes a few times before I stop her and hold her still.

"What is the matter with you? Are you going to tell me why you're pacing around this kitchen? Is this too much for you?"

Her eyes look blank. "I just need some fresh air."

I groan. "You were just outside getting fresh air and you were fine."

Julie looks sick, like she's about to lose her breakfast. "I'll just be a minute," she says and runs outside. I watch her put her hands on her knees and double over, taking deep breaths. She vomits in the bushes near the window. I turn my head away to give her some privacy.

I can feel the war waging between her head and her heart.

She turns and sees me watching her. She brushes off her t-shirt and quaintly walks back into the house, standing a few feet from me. We can hear Pearl somewhere in the house talking to someone on a cell phone, but I don't care about her right now. The person I care about wants to call this off and I'm not okay with that.

"There's something you should know." Her eyes darken. "Something that might change your mind about all of this."

"Whatever it is, I don't care." I already told her nothing will make me leave her.

She acts like my words cut her like a knife. "Oliver, just—"

I can't help myself. My entire mind blows into pieces right there. "Julie, do you want to do this or are you trying to get out of it?"

"Oliver, listen to me—there are things you don't know."

Again, I don't care.

"Yes or no, Julie? Are you in this with me or not?"

She doesn't answer me and I know I'm losing her.

I walk toward her and pull her to my chest. I hold her there until her breathing has slowed down and we're both calm. There isn't any other place in this entire world I want to be in this moment; we're standing in the kitchen of our new beginning. I push our bodies apart and place my hands on both sides of her arms, holding her steady. I fear she'll run from me when I can finally tell her how I feel out loud. It takes me a few tries in my mind to get it right. Once I feel confident enough that I won't sound like a total fool, I take my chance.

"Julie—"

Her eyes widen.

"I love you. I am in love with you."

Julie gasps and she looks as pale as a ghost.

"I want to live with you. I want to be with you. Does this really come as a surprise that I would want you to move in here with me?"

She shakes her head in silence.

"I broke the very first rule I ever promised myself, Julie. I let someone in and it turned out to be the greatest decision of my fucking life. I can't breathe without you. I know I can't think or even *live* without you." My brain hurts. I want to cry, but I don't dare even start tearing up. I finally get tired of the silence and take her sides, squeezing them gently to get her to focus. "Say something," I say to her. "Just say something—anything."

I think she's going to be sick again. Her face loses all color and her lips quiver like she needs another trip outside. I'm not going to let her go this time.

"Julie, say some—"

"I'm late," she says.

I shake my head. "Late for what? I didn't know we had anything else to do today. Why didn't you say so?"

Her face looks green and she isn't smiling. "Like as in *late*, late."

The world spins. Her voice echoes in my mind, bouncing off the walls of my skull. Her words haunt me to my bones.

She's late.

THIRTY-ONE
OLIVER

I CAN'T MOVE.

I'm frozen.

She looks at me for confirmation; did I hear what she just said?

I think I growl and nod. I'm pretty sure I do.

Do I want to run?

I want to run.

I'm not going to run.

Thirty seconds.

Thirty seconds is all it took for her to spin me back out of control. Spin me back into a web of uncertainty.

Julie.

My Julie.

You better calm the fuck down before you screw it all up.

I blow out a loud breath. I can't believe this shit. I knew the one time that I'd break my own damn rules, it would be nuclear. This shit hurts; it isn't right that I have to hurt so bad when all I want to do is love her. I can't break any more rules; I won't survive if I do.

She blinks at me, frustrated that I haven't said anything to her yet.

She wants me to answer her.

Wait, what the hell did she ask me?

No, she didn't ask me anything. She *told* me something.

Late. She's late. She. Is. Late.

"Oliver?" Her voice rips into my thoughts. "Oliver, are you okay?"

I am most *certainly* not okay. I can't believe she seriously just asked me that, no—*wait*. I can't believe she seriously just *told* me that. We're standing in the kitchen of the house I bought for her. Even though I told her I didn't, we both know the truth.

Pearl peeks her head around the corner, eavesdropping on our conversation.

"Are we okay here, kids?" She walks into the kitchen and glares at me. I know she thinks I'm the culprit for the tension around us. I squint at her and she quickly leaves the room. Julie looks at me with sad eyes—she *expected* this to happen.

Square up, Oliver. Get your head right.

I force a smile. "I'm okay. How late are you?"

Julie looks surprised. "I'm…well, just a few days late." I watch her beautiful face fall into darkness; she regrets saying anything in the first place. I step closer to her and lift her chin up with my finger. The sadness that surrounds her is suffocating. I know that I somehow have to make it right for the way I've acted.

I'm not upset that she's late. I'm upset that she surprised me with it.

"So, what should we do about this?" she asks, her voice barely there. "Should we talk about it before all of this?"

What kind of question is that?

I clear my throat. I'm hopeful that my attitude doesn't bleed straight through onto her; I know she doesn't deserve it. "I sign these papers and we go eat lunch. That's what we do." I force the smile on my face wider. Her tension doesn't ease.

I can tell she's scared—I am too—but we're standing in the kitchen of a house that's barely ours. There's an old woman eavesdropping in on us again. It isn't exactly the correct time to freak out. Julie's eyes meet mine and I hope my fake smile will convince her to give in before Pearl comes back to check on us. I know she thinks I'm apparently torturing the poor girl.

"How are we doing, kids?" Pearl comes back into the kitchen behind me. I want to tell her to get out. I also want to get it over with so Julie and I can talk about what she just dropped on me.

I turn around and face Pearl. "I'm ready to sign those papers; this is a done deal. I was just showing Julie the house before we moved things in. Do you have the paperwork with you, Pearl?" I try to get her gaze to swing toward me, but she's looking at Julie, who's clearly sick and woozy.

"Pearl? The papers?" I snap my fingers at her. She opens her suede briefcase, producing a stack of papers. I sign where each little line is marked with a pink Post-it note. "There. Last one," I say and hand her back the pen. I return to Julie and put my arm around her waist. "Thanks for meeting us here, Pearl. I assume we're done here?"

Pearl nods and looks sheepishly at me. "It was wonderful doing business with you, Mr. Jackson. If you need anything else, don't be hesitant to call my office." She doesn't even finish her sentence before walking out of the room. She bolts through the front door, closing it behind her.

Now we're alone.

The silence is overbearing.

Julie clicks her tongue softly and clears her throat. "Okay, so, what now?"

"I thought I already told you?" I snap at her. I know that I'm taking it too far, but I can't sort the feelings in my brain out.

Julie isn't buying it. "We aren't going to be able to ignore this one, Oliver." Almost like she's scolding me. "You can't just cute your way out of everything."

I disagree. I'm not even going to try to do that with her right now. I lock my jaw and my teeth clench together. "What do you want from me?"

"I want to talk about this!"

"Well, I don't! What do you want to talk about? Did you want a different reaction from me? You *surprised* me, Julie. Do you want me to ask if it's mine?" My mouth snaps shut. I don't know why I just said that.

Her eyes narrow. I know it's going to be nothing but trouble from this moment forward. Julie's ice-blue eyes catch on fire the second I meet her gaze. "I'm going to pretend you just didn't say that. Take me home, please," she demands and storms out of the kitchen. I spin my body around in a full circle. How the hell could this afternoon have possibly gone wrong?

I'm a damn mess.

"Oliver? I'd like to go home."

I close my eyes and shake my head. I walk into the living room and attempt to do what she asks. Backing halfway down the driveway—of the house our future was supposed to start in—I look up at the perfect house and growl.

Now I'm so pissed that it's hard to see straight.

Julie clears her throat. I can feel her glaring at me. "I don't know what else to say to you right now—" I grow impatient and cut her off.

"Then don't say anything."

I'm so pissed at myself that it just fuels my rage building inside. The burning, wretched ball of fire that festers inside when I know I'm so completely wrong and I can't do anything to stop it. I'm unsure of what might come spewing out of my mouth if I let it.

She gets to me first. "I'm sorry." She looks down at her lap.

I don't want to make her feel horrible.

But I'm still pretty pissed.

I gruff at her. "It's fine, I'll just get you home." The sadness that fills the air around us is suffocating. I want to do anything to make it stop; I don't want to hurt her, but it just feels so good to not care for once.

"Thanks," she squeaks. I can tell she's crying next to me. I start to reach out for her, but something inside me stops my hand from touching hers. For the first time, it actually feels wrong to touch her. Like she isn't mine—she doesn't belong with me anymore.

I know that isn't true.

I'm actually more in love with her now than ever before. Now it feels real, the stabbing pain in my chest. I can tell she's sad and there isn't anything I can do about it because it's my fault.

Randy's house isn't far, but getting there seems like an eternity. I pull up next to it and Julie instantly climbs out of the Jeep without waiting for me. At first, I don't try to go after her. After realizing how stupid that is, I nearly trip on my face as I fall from the Jeep. I catch up with her at the front door. I spin her around, breathing so heavily I might pass out.

"What?" she snaps.

My heart sinks and I frown. "I wanted to see you inside. Can I at least kiss you goodnight?"

Her tear-filled eyes close. She slowly opens them and stands on her toes to quickly kiss my lips. She turns and runs inside and locks me out. That sure as hell felt like more than just a goodnight kiss.

That felt like a goodbye kiss.

Short and sweet, like ripping off a Band-Aid.

The world spins around me. I make my way back to the Jeep in one piece, without falling on my face. I take out my phone and dial Harley's number. I let it ring three times before hanging up and calling him again.

"What's the problem?" he answers angrily on the third call. "Why are you blowing up my phone, Ollie?"

I cringe. I hate that fucking nickname.

Julie never calls me that. I love that about her.

"Meet me at The Tavern," I bark into the phone. "I think Julie and I just broke up. Again."

He sighs softly. "Are you sure?"

"She didn't say the words…apparently she's late too, but—look, I just want you to meet me at The Tavern, okay?" My voice cracks a little but I don't care. "I need to get drunk and I need you to sit with me."

I hang up the phone and slam down on the gas. I speed around the cars on the freeway, hardly caring about my safety. I open my window a little bit to let some fresh air in; it smells like her strawberry shampoo. I need to forget about that right now.

The Tavern, still in all its rustic glory, was an old college hangout for the guys and me. We never quite grew out of the atmosphere. When I was in the business of picking up women, it was always our first choice to visit. Now, I just want to pound down as much whiskey as I possibly can handle.

I park the Jeep and run my fingers through my hair a few times. I slap my cheeks to snap myself out of whatever funk Julie has just put me in.

I'm going to have fun no matter what kind of trouble it lands me in.

Harley waves to me from a stool at the bar. He shakes his head as I sit down next to him and tell the bartender what I want to drink. "Okay, what gives? Is she pregnant, really?" The first thing that comes out of his mouth, and it had to be that.

I gulp down the entire drink in front of me. "I don't know, I guess." I motion for another drink. "She just said she's late. Then I said some dumb shit and now here we are." I slurp down the second drink. He shakes his head at the bartender, who just rolls his eyes and looks annoyed at the two of us.

"So, basically, she could be pregnant with my child. I've messed it all up already and the mystery kid isn't even here yet." I slap his hand away and motion for another drink. He tries to put my hand back on the table. "I'm going to drink another one and you better let me," I growl at him. He sighs, nodding toward the bartender, who then hands me the drink. I thank him and sip on this one; my head is getting a little fuzzier than I'd planned.

Harley looks confused. "I thought you and Julie were getting along. When I talked to Casey, he said you were back to normal." He tries to catch my attention, but there's a woman with dark red hair in the corner that just smacked her lips at me. That's more exciting to me than whatever he's blabbing on about. I sip the drink some more and his voice becomes white noise; he's talking my ear off but I don't care.

Hi, she says to me with her eyes.

Hey, there, my eyes reply.

Do you want to come over here? She blinks and smiles.

I break my gaze with her and shake my head in disbelief. I'm so in love with Julie it's unreal. Then what the hell am I doing with this woman? I don't dare look back over at her. Harley's still blabbing his mouth off.

"I mean, it takes two, you know? Maybe she's just scared."

I scoff. "Yeah, maybe. But maybe I'm scared too. Why can't I just be scared and fly off the handle for once? Why do I have to always hold it together for the sake of other people?"

"What are you going to do, Ollie?"

I don't know.

I really don't know.

My eyes click with the redhead's again and she smiles. I like her smile. I like her silky, curly hair and way her legs peek out from her short skirt. Julie doesn't wear short skirts. I think about Julie's warm thighs and shake my head again. I can't do this to her.

I think Harley understands that I'm having trouble. He claps his hands and rubs them together, trying to get my attention. "I think we should get you back home—maybe Julie has come to her senses and she's waiting for you there."

I laugh. "She's not there."

Harley groans. "Don't be such a fucking idiot, Oliver. You need to talk to her."

I make my mouth into an O and widen my eyes. "You used my *actual name* for once, did you? No more Ollie? Thank fucking God for that."

"You know what?" he snaps at me and stands up. "I'm leaving now. Either you come with me or you find your own way home."

I look at the redhead, who's now boldly making her way over to me. "I can find my own way home. Scram."

Harley sees the girl and leans into me. "Don't do what you're thinking about doing. You'll not only lose Julie forever, but you'll have to live with it for the rest of your life."

I. Don't. Care.

I've already lost her. Again.

It's exhausting holding onto something you're never going to fully have as your own.

"Get out of here, man," my words slur and I push him away. I drink the remaining liquid from my glass and turn it upside down. The entire room is spinning. I swear I see Julie in the corner booth with another man until I focus and realize my sight right now is shit. The redhead is next to me now, her hand on my leg. "I'm Lucy." She bites her bottom lip.

Harley tugs at my arm. "Let's go, Ollie—you'll thank me tomorrow."

I shrug him off. "I thought I told you to fucking go?"

Her hand slides up my leg and stops a few inches up my thigh. "Can you get rid of him? He's such a bummer." The girl smacks her lips and frowns.

I agree. "Yeah, he is a bummer, isn't he?" I glare at him. "Bye now."

I turn to face the redhead and wait a few minutes before Harley finally leaves. I instantly regret letting him walk away from me. She giggles and sips some pink liquid. I see her perfectly manicured fingernails and fake designer handbag and smile.

Now this is my type of trouble.

"Do you have a girlfriend?" the redhead whispers into my ear.

Lucy. Her name is Lucy, right?

I shake my head. "I'm not really sure anymore." I let her play with my belt buckle a little before I feel a little guilty about it. "I mean, yes, I do, I have a girlfriend."

Lucy giggles. "I don't really care either way. She's not here and I am."

I nod and the room spins faster. "That's a true statement, Lucy. She's not here because all I ever do with her is fight and have some sort of drama, right? I mean, what do we really even know about each other? I can't believe I was so fucking stupid to think that I could fall in love with someone I hardly even know and now look—she's fucking pregnant?

Maybe? I mean, not that she did it on purpose…I'd never accuse her of that, but my fucking God, when does it end, Lucy? It's too hard."

Her eyes grow wide and scared. "Well, I can help you forget about…" She frowns, but swallows her confusion down. "…all of whatever it is she did to you."

She didn't do it to *me*.

I did it to *her*.

Me.

Oliver Jackson. Grade-A asshole.

I shake my head. "I can't do that to her," I say softly.

Lucy laughs. "I'd be doing it to *you*, silly. There's loopholes for everything in life, didn't you know that?"

I can't even believe I'm thinking about doing this.

I'm not this guy anymore.

I wish Harley hadn't left me alone with her.

"Your place, then?" she coos in my ear. I stand up with her and walk through the doors. The night air hits us; I would've liked some sense to be knocked into me as well. I linger at the valet station with her so she can follow me in her car. The entire thing doesn't even feel real. I see her wink at me and pull off to the side so I can find my Jeep in the parking lot.

I don't think.

I *can't* think.

I want everything to go back to normal.

I broke the first rule—*the very first rule*—that I forced myself to follow to protect myself.

I fell in love.

Hard.

The only way to come back from breaking the rules…is to start all over again.

I won't let my guard down this time.

BEFORE YOU GO...

If you enjoyed my book please take a second to leave a short review. These reviews help me as an author be found by other amazing readers like you.

Thank you so much! :)

ACKNOWLEDGMENTS

A huge thank you to all of my very first fans who have been there the whole way (in no particular order):

Ashley Short
Christina Benson
Heather Orleman
Kristena Cannon
Linda Diamond
Sara Pugh
Theresa Globoke-Fauth

ABOUT THE AUTHOR

I live in Kansas City with my husband and our son, Ryker. I have been writing for over a decade, I started out writing songs and music and then realized that those stories were too short for the tales I wanted to tell, so I switched to writing books and articles, which then blossomed into writing contemporary romance and fantasy novels. I am in indecisive person at heart, I love coffee more than a Gilmore girl and my most favorite time to write and create is during a rainstorm (with coffee!).

I love hearing from those who read my stories, I love to hear how much people relate to each character and how they are rooting for their favorites to succeed! I don't only create stories, I create entirely new worlds and people that come to life!

Wattpad
https://www.wattpad.com/user/NBenson